This house had always been Ali's home, her refuge. Yet now, as she moved from room to room, she felt nothing but emptiness.

She blamed her sadness on being forced to leave. But she knew the true cause of it was the man who had briefly shared the house with her.

The scent of him still hung in her bedroom, a reminder of that first night he'd come to her there. And when she curled up to sleep, she envisioned him braced above her there, in her bed.

She shrugged away the troubling thoughts and went back to packing.

And if she had to wipe away an occasional tear, she blamed it on the dust she was stirring up. It certainly wasn't because she was missing Garrett Miller.

She told herself she hadn't fallen in love with him, but she had – and he'd deceived her.

The Greek Tycoon's Secret Heir
by Katherine Garbera

ᮥᯪᯆᮩ

"We need to talk."

Such arrogance. She used to find it attractive. Oh, who was she kidding, she still did. There was something about a man who knew what he wanted and made no bones about it.

"Yes, we do," Ava said, trying to project a little arrogance of her own.

Christos arched an eyebrow at her. He said nothing more, and the silence built around them. Ava brushed her hands down the sides of her skirt and told herself she wasn't still the small-town girl he'd once seduced. But she felt like she was.

She tried to figure out what to say, but all the words running around in her head sounded banal. Best to be blunt.

"So…why are you here?"

"To claim your son, the Theakis heir."

Available in January 2009
from Mills & Boon® Desire™

The Texan's Contested Claim
PEGGY MORELAND

The Greek Tycoon's Secret Heir
KATHERINE GARBERA

™ MILLS & BOON®
Pure reading pleasure™

*First published in Great Britain 2009
by Harlequin Mills & Boon Limited,
Eton House, 18-24 Paradise Road, Richmond, Surrey TW9 1SR*

The publisher acknowledges the copyright holders of the
individual works as follows:

The Texan's Contested Claim © Peggy Bozeman Moreland 2008
The Greek Tycoon's Secret Heir © Katherine Garbera 2008

ISBN: 978 0 263 87086 2

51-0109

*Printed and bound in Spain
by Litografia Rosés S.A., Barcelona*

THE TEXAN'S
CONTESTED CLAIM

by
Peggy Moreland

Dear Reader,

This story centres on Ali Moran – twin sister of Jase Calhoun, the hero from *The Texan's Secret Past* – and Garrett Miller, founder and owner of Future Concepts, a billion-dollar computer company. Their story opens on the first day of January, the perfect time for all new beginnings. Ali and Garrett are the epitome of the odd couple, as she is creative, warm and friendly, and he is…well, he's a geek. A wealthy and handsome geek, but a geek nonetheless.

January is one of my favourite months – and not because of the weather! I really, really *hate* being cold! But I do like what January represents. For me, it's a new beginning, a chance to re-evaluate my life and steer it in the direction I want it to take, making any necessary changes – as well as a few resolutions I may or may not keep.

I hope you enjoy this last book in my series, and I hope you'll take the time to jot down a few resolutions of your own for the New Year. And make sure the first one is to fill your year with romance!

Happy New Year!

Peggy

PEGGY MORELAND

published her first romance in 1989 and continues to delight readers with stories set in her home state of Texas. Peggy is a winner of a National Readers' Choice Award, a nominee for *Romantic Times BOOKreviews* Reviewer's Choice Award and a two-time finalist for a prestigious RITA® Award, and her books frequently appear on bestseller lists. When not writing, Peggy can usually be found outside, tending the cattle, goats and other creatures on the ranch she shares with her husband. You may write to Peggy at PO Box 1099, Florence, TX 76527-1099, USA, or e-mail her at peggy@peggymoreland.com.

Without avid readers, where would an author be? Over the last eighteen-plus years, I've received thousands of letters and e-mails from readers all over the world, who were kind enough to take the time to write and tell me how much they enjoy my books. To each and every one of you, I dedicate this book.

One

To Garrett Miller, timing was everything, both in business and in life.

And the timing on his trip to Austin, Texas, couldn't be more perfect.

His number one goal in making the trip was to reunite his stepmother with Ali Moran, the daughter she'd given up for adoption thirty years prior. If that failed, he intended to persuade—or coerce, if necessary—Ali to give him the missing portion of the deed she held, which would enable his stepmother and her new husband to fulfill the requirements to claim a ranch they had been given.

As fate would have it, he also needed to locate

property for an expansion he was planning for his company. Since Austin was quickly establishing itself as the Silicon Valley of the Southwest, it seemed the natural choice and gave him the perfect excuse to make the trip.

The kick was, he had to accomplish it all without anyone discovering he was in Austin.

Scowling, he punched in the code for the electronic gate of Vista Bed and Breakfast, given to his secretary when she booked his reservation. If he'd known success would make him so damn popular with the media, he would've remained a geek for the rest of his life and never started Future Concepts. Who would've thought the public would care about a businessman's every move?

Or that success would make him a target for some crazy who wanted him dead?

He shoved the disturbing thought from his mind as he drove through the open gates. As far as the rest of the world was concerned, he reminded himself, Garrett Miller was currently attending a technology seminar in Switzerland, a lie his public relations department had fed the media at his request. All Garrett had to do was keep his presence in Austin under wraps, and his stalker would follow the bait to Switzerland and hopefully fall right into the trap being set for him there.

Pulling up in front of the two-story home, he

parked the rental car he'd picked up at the airport, then leaned across the seat to peer up at the house. He studied the structure a long moment, thinking of the woman inside, as well as his chances of gaining her cooperation. He'd given himself a month to find a way to convince her to reunite with his stepmother, though he doubted it would take anywhere near that long. Everyone had a price—or a weakness. It was just a matter of discovering Ali's.

He smiled smugly as he climbed from the car. He didn't doubt for a minute he'd succeed. Knowledge was power and, thanks to the P.I. he'd hired and the research he'd done on his own, he knew all there was to know about Ali Moran.

And she knew virtually nothing about him.

Perched high on a ladder, Ali stretched to snag the last ornament from the Christmas tree's uppermost branch. In spite of the cheery fire burning in the fireplace and her favorite Norah Jones CD playing on the stereo, she couldn't have worked up a smile if she had wanted to. January 1 was usually her favorite day of the year—sleeping late after celebrating the New Year with her friends, eating a huge bowl of black-eyed peas for good luck, making a list of resolutions she wouldn't keep. Best of all, January 1 marked the first day of her annual four-week vacation.

But there would be no vacation for Ali this year.

Grimacing, she tucked the ornament into the box and started down the ladder. It was her own fault, she told herself. She'd let greed get the best of her.

And who wouldn't? she asked herself in frustration. When a zillionaire calls you up and offers you four times the going rate to reserve your entire bed-and-breakfast for a month, it's kind of hard to say no. Cooking and cleaning for *one* guest, rather than the five her B&B was designed to accommodate, and getting paid four times the money for her trouble? Only a fool would turn down a deal as sweet as that.

"So quit your whining," she lectured, as she stooped to place the box of ornaments in a storage crate. The money she would earn far outweighed whatever sacrifices were required of her, including giving up her vacation.

Grimacing, she slapped the crate's flaps into place. "But that doesn't mean I have to like it," she grumbled under her breath.

The doorbell rang and she straightened with a frown. Who on earth would drop by this early in the morning on New Year's Day? she wondered. Everyone she knew would still be in bed, after partying all night—which is exactly where she'd be, if she wasn't expecting a guest to arrive that afternoon.

At the thought of her guest, she caught her lower lip between her teeth. Surely he hadn't arrived early.

She'd specifically told him check-in time wasn't until three. But who else could it be? Unable to think of a soul who'd be up and about this early on New Year's Day, she started grabbing decorations and shoving them into boxes, mortified at the thought of inviting *anyone* into her home with it looking such a mess, much less Garrett Miller.

The bell sounded a second time, setting her teeth on edge. Dropping the evergreen swag she held, she marched for the front door, telling herself he could just deal, since he had chosen to ignore check-in time.

At the door, she paused to drag the elastic band from her hair and stole a peek through the peephole. She blinked, blinked again. If she hadn't already checked out her guest on the Internet, she might not have recognized the man standing on her porch as the owner of a world-renowned company like Future Concepts. Dressed in faded jeans, a worn leather jacket and aviator sunglasses, he looked too…well, *normal.*

The bell rang a third time, making her jump. She blew out a breath, then pasted on a cheerful smile and swung open the door.

"Hi," she said and extended her hand in greeting. "You must be Garrett. I'm Ali, the innkeeper of Vista Bed and Breakfast."

He stared, the oddest expression coming over his face, but didn't make a move to take her hand.

She took a closer look at him. "You *are* Garrett Miller, aren't you?"

The question seemed to snap him from his trance-like state.

"Sorry," he said and took her hand. "It's just that you look very much like…someone I know."

A tingle of awareness skittered up her arm as his fingers closed around hers. Surprised by the sensation—and not at all sure she liked it—she broke the connection.

"You know what they say," she said, with a careless shrug. "Everyone has a twin."

He got that odd look on his face again and she inwardly groaned, thinking it was going to be a *very* long month.

"Come on in," she said and opened the door wider. "You'll have to pardon the mess," she warned, thinking it best to prepare him for the disaster that awaited them in the den. "You caught me in the middle of clearing away my Christmas decorations."

He stepped past her, trailing the seductive scent of sandalwood in his wake. "I hope my arriving early isn't an inconvenience. I had my pilot fly me in earlier than I'd originally planned."

He had his own pilot? Which probably meant he had his own plane, too. Unable to imagine that kind of wealth or the freedom it offered, she swallowed an envious sigh. "No problem." She glanced out the door toward the rental car parked in her driveway. "Do you need help with your luggage?"

He pulled off his sunglasses, looking around as he tucked them into the inside pocket of his jacket. "I'll get it later, if that's all right."

When he met her gaze again, sans the sunglasses, she felt that same tingle of awareness she'd experienced when he'd clasped her hand, only this time he hadn't touched her.

"Oh, wow," she breathed, finding it all but impossible to look away.

"Excuse me?"

"Your eyes," she said. "I didn't notice until you took off your glasses. They're brown. That rich, dark, melted chocolate kind of brown. And when the light hits them just right—" she opened and closed the door, varying the amount of light striking his face "—these little gold flecks flash like tiny explosions of light."

He reached inside his jacket. "I can put them back on, if it bothers you."

Realizing she was making a fool of herself, she offered him a sheepish smile. "Sorry," she said, as she closed the door. "I tend to get carried away about lighting. It's one of the curses of being a photographer. This way," she said, and motioned for him to follow her. "I'll give you a quick tour of the downstairs, then take you up to your room.

"Formal living room and dining room," she said, gesturing left and right as she moved down the hall. "You're welcome to use both, but most of my guests prefer the coziness of the den and breakfast room at the rear of the house. There's a beautiful view of Town Lake through the windows there."

She paused to point to a closed door at the end of a short hall. "That's the entrance to my private living quarters. It's the only portion of the house that's off-limits to guests."

He stopped beside her. "I noticed on your Web site that you cater to businessmen." He angled his head to peer at her. "I believe the blurb read something like, 'the Vista, where *all* the needs of the corporate traveler are met.'"

The emphasis he placed on "all," as well as his suggestive tone, put Ali's back up. "If you're thinking the Vista is a front for a call girl service," she informed him tersely, "you're wrong."

"I didn't say it was," he returned mildly.

"Well, just so you understand, I provide my clients with nothing more than comfortable accommodations, home-cooked meals and workspace should they need it."

"Which is all I expect," he assured her. "I was merely curious why a woman who lives alone would prefer men as guests."

She narrowed her eyes. "I never said I lived alone."

"You didn't have to. Your repeated use of 'my' and 'I' made it obvious."

When she continued to eye him suspiciously, he dropped his hands to his hips, and the corners of his mouth into a frown.

"Look," he said, clearly irritated with her. "If you're worried about your safety, don't be. You're perfectly safe with me. I'm not interested in you *or* your body. And just so *you* understand," he said, tossing her own words back at her, "if and when I'm in the mood for female companionship, I sure as hell don't need someone to arrange it for me."

She wasn't sure whether to be relieved or insulted, but one thing was certain—she'd angered her guest…something a person in her business couldn't afford to do.

"I'm sorry," she said, and meant it. "I'm usually not this defensive."

"And I'm not usually mistaken for a predator," he snapped back at her.

She squinched up her nose. "Can we hit Rewind?" she asked hopefully. "It seems we've gotten off to a bad start."

"If it makes you feel better thinking our relationship will improve by starting over—" he tossed up a hand "—then by all means consider the tape rewound."

To prove her willingness to play nice, she forced a smile. "Thanks. And to answer your question about my preference for business travelers, this is my home, as well as a bed-and-breakfast, and I discovered early on that businessmen are less disruptive to my daily life than tourists. Since they generally book only on weekdays, that's an advantage, too, as it leaves my weekends free for my other job."

He lifted a brow. "Other job?"

"Photography. I'm an aspiring photojournalist."

"A woman of many talents."

"You might want to withhold judgment until you see my work," she warned, then smiled again and motioned him to follow her. "Come on, let's finish the tour."

She started down the hall again toward the kitchen. "In the mornings, you'll find juice and coffee on the buffet in the breakfast room. I normally serve breakfast at seven on weekdays and eight on weekends, but since you're my only guest, you can choose a different time, if you like."

"Your current schedule is fine."

"The den is through here," she said, and led the way through an arched doorway. She stopped, her shoulders sagging at the amount of work awaiting her. "Welcome to the after-Christmas nightmare," she said wearily.

"Damn," he murmured, staring, then glanced her way. "Do you decorate every room in the house?"

"Pretty much. My friends accuse me of trying to make up for my dismal childhood Christmases."

"Dismal?"

"A tabletop Christmas tree and one present dispensed on Christmas Eve just before bedtime."

"Were your parents poor?"

She choked a laugh. "Hardly. More like boring." Doubting her guest was interested in hearing about her dysfunctional family, she pointed to the antique armoire, all but concealed by the wreaths stacked high in front. "Believe it or not, there's a flat screen television hiding behind that pile of greenery. You're welcome to watch TV here or in your room, whichever you prefer. I have a wireless network, so you can connect to the Internet anywhere inside the house, as well as the patios outside.

"Both the front and back doors have a keyless entry," she went on to explain. "I change the code every couple of weeks for security purposes. That's about it downstairs," she said and gestured toward a set of stairs on the far side of the room. "We'll take the rear staircase to the second floor."

When she reached the top landing, she headed for the opposite end of the hall. "You can have your pick of the bedrooms," she told him, "but since you're staying a month, I think the suite will better suit your needs. It has a separate sitting room, with a minifridge and bar. Plus, the bathroom is larger than the others, and has a tub perfect for soaking— a bonus, if you enjoy taking long baths."

She pushed open the door to the suite then stepped back out of the way. "Unless you have any questions, I'll leave you to settle in."

"Just one."

"What?"

"When my secretary made my reservations, she asked that you keep my stay here confidential."

She held her hand up like a good Girl Scout. "I haven't told a soul."

"Good. No one can know I'm here."

She teased him with a smile. "Why? Are the cops after you?"

He seemed to hesitate a moment, then shook his head. "No. I'm here to check out locations for a future expansion for my company. It's imperative that my presence, as well as my plans, remain secret until I'm ready to go public."

She drew an imaginary zipper across her mouth. "Your secret is safe with me. Anything else?"

"Not at the moment."

"Well, if you think of something, I'll be in the den dealing with the ghost of Christmas past."

Garrett shook his head as he crossed to the bathroom to put away his shaving kit, unable to believe how close he'd come to blowing his cover. When Ali had opened the door to greet him, her likeness to his stepmother had momentarily rendered him speechless. The same blond hair and blue eyes, the same delicate features. They even had similar mannerisms, which he found inconceivable, since the two had never met.

He'd almost slipped and told her his reason for staring, and would have if he hadn't been distracted by the jolt he'd received when he'd taken her hand. He'd seen the surprise that had flared in her eyes, sensed her unease in the quickness with which she had broken the contact, and knew she must have felt it, too.

He thought he'd done a decent job of recovering, then she'd made that comment about everybody having a twin and thrown him for another loop. If she hadn't appeared so genuinely guileless, he might have thought she was purposely trying to trip him up. As it was, he believed he'd successfully penetrated the enemy's camp.

Penetrated the enemy's camp?

Snorting a laugh, he tossed his shaving kit onto the vanity. Hell, he was even beginning to *think* in the vernacular of a spy.

With a rueful shake of his head, he turned for the bedroom, but stopped when he caught a glimpse of the tub she'd mentioned. Placed on a raised platform of tumbled stone tiles, it resembled an old-fashioned claw-foot in design, but its size and modern fixtures placed it solidly in the twenty-first century.

Remembering her comment about the tub being

perfect for soaking, he crossed to examine it more closely. It definitely looked inviting, he noted, with its extra long length and gently sloped ends. He glanced up at the large picture window above it. And the uninterrupted view of lake and sky it offered its occupant wasn't too shabby, either, he noted. Personally he preferred a shower, but he could see how a person might enjoy taking a long, relaxing bath in a setup like this. Add a woman to the mix and even *he* might be persuaded to forego a shower for a bath.

He squinted his eyes at the view beyond the window, easily able to imagine the scene at night. Moonlight reflecting off the lake's surface. A sky full of glittering stars. Toss in some soft piano music and a mountain of scented bubbles and it would provide the perfect setting for a seduction.

He dropped his gaze to the tub again, wondering if the Vista's innkeeper ever took advantage of the amenities the bath offered when she had the house all to herself. She seemed the bubble-bath type. Feminine. Sensual. In fact, he found it easy to picture her here, her head tipped back against the tub's rolled rim, her eyes closed, only her knees and head visible above mounds of iridescent bubbles.

Even easier—and a great deal more pleasurable— was to picture her there with *him*.

Puckering his lips thoughtfully, he dragged a finger along the rim, imagining them in the tub together, her back against his chest, her hips wedged between his thighs, his hands tracing her curves. She was stacked. He'd made that realization within seconds of her opening the door. And she had a mouth made for kissing. Full, moist lips that seemed curved in an ever-present smile.

With one memorable exception.

He chuckled softly, as he recalled her indignation when he'd insinuated the bed-and-breakfast was a front for a call girl service. She'd assumed correctly. He had thought, hoped even, that she was using the bed-and-breakfast as a front for illegal activities.

Too bad he'd been wrong, he thought with regret. If he'd been right, it would have provided him the leverage he needed to force her cooperation.

It also would have given him more reason to dislike Ali Moran.

Not that he needed more cause.

The hurt she'd inflicted on his stepmother was reason enough to wish her in hell.

Two

"Traci!" Ali shot a worried glance up at the ceiling, then lowered her gaze to frown at her laughing friend. "Get a grip, would you? He might hear you."

Traci winced guiltily. "Sorry. But when you said that about the Vista being a front for a call girl service, I had this mental image of you strutting around in skin-hugging spandex and spike heels. Can you imagine? You, a madam? Or worse, a call girl? What a hoot!"

"I could be a call girl," Ali said defensively. "Not that I ever would, but I *could*."

"Are you kidding me?" Traci said in dismay. "If

you had to depend on turning tricks for your support, you'd starve to death within a week."

Grimacing, Ali yanked open the oven door. "Well, thanks for that vote of confidence," she groused, as she shoved a basket of sopaipillas inside to keep warm.

Traci managed to snag a pastry before Ali could close the oven door. "I'm not saying you couldn't *attract* a man," she said, as she spooned honey into the pastry's puffed center. "But there's more to being a call girl than wearing skimpy clothes and flashing cleavage."

Ali gave her a bland look. "Oh, and I suppose you're an expert on the subject."

"I watch enough cop shows to teach a course. And let me tell you," she went on, warming to the subject, "the hookers they haul off the streets aren't particular about who they have sex with. They can't afford to be. *You,* on the other hand, would turn up your nose at the slightest physical flaw."

Ali's jaw dropped. "Are you saying I'm a sexual snob?"

Traci caught a dribble of honey on the tip of her finger and brought it to her mouth. "Need I remind you of Richard?"

Ali shuddered at the mention of the C.P.A. she'd briefly dated. "Please. Just thinking about his clammy hands and slobbery kisses makes me want to hurl."

"And you think the men call girls entertain are Brad Pitt lookalikes?"

"Okay, okay," Ali grumbled. "You made your point."

Traci smiled smugly. "I so love it when I'm right."

"Shh," Ali hissed, and listened, sure that she'd heard footsteps in the hallway above.

"He's coming," she whispered, and grabbed Traci by the elbow and hustled her toward the back door.

"Hey," Traci cried, juggling her sopaipilla to keep from dropping it. "Who said I was leaving? I want to meet your mystery zillionaire guest."

Ali opened the back door. "He's not my zillionaire, and you can't meet him."

"Why not?"

She gave Traci a nudge over the threshold. "I already told you. He doesn't want anyone to know he's here." Before Traci could demand to stay, she shut the door in her face and turned the lock, just in case she tried sneaking back in.

With Traci dealt with, she headed for the breakfast room where she found Garrett standing at the buffet, pouring himself a cup of coffee. He was dressed much as he had been the day before—jeans and a black pullover sweater, a casual look she found extremely sexy.

Too bad his personality kills his appeal, she thought with regret.

Forcing a smile, she crossed to greet him. "Good morning. Did you sleep well?"

He spared her a glance, before returning the carafe to the hot plate. "Not particularly."

She kept her smile in place, refusing to let his sour disposition infect her. "Well, hopefully you'll rest better tonight."

He raised the cup to his lips and met her gaze over its rim. "That remains to be seen."

Those eyes again, she thought. What was it about them that was so mesmerizing? It certainly wasn't their color. Brown eyes were as common as house flies in Texas. So why were his so compelling?

Feeling herself being drawn deeper and deeper into their dark depths, she tore her gaze away and made a beeline for the kitchen.

"Have a seat at the table," she called over her shoulder. "I'll be right back with your breakfast."

Once out of his sight, she grabbed a plate and gave herself a stern lecture, as she filled it with food. He's nothing special, she told herself. Good-looking men were a dime a dozen in Austin. And so what if he was rich as sin? She'd never considered money a positive attribute, especially in a man. All the rich guys she'd ever known were pompous jackasses, who used their money to feed their egos and need for power. Cars, boats, homes. The more attention a "thing" drew to him, the greater its appeal.

Nope, she mentally confirmed, as she pulled the basket of sopaipillas from the oven. Garrett Miller was nothing special and definitely not a man she'd want to become involved with.

Adding the basket to the tray, she returned to the breakfast room, feeling much more in control.

"I hope you're hungry," she said, as she transferred dishes from the tray. "Huevos Rancheros," she said, identifying each food item as she arranged it in front of him. "Roasted new potatoes, fresh fruit with a light poppyseed dressing and sopaipillas with butter and honey."

Tucking the tray beneath her arm, she reached for the carafe. "If you need anything," she said after topping off his coffee, "I'll be in the kitchen."

She waited until the swinging door closed behind her, then set aside the tray and headed straight for the sink, anxious to put the kitchen back in order. Elbow deep in suds, washing the pans she'd dirtied while cooking, she heard the door open behind her and glanced over her shoulder. Her eyes shot wide when she saw Garrett entering, carrying his plate and cup of coffee.

"Is something wrong with the food?" she asked in alarm.

"No. I thought I'd eat in here with you."

She blinked in surprise. "But—but guests don't

eat in the kitchen. They take their meals in the break-fast room."

He set his cup and plate on the island and slid onto a stool. "This one doesn't," he said, and opened his napkin over his lap.

She considered insisting he return to the breakfast room, then turned back to the sink with a sigh, deciding the guy had paid for the right to eat wherever he wanted.

Thinking she should try to make conversation with him, she asked, "Do you have plans for the day?"

"Nothing specific. I thought I'd take a drive later and familiarize myself with the city."

"Have you ever been to Austin before?"

"A couple of times on business, but I was in meetings and saw very little of the city."

She rinsed the soap from the pan she'd washed and set it on the drainboard. "That's a shame. There's a lot to do and see in Austin."

"Such as…?"

She wrung out the dishcloth and moved to the island to wipe down the surface. "Well, there's Sixth Street," she said, "which is a little bit like Bourbon Street in New Orleans' French Quarter. You'll find everything there from tattoo parlors to jazz clubs. It gets pretty crazy on weekends. Lots of people on the street, drinking and partying.

"The State Capitol is a must-see," she went on. "Fabulous architecture and a tremendous view of the city from the top. And if you're into history, Austin is the home of the Lyndon Baines Johnson Library, as well as the Bob Bullock Museum."

"Have you lived here all your life?" he asked.

She chuckled, amused that he would mistake her for a native. "No. I'd think my northern accent would give me away."

"Northern?" he repeated, then shook his head and speared a plump strawberry with his fork. "Trust me. Whatever accent you had was lost to a Texas twang long ago."

"Really?" she said, considering that the ultimate compliment.

"Really. Throw in a couple more y'alls and you could pass for Sue Ellen from the *Dallas* TV series."

"Wow. That really takes me back. I watched that show when I was a kid. Sue Ellen, J.R., Bobby…." Hiding a smile, she shook her head. "The Ewing family was so dysfunctional, they made mine look like the Waltons." Reaching the end of the island where the coffeemaker sat, she lifted the carafe. "More coffee?"

"None for me." He wiped his mouth with his napkin, then set it beside his plate. "You've mentioned your family several times and not necessarily in a good light."

She shrugged. "Just being honest. My parents are strange people." She carried the carafe to the sink. "If you have any food preferences," she said, changing the subject, "let me know. I try to accommodate my guests' tastes whenever I can."

When he didn't reply, she glanced over her shoulder and found him frowning at her back. "Is something wrong?"

He shook his head. "No. I...I was just wondering if you'd have time to drive me around today."

Her stomach clenched at the thought of being trapped in a car with him all day. "If you're worried about getting lost, I can provide you with plenty of maps."

"I don't need a map. It's your opinion I want, as well as your knowledge of the area. You seem to know the city well and can probably offer me insight on things I wouldn't think to ask."

"I don't know," she said slowly, while trying to think of a plausible excuse to refuse him. "I've got a lot to do today. I finished boxing up all the Christmas decorations yesterday, but I still need to carry all the crates to the attic."

"Tell you what," he said. "If you'll act as my tour guide for the day, I'll help you haul the crates upstairs. And," he added, as if sensing her reluctance, "I'll compensate you for your time."

"You'll pay me?" she said in surprise.

"Yes."

He named an amount that made her jaw drop. "That's more than some people pay for a car!"

"I assure you I can afford it." He lifted a brow. "So? Do we have a deal?"

"Well, yeah," she said, then stuck out a hand, fearing he'd try to renege on the deal later. "In Texas, a man's handshake is as good as his word."

He took her hand. "Is it the same for a woman?"

The tingle started in the center of her palm and worked its way up her arm. Wondering what it was about him that spawned the sensation, she curled her fingers into a fist against her palm.

"Yeah," she said, surprised by the breathy quality in her voice. "Same goes."

If the computer industry ever bottomed-out and Garrett suddenly found himself in need of a job, he thought he might try his luck as a private investigator. He was getting pretty damn good at this clandestine stuff. Asking Ali to chauffeur him around Austin might have been spontaneous, but it was pure genius. Not only had he finessed a large block of time in which to learn more about her, he'd also finagled a way to check out her attic. He hadn't expected to find the missing deed lying in plain sight up there—and he hadn't—but he had familiarized himself with the attic's layout, which would come in handy if Ali refused to relinquish her portion of the deed to him, and he was forced to search for it on his own.

He hoped it didn't come to that. Lying was one thing. Stealing was quite another.

"Am I driving too fast?"

He glanced Ali's way. "No. Why?"

"You were frowning."

"Was I?" He turned his gaze to the roadway again. "Just thinking."

"You must think all the time."

"What makes you say that?"

"Because you're always frowning."

"Am I?" He considered the possibility a moment, then shrugged again. "I've never noticed."

"Do you ever have happy thoughts? Things that would make you smile?"

"Like what?"

"I don't know. A pleasant memory. Maybe a funny movie you've seen that makes you laugh when you think about it."

"I don't recall the last comedy I saw."

She glanced his way. "Are you serious?"

"Why would I lie?"

Shaking her head, she turned her gaze back to the road. "So what do you do for grins?"

"I enjoy playing computer games."

She spun a finger in the air. "Whoopee."

"What do *you* do for fun?" he asked, neatly turning the tables on her.

"There's very little I do that's *not* fun. Going out

to dinner or to the movies with friends. Working in my garden. Taking pictures."

"Taking pictures doesn't count. That's a job."

"Just because it's a job doesn't mean it can't be fun."

Realizing that she had unwittingly offered him the opportunity to probe into her life for that weakness he needed, he decided to take advantage of it. "If you enjoy photography so much, why have the bed-and-breakfast? Why not be a full-time photographer?"

"At one time, that was my plan. I was going to travel the world, taking pictures, then publish them as books."

"An album of your personal travels?" he said, as if doubting there was a market for such a thing.

"It wouldn't be personal," she told him. "At least, not in the way you mean. The pictures would be of people, places and things that share a theme or tell a particular story."

"What do you mean, 'tell a story'?"

"Well, let's say I wanted to do a photographic study of an Amish family," she said. "I'd photograph them at work, at play, in their home, in their community, capturing their lives, as well as their lifestyle on film. The pictures would tell the story."

"Isn't that the same as theme?"

"In some ways, yes. But when I think of theme, I think in terms of a single topic. Take poverty for instance," she said. "If I were to choose that as my theme, I might travel around, photographing examples of poverty in different parts of the country or even the world. Poverty would be obvious in all the pictures, but the people and the settings would be different."

That she enjoyed photography was obvious in the enthusiasm in her voice, the light in her eyes. "And if you chose families as a theme, you'd photograph different families, not just one."

"Score!" she cried and held up a hand to give him a high five.

Amused, he slapped her hand. "As interesting as all that is, it doesn't explain why you're running a bed-and-breakfast and not focusing on photography."

"Long and depressing story," she said, and slanted him a look. "Sure you want to hear it?"

He opened his hands. "I asked, didn't I?"

"Oh, wait," she said, straining to look at something up ahead. "There's Callahan's. Do you mind if we stop?"

"What's Callahan's?"

"A store. I need to pick up a bag of birdseed for my feeders."

Though disappointed that the stop would interrupt what he hoped would be an enlightening view into her life, he shrugged, thinking he'd pick up on the conversation again later. "Fine with me."

"Thanks. It'll save me making a trip later." She checked the rearview mirror for traffic, then changed lanes and turned into the parking lot. After shutting off the engine, she reached over the back seat for her tote. "Do you want to come in?"

He looked at the storefront, considering, then figured what the hell. There didn't appear to be many customers. "I believe I do."

As they entered the store, Ali nudged his arm. "Aren't you going to take off your sunglasses?" she whispered.

He shook his head. "Someone might recognize me."

With a roll of her eyes, she went in search of her birdseed. He watched her walk away and his gaze slid unerringly to the sway of her hips. Yeah, she was stacked, all right, he confirmed. He watched until she disappeared from sight, enjoying the view, then turned down an aisle to explore the store's merchandise on his own.

The place reminded him of the general stores he'd seen in Western movies, carrying everything from horse tack to Western-style clothing. He paused beside a display of cowboy hats and, curious, plucked a black one from the rack. He snugged it over his head and leaned to check out his reflection in the mirror behind the counter.

"Looks good."

He glanced over and saw Ali had joined him. Feeling foolish, he dragged off the hat. "I don't wear hats."

"Really? You should. Especially a cowboy hat. You look sexy in one."

He gave her a doubtful look.

"Well, you do," she insisted. "Sort of like a bad-ass gunslinger. You know. The kind who can empty a saloon by simply walking in the door."

Hiding a smile, he ran a finger along the brim. "Maybe I should buy it and wear it to my next board meeting."

"Couldn't hurt." She took the hat from him and placed it on his head again. She studied him a moment, and he'd swear he heard wheels begin to churn in her head.

"Come on," she said and grabbed his hand. "If you're going for the gunslinger look, you're gonna need jeans and boots."

He hung back. "I was kidding."

She gave him an impatient tug. "I wasn't. Besides, you know what they say. When in Rome…"

Garrett discovered the woman was a whirlwind when on a mission. Within minutes, she had him in a dressing room, trying on jeans, shirts, boots and what she referred to as a "duster," which was nothing more than a long trench coat with a Western-style yoke and a slit up the back so that a man could sit in a saddle while wearing it.

"Aren't you dressed *yet?*" she called impatiently from the other side of the door.

He hooked the silver belt buckle at his waist, then glanced up at his reflection in the mirror. He did a double take, startled by the change the style of clothing made to his appearance. "Yeah," he said staring. "I'm dressed."

"Well, come on out. I want to see."

He plucked the black felt hat from the hook on the wall and snugged it over his head as he stepped out of the dressing room.

A flash went off, and he caught himself just short of diving for cover.

Ali slowly lowered her digital camera to stare. "Wow," she murmured. "You don't even look like the same guy."

He scowled, embarrassed that, for a split second, he'd mistaken the flash of the camera for a gunshot.

"If I didn't know better," she went on, "I'd never guess you were Garrett Miller, zillionaire entrepreneur."

"Zillionaire?" Shaking his head, he turned to study himself in the full-length mirror. "You know," he said, growing thoughtful. "This getup might be just what I need to keep from being recognized."

"Like I said," Ali said, with a shrug, "when in Rome…" She reached to tear the price tag off his shirt.

He yanked his arm back. "What are you doing?"

She spun him around to rip the tag off the rear pocket of the jeans. "Taking off the price tags. Don't worry," she assured him as she gathered from the dressing room the clothes he'd worn into the store, as well as the stack of clothing he hadn't tried on yet, "I'll give them to the salesclerk, along with these other clothes. That way you can wear your new duds out of the store and not have to change again."

Ali held the camera before her face with one hand, and directed Garrett with the other. "A little to the left. A little more. Stop! Perfect." She clicked off a half-dozen or more shots, then dropped the camera to swing from her neck. "Now let's try a few with you standing with one boot propped on the boulder."

He dropped his hands to his hips in frustration. "I'm not a damn model, you know."

"No," she said patiently. "And I'm not a chauffeur, yet I've been driving you around all day like I was."

"A duty you're being well paid for," he reminded her.

She wrinkled her nose. "Oh, yeah. Right. Tell you what," she said. "Pose for a few more shots, and I'll give you a full set of prints, no charge."

"'A few shots' is all I agreed to when you talked me into this nonsense more than an hour ago."

"Can I help it if you're such a handsome model?"

"Flattery will get you nowhere," he said dryly.

"Okay. How about this? You let me take a few more pictures, and I'll chauffeur you around the whole month you're in town."

He frowned a moment, as if considering, then nodded. "All right. You've got yourself a deal."

Grinning, she drew the camera before her face again. "Boot on the boulder," she instructed. "Forearm braced on the knee. Now look off into the distance and make that face you make when you're thinking really hard. Great!" she exclaimed, and clicked away. "Man, you should see this. The sun is setting just behind your left shoulder and creating perfect shadows on your face.

"Give me a forlorn look," she said, continuing to click off shots. "You know. Like you've been running from the law for months, and you're missing that pretty little saloon girl you met up in Dodge City."

"A saloon girl in Dodge City?" He dropped his head back and laughed. "Damn, Ali, where do you get this stuff?"

The transformation laughter made to his face almost made her drop her camera, but she managed to hold on to it and keep clicking. "Part of the job," she told him. "Just part of the job."

Shaking his head, he dragged his foot from the boulder. "You should be a writer, not a photographer." When he realized she was still taking pictures, he held up a hand to block her view. "Would you stop," he complained. "You must've taken a hundred pictures or more."

She reluctantly lowered the camera. "I'll be lucky if a third are worth anything."

He went stock-still. "You didn't say anything about selling these pictures."

"Would you lighten up?" she said, laughing. "I took the pictures for fun, not to sell. Kind of a souvenir for you of your trip to Texas."

"Oh," he said in relief. "Which reminds me," he said, and plopped down on the boulder, stretched out his legs. "You were going to tell me why you're running a bed-and-breakfast, rather than focusing on a career in photography."

Gathering up her tote, she crossed to sit beside him. "Are you sure you want to hear this?" she asked, as she pulled her camera over her head. "It's really boring."

"I wouldn't have asked, if I didn't."

With a shrug, she tucked the camera into her tote. "It goes back to when I dropped out of college during my junior year and moved to Austin."

"Why did you drop out?"

"My parents come from a long line of doctors and they expected me to follow in their footsteps. Carry on the family tradition. That kind of thing."

"And you didn't want to?"

"Not even a little. I did try," she said in her defense. "But I hated all the science courses I was required to take and my grades proved it. I tried to talk my parents into letting me change my major, but they wouldn't listen. They kept saying I wasn't applying myself. That being a doctor was an honorable occupation, a duty even. We argued about it all during Christmas break, and I finally told them that they couldn't force me to become a doctor, that I was going to sign up for the courses *I* wanted to take."

"And did you?"

She grimaced. "For all the good it did me. When they received the bill from the university for my spring tuition and saw what courses I'd signed up for, they refused to pay it. When that didn't whip me into line, they closed the checking account they'd set up for me to pay my college expenses, which left me with no money and no way to pay for my housing, food. Nothing."

"So how did you end up in Texas?"

"Claire Fleming. She and I met our freshman year in college and became best friends. She knew my parents had cut me off and how bummed I was. To cheer me up, she invited me to go to Austin with her to visit her grandmother. I had nothing better to do, so I tagged along.

"To make a long story a little shorter, the Vista belongs to Claire's grandmother, Margaret Fleming. It was a wedding present from her first husband. Sadly he died after they'd been married only a few years. She remarried several years later to some oil guy and moved to Saudi Arabia, but she held on to the house. Said selling it would be like cutting out her heart.

"She came back to the States several times a year

for month-long visits and always stayed at the house. As she got older, it became harder for her to travel and she wasn't able to come as often. You can imagine what happened to the house. What the vandals didn't destroy, varmints did. It was a mess. She'd always hoped that Claire would want the house someday, but Claire fell in love with an Aussie and was planning to move to Australia right after graduation, which she did, by the way. So the grandmother decided to make one final trip to Austin before selling the house. Claire was to meet her there and help her pack up what personal belongings she wanted to keep.

"What I didn't know was that Claire and her grandmother had already discussed my situation, and they'd decided to offer the house to me." She held up a hand. "And, yes, I know it sounds too good to be true. At the time, I thought so, too. But Mimi—that's Claire's grandmother—was dead serious. She really loved the house and didn't want to sell it, and she definitely didn't need the money. So she offered it to me. All she asked in return was that I take care of it and love it as much as she did."

"Sounds like the perfect arrangement."

"It was a sweet deal, all right, but it only resolved my need for housing. I was still broke and without a job. Mimi, Claire and I brainstormed ways I could earn money to cover my expenses and still have time to go to school, and we came up with the idea of renting out the extra bedrooms to college students. It was the perfect setup for me. Since the house is on Town Lake and relatively close to the university, I never had a problem leasing the rooms, which meant I could be really selective about who I leased to."

"If it was such a success, why the change to a bed-and-breakfast?"

She lifted a brow and looked down her nose at him. "Have you ever lived with twelve college students?" She shuddered, remembering. "It was bedlam even on the best day. And there was absolutely no privacy. After I graduated, I decided I wanted the house to be more like a home than a dorm, and I came up with the idea of turning the Vista into a bed-and-breakfast."

"And the grandmother was okay with the change?"

"More than okay. In fact, she gave me the house."

"*Gave* it to you?" he repeated.

She nodded. "I think she'd reconciled herself to the fact that Claire was never going to want it, and she definitely didn't want her son to get his hands on it, so she decided to give it to me."

"Gave it to you," he repeated, doubting her story, since his research had indicated the only property Ali owned was her car.

"It's not official yet," she was quick to tell him. "She only told me about her decision last summer, then she caught pneumonia and passed away just before Thanksgiving. Her estate was sizable, to say the least, so it'll probably take a while for her lawyers to get everything prepared for probate and the necessary papers filed to transfer ownership to me."

She glanced around, and was surprised to see it was getting dark. She hitched the strap to her tote over her shoulder. "I had no idea it was getting so late. We'd better go."

He stood, and offered her a hand.

When she grasped his hand, she felt that now familiar spark of electricity between their palms and watched his face as he pulled her to her feet, wondering if he felt it, too.

"Did you feel that?" she asked.

"What?"

"That sparkly thing when our hands touched."

"Sparkly thing?" He shook his head. "No, can't say that I did."

"Really?" she said in surprise, then frowned and rubbed thoughtfully at her palm. "That's weird. I feel it every time we touch."

Three

Sparkly thing?

Garrett snorted as he climbed into bed. How about a hundred volts of electricity shooting up his arm?

But he sure as hell wasn't going to admit that to Ali. If he'd learned nothing else during his thirty-six years of living, it was never reveal your weaknesses to your enemy.

Enemy?

Frowning thoughtfully, he folded his hands behind his head, and stared up at the ceiling, unsure if that tag still fit. If the stories Ali had told him today were true, she was looking more like a victim, than the enemy.

Her dropping out of college up north and finishing her education in Texas was true enough. He'd unearthed that nugget about her past while doing his own research prior to making the trip to Austin. But nothing he'd found had indicated her move to Texas was due to her parents cutting her off. He might've dismissed her story as exaggeration, if he hadn't already heard his stepmother describe her adoptive parents as cold and heartless people. But in Garrett's opinion, what Ali's parents had done to her was inexcusable. Imagine, a parent who would knowingly leave his child with no money, no job and no prospects…

He shook his head ruefully. Ali was just damn lucky she'd had a fairy godmother waiting in the wings. No telling what would've happened to her if Mimi and Claire hadn't come along, offering her a place to live, as well as the means to support herself.

He frowned, more than a little surprised by the level of compassion he felt building toward Ali. He was going to have to be careful, he told himself. Prior to coming to Austin, he'd had a laundry list of reasons to despise her. He couldn't allow a hard-luck story blind him to the hurt she'd caused his stepmother or allow it to distract him from his purpose for being in her home.

Her life might resemble Cinderella's, but he sure as hell was no Prince Charming, prepared to charge onto the scene to rescue her.

If anything, he'd come to destroy her.

To prove it, he reached for his cell phone and punched in the number of his lawyer.

"Hey, Tom. Garrett. Sorry to call you at home and at such a late hour, but I need you to do some research for me. See if you can locate information on a woman by the name of Margaret Fleming. Her last address was in Saudi Arabia, but she owned property in Austin, Texas.

"No," he replied to Tom's question. "This doesn't have anything to do with Future Concepts' expansion. This is…personal. The woman passed away last November. I want to know who inherited the house she owns in Austin."

He visited a moment longer, then disconnected the call and settled back on the bed.

Ali may not have realized it, he thought in satisfaction, but there was a strong possibility she'd given him the "price" he needed to win her cooperation. That she loved the house was obvious, and Garrett would bet his controlling shares of stock in Future Concepts that she didn't own it.

But *he* would before the month was out.

After chauffeuring Garrett around for three days, Ali had decided two things about her current guest. He had more mood swings than a pregnant woman, and he was the most impatient man she'd ever met in her life.

Most people would just kick back and relax, while riding in a car. Not Garrett. God forbid the man waste a second of his precious time. At the moment, he had his BlackBerry in his hand and was checking his e-mail, a task he had conducted at least four times during the day. It was almost ten o'clock at night, for heaven's sake! Was his correspondence so important he had to check it even at night?

Noticing the brake lights coming on ahead of her, Ali slowed, adjusting her speed to the long line of cars in front of her.

"Uh-oh."

Garrett lifted his gaze from his BlackBerry. "Uh-oh, what? Why are you stopping?"

She tipped her head at the traffic in front of them. "Construction. I forgot the highway crew closes down all but one lane at night so they can work on the interstate when there is less traffic."

Scowling, he closed his BlackBerry and began to drum his fingers impatiently on the console.

After sitting for five minutes at a standstill, he swore. "Dammit! This is ridiculous. There's got to be an alternate route."

She shook her head. "There's not. And even if there was," she added as she looked in the rearview mirror at the long stream of headlights behind her, "there's no way we can get off the interstate now. We're trapped between exits."

His scowl deepened.

The headlights on the cars ahead of her began to blink off, an indication that the drivers had resigned themselves to the delay and had turned off their engines. Ali followed suit, but left the radio playing.

He whipped his head around to peer at her. "Why did you turn off the car?"

She lifted a shoulder and slid down in her seat, making herself more comfortable. "No sense wasting gas. These delays can last up to a half hour or more."

"A half hour!"

"Would you lighten up?" she said with a laugh. "A little delay isn't going to kill you."

He burned her with a look, then turned his gaze back to the windshield to glare through the darkness at the stalled traffic.

Deciding he needed a distraction, she twisted the dial to an oldies' station and cranked up the radio to an earsplitting level.

He clapped his hands over his ears. "What the hell are you doing?" he cried.

She opened her door. "Creating a diversion," she replied as she climbed out. Rounding the hood, she opened the passenger door and grabbed his hand. "Come on, Garrett. They're playing our song."

"What?" he said in confusion, as she all but dragged him out of the car.

"Music. Dance. Get it?" She dropped her hands

to her hips, with a disgusted huff. "Don't tell me you don't know how to dance."

"I know how."

She placed a hand on his shoulder and stepped in close. "So dance with me."

Garrett shot an uneasy glance around at the cars behind them, sure that everyone was staring at them and laughing. "This is ridiculous," he muttered.

"No," she informed him. "It's spontaneous. Fun. Something I don't think you have nearly enough of."

He probably could've resisted, was sure he would have climbed back into the car, if she hadn't pressed her body against his and begun to sway to the slow beat of the Righteous Brothers' song pumping from the car's speakers.

Without conscious thought, he began to sway, too, his body moving in rhythm with hers. A heartbeat later he was guiding her in a slow dance around the car. Later he would be grateful for the darkness, the lack of headlights, would probably curse himself for the chance he had taken in exposing himself to the public eye and the danger he might well have put himself in. But at the moment, all he could think about was how perfectly her body melded to his, how naturally they moved together, how utterly *free* he felt dancing in the middle of an interstate highway with hundreds of people looking on.

The song ended and he swayed slowly to a stop. Instead of releasing her, he turned his face against her hair, painfully aware of every point where their bodies touched. He felt the quickening of her breath against his neck, the tremble of her fingers within his. One smooth glide of his lips over her hair and his mouth was on hers. The pleasure, the taste of her was like taking a fist in the gut, totally unexpected and hitting low and hard.

Her lips were pillows of satin beneath his, her taste an aphrodisiac that streamed through his bloodstream like fire. A part of him knew he should stop, that kissing her was a mistake, that he was chancing blowing the mission he'd come to Austin to accomplish. But he couldn't stop. It took the impatient sound of a car horn to force his mouth from hers. Even then he didn't release her. With his eyes on hers, he searched her gaze, found the same heat in them that fired his veins.

It was Ali who made the first move, taking a step back and hugging her jacket more closely around her. "Uh. Looks like traffic's starting to move."

He glanced toward the cars lined in front of them and saw that headlights were blinking on, engines were starting. "Yeah," he said dully, wondering what had come over him. "Let's get out of here."

Ali didn't know what had happened to Garrett overnight to put him in such a grumpy mood, but if it was because of the kiss they'd shared on the inter-state, he could darn well get over it.

She just hoped she could.

She slid a glance his way. Who'd have thought he could kiss like that? Not her, that was for darn sure. In the blink of an eye, he'd turned a spontaneous street dance into a lustfest…and with very little effort on his part.

And she'd thought the tingles she'd felt when they touched were something. Ha! They were nothing compared to the kick she'd received when his lips had touched hers. She released a slow breath, the reminder alone enough to make her want to whip the car over to the shoulder and jump him.

She slanted him another look. So why wasn't he similarly affected? From the moment he'd appeared for breakfast, he'd done nothing but scowl. And as for conversation… Well, there wasn't any. They'd been driving all morning, with him giving two-word commands—turn right, turn left, leaving her with no sense of where he wanted to go or exactly what he was looking for.

And as far as the kiss went… Well, he hadn't said a word about *that*.

She firmed her lips. Well, if that's the way he wanted to play it, she could pretend it hadn't happened, too.

"Maybe if you told me what kind of property you're interested in," she said, "I could be of more help."

He continued to frown at the map displayed on the screen of his portable GPS. "A minimum of ten acres, preferably more."

"What about accessibility to public transportation?" she asked, hoping to narrow the parameters somewhat. "Wouldn't that factor into where you'd want to build?"

"Not necessarily."

"Great," she muttered under her breath. "Another irresponsible employer adding to Austin's already burgeoning traffic problems."

He glanced her way. "I'm not irresponsible."

"If you build where there's no access to public transportation, you are," she informed him. "You'd be adding to traffic and that's irresponsible in my book."

Scowling, he turned off the GPS. "For your information, I consider the effect my company has on a city's traffic, as well as its effect on the environment."

"How?" she challenged, doubting that he considered anything but profits when he made decisions regarding his company.

"At the current facilities on the East Coast, we offer a shuttle service from specified locations around the city. Employees who take advantage of the shuttle, and those who ride in a carpool with a minimum of two other employees, receive monetary rewards for their efforts. If I build a complex in Austin, I'll implement the same policy here."

"If?" she repeated. "I thought building here was a foregone conclusion."

"Only if I'm able to find a suitable site."

"Oh."

"Yeah. Oh."

Having had enough of his sour disposition, she tightened her hands on the wheel. "Why are you in such a bad mood?"

He set the GPS on the floorboard at his feet. "I'm not in a bad mood."

"Well, you darn sure look like you are." She held up a hand. "Oh, wait. I forget that expression is normal for you."

He nailed her with a look. "Are you purposely trying to tick me off? If so, you're doing a damn good job."

That's it, she thought angrily and whipped the car to the side of the road. She'd had all she was going to take of his sour attitude. Ramming the gearshift into Park, she spun on the seat to face him. "Don't try blaming your bad mood on me," she warned. "You were grumpy when we started out this morning."

"Well, maybe if I could get a good night's sleep, I'd be in a better mood," he shot back at her.

"And you're not sleeping is my fault?"

"It is if you're the one responsible for putting that lousy mattress on the bed."

Her jaw dropped. "There's nothing wrong with that mattress! It's top-of-the-line and almost new."

"It sags on one side."

"So sleep on the other! Better yet, sleep in a different bed. You leased the entire house. Pick another one to sleep in."

"Fine. I want yours."

She gaped. "You *what?*"

"I want yours. You said I could have my pick."

"I didn't mean mine!"

"Why not? You said I could have my pick."

"Of the rooms you *leased*," she informed him.

"Too late. You already said I could have my pick, and I choose your bed."

She fought for patience. "If you want to sleep in one of the other rooms upstairs, fine. You certainly paid for the right to sleep wherever you want."

"I certainly did," he agreed, "and I choose to sleep in your bed."

She started to respond, then closed her mouth and narrowed her eyes in suspicion. "You're just trying to avoid the real issue, aren't you?"

"And that would be…?"

"Kissing me last night. Well, let me tell you something, buddy," she went on before he could say anything. "It was no big deal. Okay? As far as I'm concerned it's forgotten. Over. Done with. Never happened."

"Oh, really?"

"Yeah, really. I—"

Before she could finish, his mouth was on hers, smothering her words. There was no slow buildup to *this* kiss. His mouth came down hard on hers, forcing her head back against the seat and her pulse into a gallop. She tasted the anger in him, the heat. A split second later his lips softened, sweeping over hers with a seductive slowness that stole her breath, before he nipped at her lower lip and withdrew. She opened her eyes to find he'd settled in his seat again, his gaze on the windshield.

"Let's check out the area around Bastrop."

She stared, wondering if she'd imagined it all. "B-Bastrop?"

"Yeah. From the map I was looking at, it appears to be near Austin, yet far enough away that parcels of land are probably still sold by the acre, rather than by the square inch."

She straightened and pulled the gearshift into Drive, her hand shaking a bit. "B-Bastrop's a nice town," she said, anxious to prove she was as unaffected by the kiss as he seemed to be. "Lots of history and beautiful old homes. I would imagine their tax base is lower than Austin's, which would be a bonus for your company and whatever employees might choose to live there."

He pointed to a convenience store up ahead. "Pull over and I'll buy a paper, so we can check out what's for sale."

She turned into the parking lot and pulled up alongside the newspaper rack, her pulse rate almost back to normal. "Wouldn't it be easier to just call a Realtor?"

"It would," he agreed, as he climbed from the car, then ducked his head back inside. "Better yet, why don't I just rent a billboard and announce to the whole world I'm here looking for land?" Muttering under his breath, he slammed the door and strode for the newspaper stand.

Jerk, she thought resentfully as she watched him feed coins into the slot. His paranoia about keeping his presence in Austin a secret was wearing thin. She could see how it made good business-sense for him to play his cards close to his chest. But wasn't he carrying this a little far? He never took a step out of the house without those stupid sunglasses. And earlier, when she stopped at the window of a fast-food joint to order sodas, he'd slumped down in the seat and kept his face averted, like he was afraid someone was going to recognize him, which was totally nuts. It wasn't like he was a movie star or something. He was a business-man, for cripes' sake! Prior to him coming to the Vista, if she had passed him on the street, she wouldn't have even given him a second look.

Unfortunately he chose that moment to bend over to pull a newspaper from the rack, giving her a full view of his nicely shaped butt, and her mouth went dry as dust. Okay, she admitted, wetting her lips. Maybe she would've looked twice. But she doubted she would've recognized him. And even if she had, it wouldn't have occurred to her that he was in Austin to buy property. For all she'd know, he could be on vacation. All this hush-hush, top-secret stuff was ridiculous.

He jumped into the car and slid down in the seat as he slammed the door. "Drive!"

She blinked in surprise. "Excuse me?"

He lifted his head slightly to peer out the rear window, then dropped back down. "I think the guy at the gas pump recognized me."

"So?"

"So get the hell out of here!" he shouted.

She stomped on the accelerator and careened onto the highway, sending the rearend of the car fishtailing crazily.

"Is he following us?" he asked.

She looked in the rearview mirror and saw that the truck had indeed pulled onto the highway behind them. "I don't know that he's following us, but he is behind us."

"Speed up."

Though she wasn't sure the rental she was driving could outrun the truck, she pressed down harder on the accelerator.

"Is he still there?" he asked after a minute.

She glanced in the rearview mirror again. "Yeah. About four car-lengths behind."

"Faster."

She shot him a look. "Are you crazy? I'm already going thirty over the speed limit."

"So go fifty! Just lose him."

She glanced in the rearview mirror again. "Uh-oh," she murmured, and lifted her foot off the accelerator.

"What are you doing?" he yelled. "I said speed up, not slow down!"

"I don't know what whirling red lights mean where you're from," she told him, "but in Texas, they mean pull over."

He sat up and looked out the rear window. "Ah, hell," he groaned, then turned to scowl at her. "You might have told me the cops around here drive unmarked vehicles."

"And ruin your fun?" she said sweetly. She hit the button to lower the window and greeted the patrolman approaching the car. "Good morning, Officer."

He touched a finger to the brim of his hat. "Morning, ma'am. Is there a reason you were driving forty-five miles per hour over the speed limit?"

"Only one," she replied, and hooked a thumb over her shoulder at Garrett. "Him."

Garrett hissed a breath between his teeth, then yanked off his sunglasses and leaned around Ali to look up at the policeman. "My fault entirely," he said. "I didn't realize you were a police officer."

"Ah," the patrolman said, nodding. "So speeding's all right, so long as the law isn't around."

"No, no, no," Garrett replied in frustration. "That's not what I meant, at all. I was buying a newspaper and saw you watching me. I thought you'd recognized me, so I told Ali to lose you."

"Why don't you dig yourself a little deeper?" Ali said under her breath.

Garrett burned her with a look, then shifted his gaze to the police officer again. "I'm Garrett Miller," he said, as if that explained everything.

The officer looked at Ali. "What? Is he some kind of rock star or something?"

Ali rolled her lips inward, to keep from laughing. "Uh. No, sir. He owns Future Concepts, a computer company."

When the officer's expression remained blank, she looked over at Garrett and shrugged. "Your turn."

"It's not funny," Garrett snapped as he flopped down on the sofa.

"No, it's not," Ali agreed, trying her best to hide her smile. "But if you could have seen your face when Officer Wilhelm told you to put your hands on the trunk of the car and spread 'em…." She sputtered a laugh, unable to help herself. "Now *that* was funny!"

Scowling, he folded his arms across his chest. "Well, I'm glad you found it humorous. Being frisked like a common criminal certainly isn't my idea of fun."

"I'd think you'd be relieved," she said, feigning wide-eyed innocence. "You told him everything about yourself except your favorite color of underwear and he still didn't have a clue who you were."

"No, but the dispatcher recognized my name."

"Which is all that saved you from taking a ride in the backseat of a patrol car," she reminded him.

"You're really enjoying this, aren't you?"

She didn't even try to hide her smile. "Uh-huh."

"Why?"

"Honestly? Because I think you place way too much importance on yourself."

He lifted a brow. "Oh, really."

"Yes, really. You need to lighten up. Forget you're a zillionaire for a while. Kick up your heels and have some fun for a change."

He snorted. "You don't have a clue what it's like to be me."

"Other than boring, no."

"Boring?" He pushed to his feet, his jaw clenched in anger. "Let me tell you what it's like to be me," he said, bearing down on her. "Money attracts people, including crazies and crooks. And unlike our friendly police officer this morning, most people recognize my name, if not my face, which causes problems for me. Because of my success, I haven't been able to fly commercially in years. I can't go to a movie theater or a restaurant, or anywhere for that matter, without

drawing attention. If I do venture out to a highly pub-
licized event, I'm forced to take a bodyguard along,
just in case some lunatic decides to try to kidnap me
for ransom.

"And as for having fun," he continued, "unless it can
be boxed and delivered for me to enjoy in the privacy
of my home, I can forget it. Going out in public is a
freedom I lost the day I made my first million."

By the time he finished his tirade, he was standing
nose to nose with Ali, so close she could feel the
warmth of his breath on her mouth.

"I—I had no idea," she stammered.

"Most people don't. They envy my success, even
try to emulate it, but they don't know what success
has cost me, what it would cost them if it was theirs."
Hiding a smile, he turned away. "But you'll get a
taste of it soon enough."

She tensed. "What do you mean?"

"Our good friend Officer Wilhelm gave us his
word he wouldn't tell anyone about seeing me, but
I'll bet you money he tells someone. Or the dispatcher will. And if one of them does tell, you can
expect the media to start arriving by morning."

Her eyes rounded. "Here?"

"Here and anywhere we dare venture. Media
hounds are like fleas on a dog. Irritating as hell and
all but impossible to get rid of."

* * *

Ali paced the living room, stealing an occasional peek through the blinds she'd closed. So far, so good, she thought. Not a person or a car in sight.

Confident that Officer Wilhelm had been true to his word—or Garrett had exaggerated his own importance, which is what she felt was more the case—she abandoned her watch and went to the kitchen for something to drink.

"I'm getting a glass of wine," she called to him in the den. "Do you want one?"

"Yes, please."

She filled two glasses and carried them to the den. She glanced over her shoulder at the television as she handed Garrett his drink. "What are you watching?"

"Jeopardy."

Figures, she thought, biting back a smile, as she sank down on the sofa beside him. "Who's winning?" she asked.

"Guy on the left. They're about to start Double Jeopardy, though, so that could change things."

A commercial came on and he lifted the remote to surf through channels.

"Do you have something against commercials?" she asked in frustration.

"Other than being an utter waste of my time?" He shook his head. "Not particularly."

"You advertise," she reminded him.

"Some."

"Hypocrite."

"Why? Because I refuse to watch a boring commercial?"

She opened a hand. "If the shoe fits…"

"It's marketing's responsibility to capture the attention of the consumer. If they fail—" he clicked the remote "—which my company's commercials seldom do," he informed her, "I change channels until I find something that does catch my attention. Like that," he said and set the remote aside.

"The stock market report?" She fanned her face. "Stop. Please. I'm not sure my heart can take the excitement."

He shot her a scowl. "Why don't you go spy on the reporters lurking outside some more?"

She tucked her feet beneath her and took a sip of her wine. "There's nobody out there."

"There will be by morning."

"You're full of bologna. No reporters are coming here."

"Wanna bet?"

"As a matter of fact, I do," she said.

"Five hundred says they'll be here by morning."

She considered, then shook her head. "Too rich for my blood."

"Okay, if you don't want to gamble cash, put up some of your photography of equal value."

She hesitated a moment, then stood and stuck out her hand. "All right, you've got yourself a deal."

He took her hand, but instead of shaking it, he used it to haul himself to his feet. "I prefer photos of landscape, rather than people."

She lifted a brow. "Kind of confident you're going to win, aren't you?"

He shot her a wink and turned away. "When it's a sure thing, I can afford to be."

She frowned at his back. "Where are you going?"

"To bed."

"Hey, wait a minute!" she cried, hurrying after him. "That's the way to my room."

"I know. Remember? I chose your bed to sleep in tonight."

"You're not sleeping in my bed!"

He opened the door to her private quarters. "Yes, I am."

She ran after him, praying she hadn't left underwear or any other equally embarrassing items lying around. "Garrett, really," she pleaded. "You can sleep in any bed you want. Just not mine."

He sank down on the side of her bed and bounced a couple of times, as if testing the mattress. "I prefer this one," he said, and stood, pulling his sweater over his head.

Ali stared, unable to tear her gaze away from the oh-so-sexy chest he'd exposed. Who'd've thought?

she thought, as heat crawled up her neck, threatening her air. She'd been pressed against his chest the night before when they'd kissed, but they had both had on jackets, which had done a heck of a job of concealing what proved to be a wonderfully muscled and toned body.

"You win," she managed to say, and darted for the adjoining bath. "Just let me get my stuff."

She grabbed her pajamas and toothbrush and hustled back out, careful to keep her gaze fixed straight ahead, fearing he'd stripped completely while she was out of the room. In the doorway, she groped blindly behind her for the knob, to pull the door closed behind her.

"Ali?"

She stopped, but didn't dare turn around. "What?"

"Since you enjoyed kissing me so much, I thought you'd want to sleep with me, too."

Setting her jaw, she slapped a hand against the wall switch, turning off the light, and yanked the door closed behind her.

She wasn't sure, but she'd swear she heard him laughing as she stalked to the den.

Score one for the home team, Garrett thought, chuckling, as he climbed into bed. Judging by Ali's fast exit following his comment about her sleeping with him, it appeared he'd succeeded in getting even with her for the hard time she'd given him over his run-in with the law and Officer Wilhelm.

He punched up his pillow and lay back, wondering where she would sleep. There were plenty of empty beds to choose from, including the one he'd slept in prior to claiming hers. He'd blamed his inability to sleep on the sagging mattress, which was what had started the whole where-will-Garrett-sleep debate. But Garrett's sleeplessness wasn't due to a sagging bed.

It was due to the Vista's innkeeper.

His smile faded. He hadn't intended for it to happen, had done everything within his power to prevent it, but it was true.

Ali Moran had gotten under his skin.

It had started with the stories she'd told him of her past and his growing suspicion that she was more victim than enemy, and had quickly escalated to a physical attraction that grew stronger each day he spent with her.

He dragged his pillow over his face to smother a groan. What the hell was he going to do now? he asked himself in frustration. He'd arrived in Austin prepared to despise her, ruin her if necessary, and now all he could think about was sleeping with her? She was his stepmother's daughter, for God's sake!

He could handle this, he told himself. It was simply a matter of refocusing his goals, keeping a respectable distance from her.

He drew in a deep breath, telling himself he could do this. He'd maintained his objectivity in tougher situations.

He was immediately proved wrong. That one breath had filled his senses with her scent, evoking images of her. Lying in this very bed. The two of them together. Her nude body wrapped around his like a vine.

Groaning, he rolled to his stomach and buried his face in the pillow.

"Focus," he told himself sternly. "Just focus on the damn goal."

He'd call his lawyer tomorrow, he promised himself. Find out if Tom had discovered who owned the Vista yet. Knowledge was power and power was what he needed to keep the scales weighted on his side…and hopefully his mind focused on his goal and not on the Vista's innkeeper.

Ali tiptoed into her bedroom and cautiously approached the bed. She really didn't want to wake Garrett—or be in the same room with him after the crack he'd made about her sleeping with him—but she preferred both to calling the police.

At the side of the bed, she leaned to touch his shoulder. The next thing she knew, she was flat on her back on the mattress and Garrett was straddling her, his fist reared back, like he was going to slug her.

"Garrett! It's me! Ali!"

He blinked, then rolled off her, swearing. "Dammit, Ali! Don't ever slip up on me like that again."

Eyeing him warily, she dragged herself up to a sitting position. "Don't worry. I won't."

He twisted around to switch on the bedside lamp, then slumped back against the headboard, scowling. "Sorry," he muttered, then glanced over at her. "I didn't hurt you, did I?"

"N-no. Scared me plenty, though." Realizing the skill and strength required to accomplish a move like the one he'd just performed, she asked, "Where'd you learn to do that?"

"Self-defense class." His scowl deepened. "When your life has been threatened as many times as mine, you take what precautions you can."

"Threatened?" she repeated.

"Yes, threatened." He slanted her a look. "Why were you sneaking around in my room, anyway?"

"I'd remind you it's *my* room, but we've got more pressing matters to worry about."

"Like what?"

"Like the men outside."

He shot up from the bed and ran to peer out the window.

The sight of him standing there in nothing but black silk boxer shorts was almost enough to make her forget about the men she'd seen skulking around outside.

Almost.

"You can't see them from there," she told him. "They're out front. On the street side of the rock wall."

He dove across the bed for the lamp and switched it off, plunging the room into darkness.

"What are you doing?" she cried.

He clapped a hand over her mouth. "Shh," he whispered. "We don't want them to know we're awake."

She shoved his hand away. "Why not?"

"If they think we're asleep and unaware of their presence, hopefully they'll stay where they are and wait for daylight before approaching the house."

"But I thought you didn't want them here?" she said in confusion.

"I don't." He dropped his elbows to his knees and his head to his hands. "We've got to think of a way to get out of here without them seeing us."

"*We?* As in you and me?" She shook her head. "Uh-uh. Sorry, buddy. But I'm not going anywhere with you."

"You have no choice."

"Oh, I have lots of choices," she informed him. "The most obvious is staying right here in my own house."

"You can't. It's no longer safe."

The somberness of his tone turned her blood to ice. "What do you mean, it's not safe? We're talking men toting cameras here, not Uzis."

"There's something I need to tell you," he said

hesitantly. "I wasn't completely honest with you about why I wanted my presence here kept a secret."

She dropped her head back with a moan. "I really hate middle of the night confessions."

"My life's been threatened."

She snapped her head back up to stare. "Somebody wants you dead?"

"It appears that way."

"But…why?"

"If I knew that, I'd probably know who wanted to kill me."

"And you think whoever that person is, is outside my house right now?"

"No. I'm fairly confident it's only photographers out there. But once they make my presence here known," he added, "I can almost promise you the person who threatened me will come here looking for me."

She stared, trying to make sense of what he was telling her, then held up a hand. "Wait a minute. Just because somebody wants you dead, doesn't mean I'm in danger."

"I'm afraid it does. If he comes here and finds me gone, he may take you."

"Me?" She choked a laugh. "Like anyone would want me," she said wryly.

"He would, if he thinks you're important to me."

Her heart faltered, then kicked hard against her chest. "You mean he might use me as a hostage?"

"It's possible and it's a chance I'm not willing to take."

Vivid images of every movie or news clip she'd seen involving hostages filled her mind. And not a one of them were pretty. "Oh my God," she whispered. "What are we going to do?"

"We're getting out of here." He rolled off the bed and snatched up his jeans, tugged them on. "I'm going upstairs to pack my stuff and make some phone calls. You'll need to pack a bag, too. Enough to hold you for a couple of weeks."

"A couple of weeks!" she cried. "I can't be gone a couple of weeks!"

"Hopefully you won't be," he told her. "And no lights," he warned, as he headed for the door. "We don't want them to suspect we're up to anything."

Garrett took the rear stairs two at a time and broke into a run when he reached the second floor. Getting out of Austin was imperative, but where to go was a problem. He couldn't call for his private jet. It would take too much time for his pilot to fly to Texas. Public transportation was out, as it made him too visible. That meant finding some place close to hide out for a while, somewhere no one would think to look for him.

He knew of only one place that fit his needs: his stepmother's son's ranch.

Muttering a curse, he paced his room. He didn't

want to call Jase. Calling him meant explaining where he was, what he was up to, and his stepmother had made them promise they wouldn't search for Ali, that they would respect her request for privacy and leave her alone.

But *he* hadn't promised, he reminded himself. Jase and Eddie, Jase's father, had promised.

Admonishing himself of any guilt for his actions, he pulled his cell phone from his briefcase and scrolled through the address book until he found Jase's home number.

Mandy, Jase's wife, answered on the second ring.

"Hello?" she said sleepily.

"Mandy, it's Garrett."

"Well, hey, Garrett," she said, sounding surprised to hear from him. "What are you doing calling me in the middle of the night?"

"I'm in a jam. Is Jase there?"

"He's in Washington visiting his mother. Haven't you seen him?"

"No, and I really need his help."

"Call him at Barbara's. I'm sure he'll do whatever he can to help you out."

"I can't call him at Barbara's," he said in frustration. "You'll have to help."

"You know I'll do whatever I can, but wouldn't it make better sense to just call Jase, since he's in Washington and I'm in Texas?"

"That's just it. I'm in Texas, too."

"What!" she cried. "Where?"

"Ali Moran's house."

A pregnant pause followed his announcement.

"You're at Ali's?" she said.

"Yes. I'll explain later, but we need a place to hide out for a couple of days. I was hoping we could stay in one of the hunting cabins."

"Of course you can," she told him, then asked hesitantly, "Does Ali know you're Barbara's stepson?"

"No, and you've got to promise me you'll keep it that way."

"Are you sure you know what you're doing?" she asked doubtfully. "Barbara made y'all promise you'd leave Ali alone."

He felt a stab of guilt and quickly shrugged it off. "Jase and Eddie promised. I promised nothing."

"That's splitting hairs, don't you think?"

He drew in a breath. "We can discuss this later, okay? Right now I've got to get us out of Austin."

"Okay. But when Barbara finds out about this, I'm pointing all ten fingers at you, buddy. Understand? I'm not chancing getting on my mother-in-law's bad side just to save your butt, even if it is a cute one."

The next call Garrett made was to the head of his company's security department.

"Joe, it's Garrett. We've got a problem."

Four

The plan Garrett devised for his and Ali's escape included every mode of transportation, with the exception of air. He probably would've considered that, too, if he or Ali had known how to fly.

Their adventure started on land, with them sneaking down to the pier and climbing aboard the rowboat Ali kept on hand for her guests to use. With moonlight as their only illumination, they'd rowed across the lake and docked near the shoreline of the Hyatt Regency. From there, they'd grabbed a taxi for the airport, where Garrett had insisted Ali rent a vehicle, claiming if he rented it he would be leaving a paper trail that could easily be followed.

After loading their luggage into the rental, they'd left Austin, with Ali behind the wheel. She had thought he would insist on driving, had even suggested it, but he had reminded her she had rented the car and had listed herself as the sole driver, a legality Ali was willing to overlook in exchange for some much needed sleep. Apparently Garrett wasn't.

Though she'd repeatedly asked him their final destination, the most she had been able to get out of him was that he'd arranged for them to stay in a friend's hunting cabin.

"I feel like I'm playing connect the dots," she said wearily, as she made the turn off the highway that carried them beneath an iron arch bearing the brand CCC. "Turn here, turn there. Go straight. At least tell me if we're getting close."

"We're almost there. Keep driving until you see a small wooden arrow on the right that says 'Hunting Cabins.'"

"Are you sure these people are expecting us?" she asked uneasily. "It's four o'clock in the morning. I don't want somebody shooting at me, thinking I'm a trespasser."

"They know we're coming."

"Have you been here before?"

"Once." He pointed ahead. "There's the sign."

Ali made the turn, slowing when her headlights illuminated a road that was little more than a path. "Now I know why you told me to request an SUV from the rental agency."

"Pointless to hide, if you're going to make yourself easily accessible."

"I shouldn't even be hiding," she said petulantly. "I should be at home asleep in my bed."

"If you were home, I guarantee you wouldn't be sleeping. You'd be listening to your doorbell and phone ring off the wall. And if those guys hanging around outside have figured out a way to scale the rock wall that borders the street-side of your property, you might find yourself staring at a stranger's face in your window—or worse, the lens of a camera. And when daylight arrives, you can bet at least one helicopter will be hovering over your house, taking aerial shots." He waved a dismissive hand. "But once those pictures hit the papers, you wouldn't have time to worry about the cameras any longer. You'd be too busy trying to stay alive."

"Okay, okay," she snapped. "I get your point."

"Good. I really don't want to have this conversation again."

She saw a large shadow looming ahead and hit the bright lights. "Is that the cabin?" she asked.

"One of them."

"How many are there?"

"Six, as I recall. They've left the cabin on the far end open for us."

She'd driven past two, when he said, "It's the next one"

"But you said there were six," she said in confusion.

"At least that many. But there are only three on this particular road."

She pulled to a stop, and glanced in the rearview mirror at the path they'd followed, barely visible in the red glow of her brake lights. "You call that a road?"

He climbed from the vehicle. "Accessibility," he reminded her.

"Yeah, yeah," she grumbled, as she trudged toward the rear of the SUV to help him with the bags. An eerie howl sounded in the distance and sent her scurrying to Garrett's side. "Did you hear that?" she asked in a nervous whisper.

"Hear what?"

The howl sounded again. *"That,"* she said, with a shudder.

He pushed her tote against her chest, forcing her to take it. "Probably a coyote."

"Probably?" With her gaze fixed on the darkness, she eased closer to his side. "You aren't sure?"

He pulled out her suitcase and set it on the ground. "You're the one from Texas. Don't you know a coyote when you hear one?"

"Sorry," she said dryly, "but we don't have many coyotes roaming the streets of downtown Austin."

He closed the rear hatch and the interior light blinked off, leaving them in inky darkness. He tried to turn, but with Ali on one side and her suitcase on the other, he was trapped.

"If you'll give me some room," he said in frustration, "I'll lead the way to the cabin."

She grabbed the handle of her suitcase and dragged it out of his path, but remained where she was. "No way, buster. You're not leaving me to bring up the rear. The last person on the trail is always the one plucked off and never seen again."

He heaved a sigh. "I'm sure there's logic in there somewhere, but I'm too damn tired at the moment to reason it out."

With Ali sticking to him like glue, he made his way to the cabin. Once inside, it didn't take Ali long to figure out the cabin had only one bed, which she was quick to point out to Garrett.

"So we'll share," he replied. "It's a king. It's certainly big enough."

"Both of us in the same bed?"

He shrugged off his jacket and tossed it to a chair. "If you have a problem sharing, you can sleep on the couch."

She glanced through the doorway at the couch in the other room, thinking about the eerie howling she'd heard, as well as the lunatic who supposedly wanted Garrett dead. Deciding that sleeping on the couch held about as much appeal as being the last person on the trail, she snatched up pillows and began erecting a wall down the center of the bed.

"Line of demarcation," she warned him.

Ali didn't expect to sleep a wink. Not with the threat of an assassin on her mind and Garrett on the other side of the bed. To her surprise, within minutes of closing her eyes, she slipped into a deep sleep and didn't stir until hours later, when sunlight flooding through the bedroom window pricked at her eyelids. In an effort to block the sun, she folded an arm over her head and snuggled deeper into the cocoon of bedding.

Her mind slowly registered a difference in the firmness of the wall of pillows at her back, as well as the heat it was producing. Praying the cause wasn't what she feared, she cautiously pushed her buttocks against the wall and froze when she met the unmistakable shape and resistance of an erection.

"Don't panic," a sleepy voice said from behind her. "Men wake up like this all the time."

She twisted around to find Garrett directly behind her. "And that's supposed to make me feel better?"

"Only if you considered it a threat." He lifted a shoulder. "But if you prefer to claim ownership for producing it…."

"Claim ownership?" she repeated, then sputtered a laugh and rolled from the bed, pleased to discover he had a sense of humor. "As if."

"Where are you going?" he called after her.

"To get dressed."

"Don't you want to finish what you started?"

She fluttered a hand, but kept walking. "No, thanks."

After dressing, Ali went to the kitchen in search of food, and found Garrett sitting at the table in the breakfast nook, working at his laptop. "Have you eaten?" she asked, as she passed him on her way to the refrigerator.

"Nibbled."

"Well, nibbling's not going to cut it for me. I'm starving." She opened the refrigerator and was surprised to find it fully stocked. "Wow. Your friends really know how to make a person feel welcome."

"Mandy likes to play mother."

She froze, her hand on a bowl of fruit. *Mandy?* Forcing the tension from her shoulders, she pulled out the bowl of fruit. "I, uh, assumed your friend was a male."

"Mandy is Jase's wife. They're both friends."

A pitifully brief explanation, but at least she now knew this Mandy person wasn't a romantic interest of Garrett's.

Not that she cared, she told herself.

She dropped down on the chair opposite him and plucked a grape from the bowl. "What are you doing?" she asked curiously.

"Checking my e-mail."

"You can get Internet access in the boonies?" she asked doubtfully.

He tapped a finger against the side of his laptop. "Thanks to a wireless card from my cell phone provider. Anywhere I can receive cell phone reception, I can access the Internet."

"Wow!" She popped the grape into her mouth, chewed. "So? Any word on the guy who's threatened you?"

"No."

"Have you checked to see if you've made the news?"

"No mention, yet."

"Well, that's good, isn't it? It means we're safe here, right?"

"For the time being."

Grimacing, she fished a strawberry from the bowl. "You could've lied, you know," she informed him, as she sank her teeth into the strawberry. "I could use some reassurance here."

"I'm not going to lie just to ease your mind." He closed the lid of his laptop and met her gaze. "But if it'll make you feel better, the more time that passes without my whereabouts making the news, the more likely it is the person who's threatening me will fall into the trap my security team has set for him."

"You consider that reassuring?" With a woeful shake of her head, she rose. "If that's the best you can do, I'm pulling a Scarlett O'Hara."

"What's a Scarlett O'Hara?"

"Putting off until tomorrow what I don't want to think about today."

"What does that resolve?"

"Nothing for you, maybe," she told him as she moved to the den, "but it works wonders for me." She stopped before the fireplace to look at the portrait hanging above it. "Who're they?" she asked curiously.

"Jase's parents."

"They look nice," she said.

"I wouldn't know. I never met them."

"Sometimes you can tell a person's personality just by looking," she said, studying the couple's faces. "Look at her smile. It's not just on her lips, it's in her eyes. And him," she said, pointing. "The way he's holding his arm around her, his stance? He obviously adores her and is very protective of her."

"That's quite a lot to assume from a simple photograph."

"Some things can't be faked." She ambled on, smoothing a hand over the supple leather of the sofa's back, as she looked around. "This is a cool place.

Rustic, yet comfy. Much nicer than what I'd expect a hunter's cabin to look like."

"This was Jase's home."

She glanced back to find Garrett had moved to stand in the doorway between the kitchen and den, and was watching her.

"Why'd he move?" she asked.

"It was Mandy's idea. After they married, she wanted to live in the family home."

"Family home?" Her imagination conjured a big rambling house full of kids and laughter. "I guess his brothers and sisters didn't have a problem with that?"

He seemed to hesitate a moment, then shook his head. "Jase was the Calhouns' only child. He inherited their entire estate after their deaths."

"Wow," she said and crossed to peer out the front window. "He inherited all this?"

"Yes."

"How big is it?"

"I have no idea. Huge, I would imagine. I know he raises cattle and has a large pecan orchard business, plus he leases hunting rights and cabins to hunters during hunting season. I'd think all that would require a substantial number of acres."

"Probably." She turned to him. "Do you think he'd mind if I wandered around and took some pictures?"

"Of what?"

"Nature, silly," she said, laughing. "There are

some gorgeous old trees behind the cabin, and woods are usually full of all kinds of interesting vegetation."

"I don't think he'd mind, as long as you didn't stray too far."

"Cool!" She started for the bedroom to get her camera, then stopped, remembering the coyote she'd heard howling the night before. "Want to come along?" she asked hopefully.

He pushed away from the wall. "Why not? There's nothing else to do."

She beamed a smile. "Great. I'll get my camera. Won't take a second."

When she returned, Garrett was standing before the gun case, studying its contents. Her blood chilled, as she watched him take out a handgun.

"Uh, what are you doing?" she asked uneasily.

He spun the cylinder, checking the chambers for bullets. "Never know what you might run into in the woods."

"Do you think the guy who's after you will come here?"

He shrugged. "Best to be prepared."

She gulped, wishing she hadn't asked. "Do you know how to shoot a gun?"

He tucked the pistol into the waist of his jeans. "I rescued Zelda."

"Zelda? The video game?"

At his nod, she choked a laugh. "Just my luck. Of

all the men in the world to get marooned with, I get stuck with a computer nerd who thinks he's embodied with super powers."

Garrett sat on a log, watching Ali stroll alongside the creek, snapping pictures.

In spite of the danger lurking somewhere beyond the boundaries of the ranch, he felt surprisingly relaxed, calm even. He'd been living with the threat of his would-be assassin long enough to know that his current mood wasn't normal. He also knew Ali was responsible for the change. She had a way of dealing with adversity that reduced its importance, made the most dire situation seem almost comical.

Pulling a Scarlett O'Hara.

He shook his head in amusement. Leave it to Ali to come up with something like that. But as ridiculous as her method sounded, he couldn't argue its success. Caught in a similar situation, another woman would be wringing her hands and wailing about her plight. Not Ali. In spite of the danger they might be in, she was seemingly having the time of her life, crawling over rocks and stumps, taking pictures of plants and bugs, and all because she refused to think about their problem.

Some might consider her method of dealing with adversity a form of denial, foolish and nonproductive. A week ago, Garrett would have thought the same damn thing. But after spending time with her and experiencing, if only by association, the benefits of her methodology, he was beginning to believe the whole world would be a better place if more people took Ali's approach to life.

"Careful," he called to her, as her foot slipped on a rock. "That water might not be deep, but I'll bet it's cold."

"And icky," she said, making a face, as she looked through the viewfinder. "Lots of moss and slime. Oh!" she squealed. "There's a turtle."

"In the water?"

"Hiding under a rock." She lowered the camera and motioned for him to join her. "Come look."

"Thanks, but I've seen a turtle before."

"Not one this big. He's huge!"

Heaving a sigh, Garrett pulled the pistol from his waistband and set it on the log, before crossing to her.

She lifted the camera strap over her head and dropped it over his. "You can see him better through the zoom lens," she explained. "Hunker down here," she said, pointing to the spot where she'd been standing. "He's on the far side of the creek."

Garrett squatted down and brought the camera before his face. "I don't see anything."

She stooped behind him to peer over his shoulder. "Move the camera a little bit to the left. A little more. Do you see it now?"

He lowered the camera in disgust. "I don't see anything but rocks and muddy water."

"Oh, for heaven's sake," she fussed, and reached over his shoulders to bring the camera before his face again. Placing her cheek next to his, to align their vision, she nudged the camera a fraction to the left. "There. Do you see him now?"

See what? Garrett wasn't sure he hadn't been struck blind. He'd heard of sensory overload before, but he had never personally experienced its debilitating powers. With Ali's breasts hugging the back of his neck like a cushioned collar, her cheek chafing like silk against his, and her strawberry-scented breath teasing his nostrils, all he could think was, with a slight turn of his head, he could taste her strawberry-flavored lips. A quarter turn more, and he could bury his face in the pillowed softness of her breasts.

"Well, do you?" she asked impatiently. She glanced his way, and drew back with a start, when she found him looking at her and not the turtle. Her eyes rounded. "You're feeling it, aren't you?" she cried. "That sizzle of sensation?"

He considered lying, but it seemed pointless to continue to deny what must be obvious.

"Makes you want to test it, doesn't it? See how far we can push it without getting burned."

"Yeah," she breathed, and wet her lips.

Without allowing himself time to think of consequences, he turned on the balls of his feet, caught her face between his hands and stood, bringing her mouth to his. He tasted the strawberries that had teased him moments before, found the lingering sweetness of grapes, before her lips parted beneath his on a sigh, inviting him to deepen the kiss. He did so gladly, exploring the secret crevices, teasing her tongue until it danced with his.

"Sizzling yet?" he murmured against her lips.

"Oh, yeah," she breathed. "How about you?"

He slipped his hands inside her jacket and smoothed his hands up her ribs. "I'm not sure. Describe the sensation to me."

Her breath caught as his thumbs bumped over the fullness of her breasts. "Can't," she said, releasing the breath on a shuddery sigh against his lips. "Brain's fried."

He was afraid his was, too. The curves his hands traced were soft and utterly feminine, her body's response to his touch sensual and arousing. Desire stirred his loins, a none too subtle reminder of how long it had been since he'd been with a woman.

Refocus on the goal. Keep a respectable distance.

He drew back at his conscience's reminder, telling himself he would do both, but one look at her passion-glazed eyes, the moist, swollen lips still poised for a kiss and he knew keeping a distance was no longer an option.

Given time, he probably could've come up with a better way to express his needs, prettier words with which to seduce her. But at the moment, only the simplest came to mind.

"I want you. Now."

A trail of coats, boots, jeans and sweaters stretched from the front door of the cabin to the foot of the king-size bed. Lust left no time for modesty or tidiness. It carried them straight to the bed, where they fell, their mouths welded, their bodies so closely entwined it was impossible to determine where one started and the other stopped.

For Ali it wasn't close enough. She'd never wanted a man as badly as she did Garrett at that moment. Awakening that morning with him spooned at her back probably had a lot to do with her ravenous hunger. But, if she were honest, it had been building since the morning she'd opened her door, taken his hand, and felt that first ripple of awareness crawl up her arm. His appeal had taken a jump the day she was photographing him in his Western gear and she'd seen what a smile did to his face. And the night he'd kissed her in the middle of Interstate 35…well, his lust factor had shot off the charts.

Desperate to touch him, explore every inch of his body, she swept her hands down his back, over his buttocks, dragged them up his arms, marveling at the strength she sensed within each tightly corded muscle. And his chest…oh, his chest, she thought with a shiver, as she splayed her hands over the expanse and pressed a kiss against its center, inhaling the scent of sandalwood. She'd carried the image of his bared chest to bed with her the night before when he'd commandeered her bedroom and had spent sleepless hours awake and yearning.

But there was no need to yearn any longer.

Knotting her fingers in his hair, she returned her mouth to his and teased his tongue into a dance, all but begging him to take her. As if in response to her silent request, he slipped a hand between her thighs, and she had to clamp her knees together to keep from shattering right then and there.

"Let me touch you," he whispered against her lips.

At his urging, she let her legs part and closed her eyes, focusing on each new sensation he evoked as he stroked the velvety folds of her femininity.

No more words passed between them. There was no need for talk. They communicated with their hands, their eyes, conveyed their impatience with low, guttural groans, their pleasure with long, breathy sighs.

She pressed her lips to his throat, his shoulder, his chest, and savored the salt on his skin, his very maleness. Stroked her hands over his back, his arms, his buttocks, and wondered at his endurance. Everywhere their bodies touched burned as her need for him spiraled higher and higher, until she feared it would consume her. Growing impatient, she cupped his buttocks and urged his hips to hers. His sex brushed her center, and she arched, then melted, her womb softening to accept him.

Braced above her, with his eyes locked with hers, he pushed inside. He held himself there for a heartbeat, two, then began to move, each thrust taking him deeper and deeper inside. She watched the passion build on his face, touched her fingers over the flush of it, then dragged her fingertips down to his lips, his chest. With a groan, he dropped his mouth to hers, mimicking with his tongue the thrust of his sex inside her. It proved to be too much for her.

Desperate for the release that teased her, she arched high and hard. Her body seemed to implode, folding in on itself to envelop him, absorbing the tremors that shook him. She closed her eyes and inhaled deeply, sure that she would die from the sheer pleasure of it all. Seconds, maybe hours passed as she floated, completely sated. A hand cupped her cheek and she opened her eyes again to find him looking down at her.

"Ali."

Her name was hardly more than a whisper that slipped past his lips, but the sound of it, the wonder in it, squeezed at her chest. Emotion rose to fill her throat and released a single word to drift through her mind, wing its way to her heart.

Love.

No, she told herself, and squeezed her eyes shut, telling herself it wasn't possible—she couldn't be falling in love with Garrett. She barely knew him. But when she opened her eyes and met the warmth of his, saw the tenderness, the utter contentment of his expression, she knew there was no way she could deny her feelings.

"You okay?" he asked in concern.

She forced a smile and nodded. "Yeah. Fine."

He lowered himself over her to touch his mouth to hers, then nestled his face in the curve of her neck.

Five

It took a moment for Ali's pulse to slow, her mind to clear enough to absorb the magnitude of what had just transpired.

She, Ali Moran, lowly innkeeper of Vista Bed and Breakfast, had just had sex with *the* Garrett Miller.

Not just sex, she thought with a shiver. Mind-blowing, toe-tingling, life-altering sex.

And it had started with nothing more than a kiss. In a matter of seconds the kiss had escalated to a sexual encounter that had blinded her to the fact that Garrett was essentially a stranger. Under normal circumstances, that fact would have kept her from tumbling into bed with a man.

Which further proved her current circumstances were anything but normal. Hiding from a would-be assassin on a ranch God-knew where with a man with whom she had about as much in common with as she did…well, she didn't have anything in common with him, which was exactly the point, and just one more reason to question why she'd all but raced him to bed.

A hand touched her cheek, and she jumped, startled, and turned her gaze to find Garrett looking at her.

"I—" He stopped, then shook his head. "I don't know what to say."

Assuming by his hesitancy, his expression that what he wanted to tell her was that he regretted making love with her, she tried to sit up. "You don't have to say anything. Really. I understand."

He pressed a hand to her chest, stilling her. "No. I don't think you do." He leaned to touch his lips to hers in a kiss so sensual it sent a shiver chasing down her spine. "That was a…surprise."

His voice was husky, the stroke of his thumb along her cheekbone as mesmerizing as the eyes that held hers.

She melted back against the pillow. "Yeah. It was."

"I probably should apologize for taking advantage of you, but if I did, it would be insincere. I'm not one damn bit sorry."

"It wasn't like you forced me."

His mouth curved in a smile. "Which makes it all the more interesting."

"Garrett," she began, then stopped, her mind going blank as he stroked his hand down her throat, cupped a breast.

He lifted a brow. "You know, I think this is the first time I've ever seen you at a loss for words."

She choked a laugh. "You may be right."

"In that case—" he draped an arm over her waist and drew her hips to his "—I know something we can do that doesn't require words."

Of the same mind, she looped her arms around his neck. "I'm game."

A muffled ring had Ali sleepily lifting her head. Realizing it was her cell, she scrambled from the bed, where she and Garrett had spent the greater part of the last two days, and dug her phone from her tote bag. "Hello?"

"Where *are* you?"

Wincing, she sank down on the foot of the bed. "Hey, Traci."

"Don't 'hey, Traci' me. Where are you?"

"I'm—" She glanced at Garrett, who was awake, too, and listening. "Out of town," she finished vaguely.

"Well, you might have told me you were moving," Traci said, with a sniff. "I am your best friend, after all."

"Moving?" Ali repeated in confusion. "I didn't say anything about moving. I said I'm out of town."

"Then why is there a For Sale sign in front of your house?"

Ali shot up from the bed. "What?" she cried.

"A For Sale sign. I saw it when I went over there this morning. After you didn't show up for yoga class," she added.

Ali dropped her head to her hand. "Oh God, Traci. I'm sorry. I totally forgot about yoga."

"Along with telling me you were moving," Traci said, sounding hurt. "And what is it with all those people hanging around your house? When I went by to check on you, these guys rushed my car. Scared me to death. I took off so fast, it's a wonder I didn't run over somebody."

Ali flattened her lips. "As far as I'm concerned, you could have run them all down. They're tabloid photographers."

"No kidding? Are they there because of your mystery guest?"

"No," she said wryly, "they want pictures of me." She dragged a hand over her hair. "Back to the For Sale sign," she said refocusing the conversation. "Some kid must have put it there as a prank."

"Juvenile delinquents," Traci said testily. "You'd think they'd have something better to do with their time, than terrorizing the neighborhood."

"I probably should call the Realtor and let them know. Do you remember the name of the company on the sign?"

"It was one of those national chains. Century 21, I think."

"Great," Ali muttered. "There's probably a dozen or more Century 21 offices in Austin."

"I'd offer to drive by and get the name for you, but those guys who are hanging around scare me."

"Me, too," Ali agreed, then shook her head. "Don't worry about it. I'll make a few calls and see what I can find out."

"Allbright," Traci blurted out. "I remember now. It was Allbright Century 21."

"Well, that's handy. You just saved me making a dozen calls."

"What about your houseguest?" Traci asked. "Did you just leave him at the house to fend for himself?"

"Uh, no." Ali shot a glance over her shoulder at Garrett. "He's with me."

"What! You mean y'all are *together?*"

Ali rose and walked away from the bed. "Sort of," she said in a voice low enough she hoped Garrett couldn't hear.

"Details, girlfriend. I want details."

"Later. I have to go."

"No!" Traci cried. "Not until you tell me where you are."

"Sorry. No can do."

"Ali Moran, don't you dare—"

Ali disconnected the call, cutting Traci off, then blew a breath up at her bangs.

"Problem?"

She turned to find Garrett sitting up in bed, the covers bunched at his waist. How he could look so mouthwateringly *good* after so many days of nonstop sex was beyond her. Personally she felt—and probably looked—like a rag. She crossed to crawl onto the bed. "Traci's mad at me because I didn't show up for yoga."

"Traci?"

"Girlfriend."

"What was that I heard about moving?"

"When I didn't show up for yoga, she went by the house to check on me and saw a For Sale sign out front." She lifted a shoulder as she settled at his side. "School's out for the holidays, so it was probably some kid pulling a prank."

"You should notify the Realtor."

"I will."

"I take it our friends are still hanging around?"

She hid a smile. "Traci said she was afraid she'd run over one of them."

"Too bad she didn't."

"I'll tell her to work on her aim." Her smile slowly faded, as she wondered what their presence meant. "Since they're still there, does that mean we're safe?"

"It's best to assume we're not." Her expression must have revealed her disappointment, because he gave her leg a reassuring pat. "Tell you what. You call the Realtor about your For Sale sign, and I'll call my security chief and check to see what's happening in Switzerland."

"Deal."

While Garrett went for his phone, Ali called directory assistance for the number of the realty company, then waited for the connection.

"Allbright, Century 21. May I help you?"

"I hope so," she said, heaving a sigh. "One of your For Sale signs is in front of my house. A kids' prank, I'm sure, but I thought your company would want to know so they can return it to the property it was taken from."

"Yes, we certainly do, and I'm so sorry for the inconvenience. The address?"

Ali rattled off the Vista's street address. "Kids," she said, and chuckled. "They do the darnedest things."

"By chance are you Ali Moran?"

"Well, yes," Ali said in surprise. "How did you know?"

"I just checked our database, and we have that property listed for sale. Your name is listed as the contact."

"No. You're mistaken. I'm not selling the Vista."

"You may not be, but the owner is. Mr. Ronald Fleming. In fact, the listing agent has been trying to reach you all morning to make arrangements to show the property. If you'll hold, I'll connect you with Diane. She's the listing agent."

Ali dropped the phone to her lap, breaking the connection. No, she told herself numbly. This had to be a mistake. Ronald Fleming didn't own the house. Ali did. Mimi had given it to Ali, because she knew her son didn't care a flip about the house and would sell it at the first opportunity.

"Ali?"

She looked up to find Garrett looking at her in concern.

"What's wrong?" he asked. "Did you talk to the Realtor?"

She nodded, not trusting her voice. "She said it wasn't a prank. Mimi's son listed the house."

He sank down on the edge of the bed. "But you said Mimi gave you the house."

Tears filled her eyes. "I thought she did."

He stared at her a long moment, then squeezed her knee. "It's probably just a misunderstanding. Why don't you call her attorney. I'm sure he can straighten it out."

She shook her head. "I don't know her attorney's name. The only person I know to ask is Claire." She glanced at the bedside clock and her shoulders drooped. "And I can't call her now. It's the middle of the night in Australia."

She drew in a steadying breath, refusing to believe there was even a chance her house was about to be sold out from under her. "I'm sure you're right," she said, trying to think positively. "It's probably just some crazy misunderstanding." She forced a smile. "So? What did you find out from your security guy?"

"The trap is set. They're just waiting for him to take the bait."

"And when will that happen?"

"Hopefully within the next forty-eight hours."

She gave him a hesitant look. "They're sure he's in Switzerland and not on his way to Texas?"

"He was seen entering a Swiss hotel less than two hours ago."

"And they'll let you know if there's a change, right?"

"Without question." He gave her knee another pat and rose. "I don't know about you, but I'm starving. Let's get something to eat."

She had a feeling his mention of food was just a ruse to get her mind off the danger they were in, as well as her uncertainties concerning the ownership of the Vista, but she was grateful for the distraction.

"It's nice out," she said, and scooted from the bed. "Let's make a picnic lunch."

Garrett didn't know whether to curse himself for not following up with his lawyer concerning ownership of the Vista or breathe a huge sigh of relief, as he and Ali hiked through the woods.

He ended up breathing a sigh of relief.

If he *had* followed up and discovered the property was owned by Ronald, he would have instructed his lawyer to purchase the Vista, which meant that he would be the current owner, not Ronald and he would be the one responsible for Ali's earlier state of despair.

That he would care about Ali's feelings or that he was responsible for them was new and a complication he refused to think about…for the time being, anyway.

Setting the thoughts aside, he spread the blanket over the ground at the picnic spot Ali had chosen. "Hard to believe it's January," he said, as he spread the blanket over the ground. "At home they're shoveling snow."

Ali sank down and began removing items from the basket of food she'd packed for them. "I can't say I miss winters up north."

He shrugged off his jacket, before joining her on the blanket. "It's got to be close to seventy degrees."

"Probably." She popped a strawberry into her mouth and smiled, as she chewed. "And tomorrow could be below freezing. It's best not to question Mother Nature, just enjoy her idiosyncrasies."

Chuckling, he stretched out, propping himself up on an elbow. "Which is my policy with most women."

She held a grape before his mouth. He caught the

fruit between his teeth, nipping at her fingers before drawing it into his mouth. "Wasn't Nero merrily eating grapes while Rome burned?"

"Worse. He was playing the fiddle. Men," she said, with a dramatic roll of her eyes. "They're clueless."

"I resent that remark."

She teased him with a smile. "With the proper persuasion I might be convinced to make you an exception."

He cupped a hand behind her neck and brought her mouth to his.

Humming lustfully, she slowly withdrew. "Okay. You get a pass."

Grinning, she handed him a plastic wrapped sandwich, then selected one for herself. She took a bite, chewed. "Tell me about your family," she said.

"Like what?"

"Like mother, father, siblings." She teased him with a smile. "Or were you hatched?"

"Although I've been accused of being inhuman on more than one occasion, I did have a mother and father. Both of whom are now deceased."

She gave him a sympathetic look. "Sorry. Was it recent?"

"My mother died years ago. I have no memory of her. My dad died about three years ago. Cancer."

"Siblings?"

"An only child."

She lifted a brow. "Really? Me, too." She licked mayonnaise from her finger, before lifting the sandwich for another bite. "So were you and your dad close?"

"No."

His clipped, one-word response had her lowering the sandwich to stare. "Did he beat you or something?"

He snorted. "That would've required him to get near me, and I don't recall him ever being within an arm's reach."

She set her sandwich aside. "Seriously?"

"Seriously."

"But—" She stopped, frowned. "He was your only parent. Who took care of you?"

"The first couple of years after my mother died, baby-sitters. When I was six, he remarried."

"What was your stepmother like?"

"An angel."

She blinked, surprised by the transformation in his face as well as his voice, when he spoke of his stepmother. "Tell me about her."

"Kind. Selfless. Intelligent." He lifted a shoulder. "I'd do anything for her."

She stared, not doubting for a minute that he would and wondering what kind of person instilled that kind of devotion. Shaking her head, she picked up her sandwich again. "You were lucky."

"Lucky?"

She took a bite, chewed. "Yeah. I mean, bummer about your dad, but at least you had a good stepmother."

He dropped his head back and laughed.

She lowered her sandwich. "What?"

"Bummer?" He laughed even harder. "I've received all kinds of reactions to my dad's unfatherlylike behavior, but never 'bummer.'"

She jutted her chin. "If you're expecting pity from me, you won't get it. Your father may have been emotionally handicapped, but your stepmother obviously knew a thing or two about parenting and you were darn lucky to have her."

"No one knows that better than me. It's just that your response was so unexpected, so polar opposite of how most people react to hearing about my childhood…. It just struck me as funny."

Pursing her lips, she picked up her soda. "Well, I'm glad you find me entertaining."

He reached to cover her hand with his. "I'm not laughing at you, Ali," he said quietly. "Quite the opposite in fact. I find you refreshing. Fascinating. Intriguing."

She rolled her eyes. "Oh, please. Much more of your bull and I'll need boots."

"That was no bull. It's the truth. You're all those things and more."

She frowned at him, trying to decide if he was

serious. Finding nothing but sincerity in his eyes, she drew her hand from beneath his. "Don't complicate this any more than it is," she warned.

"What do you mean?"

"I *mean,* this situation is already packed with enough drama to keep a soap opera's scriptwriters in material for a year. Being stalked by the media," she said, ticking off items on her fingers. "Marooned in a secluded cabin in the woods. A would-be assassin on the loose. Living with the possibility of having my house sold out from under me at any moment."

"And me finding you fascinating complicates those things?"

"Well, of course it does!" she cried. "I'm at my most vulnerable right now. Falling for you would be a huge mistake."

"Why?"

"You need to ask?" she asked incredulously.

"Obviously I do."

"Because you're a zillionaire, and I'm an innkeeper who might not even have an inn to keep when and if I make it back home. You live on the East Coast, I live in Central Texas. You're left-brained, I'm right. Making love with you is absolutely incredible. February 1, you're gone."

"Obviously you've given this some thought."

Embarrassed because she had, she dropped her

gaze. "If I don't allow myself to believe something is possible, then I can't be disappointed when I'm proven right."

"Ah, Ali," he said softly. "Only you could come up with a rationale like that."

"There's nothing wrong with my reasoning."

"No," he agreed, "not a thing." He sat up and tugged her over, burying his face in the curve of her neck. "So what's the plan?"

Distracted by his sensual nibbling at her neck, she asked weakly, "What plan?"

"For the remainder of the month. For us."

She turned in his arms. "Enjoy every minute of every day." Smiling, she pressed her mouth to his and forced him back to the blanket. "And *you*."

Garrett couldn't argue with Ali's plan. The company of a beautiful and fascinating woman, and the promise of unlimited and unbelievable sex for a month, with absolutely nothing expected from him in return? Hell, it was every man's fantasy!

He did suffer a moment's concern when he considered the future. Ali was his stepmother's daughter, after all. What would happen when the month was over and she discovered his stepmother was *her* mother?

He pushed the worrisome thought away, telling himself he'd deal with that problem later. It wasn't as if she had any expectations of a future with him, he reminded himself. She, herself, had offered up a laundry list of reasons as to why a relationship with him would never work. She'd even told him she intended to enjoy the time they had together. So why should he feel guilty about taking advantage of what she so freely offered?

He glanced over his shoulder at the cabin where Ali was inside placing a call to her friend Claire in Australia. He didn't even want to think how that conversation would affect Ali. Her love for the big, rambling house was obvious. She'd spent, what, ten years in the house? Caring for it, maintaining it, building a business around it. She was bound to take losing it hard, especially after thinking it was hers. What bothered him was how she would take the news.

So why was he standing outside, avoiding going inside the cabin? he asked himself. The answer was so clear, a blind man could have seen it. He didn't want Ali hurt, didn't want to see the heartbreak in her eyes, on her face. Didn't want to see any more evidence of the victim he'd begun to believe she was.

Heaving a sigh, he forced himself to take that first reluctant step toward the cabin.

Ali tugged up the hem of her shirt to mop her eyes. "It's okay," she assured Claire tearfully. "And please don't think I blame Mimi. It's not like she knew she was going to die. She probably thought she had plenty of time to change her will."

"But you know she didn't want Dad to have the house," Claire argued stubbornly. "She knew he didn't care anything for it, would just sell it. That's why she wanted you to have it."

Ali gulped back tears, nodded. "I know, and I wish it was mine. I hate to see it sold, as much as Mimi would if she were here."

"Oh, Ali," Claire cried softly. "If there was any way I could stop him, you know I would."

"I know, Claire. I know. But what's done is done. There's no use either one of us crying over it now."

"Why don't you buy it?" Claire said impulsively.

"Me?" Ali choked a watery laugh. "Don't I wish. But you know what property values are like in Austin, especially those around downtown. I could never afford to buy the Vista." She drew in a steadying breath, searching for the positive thoughts she needed to get her through this. "I've had ten wonderful years at the Vista, thanks to you and Mimi. For that I'll always be grateful."

"Oh, Ali," Claire wailed. "I could just wring Dad's neck. He's so heartless, so *mean*."

"Don't blame your dad," Ali scolded gently. "He can't help being the way he is."

"Like hell he can't," Claire muttered bitterly. "You'd think he would've inherited at least *some* of

Mimi's heart. But, no, he's just like Papa Fleming. Selfish and mean to the bone."

"I guess it skipped a generation," Ali said. "You definitely have Mimi's heart." She drew in another breath. "I better go. I've kept you on the phone long enough."

"I'm so sorry, Ali-Cat," Claire said miserably, falling back on the nickname she'd given Ali during their college years. "If there's anything I can do, just let me know, okay?"

"I will. Love you," she said and quickly disconnected. Dropping the phone, she buried her face in her hands and gave in to the tears she'd suppressed.

She'd cry just this once, she promised herself. Grieve for the house she'd grown to love, the home it had become for her, the living it had provided her. Then she'd put it behind her. Not think about it again. Pull herself up by the bootstraps and figure out what to do, where to go. But she needed this moment of self-pity, this opportunity to rail at the fates who seemed to have had it in for her since birth.

What had she done to deserve so much disappointment, so much grief? she asked herself, letting the tears fall. Conceived by parents who didn't want her and given to parents who only wanted someone to carry on their precious family tradition of becoming doctors. And when her adoptive parents had turned their backs on her and all but kicked her out on the streets, had she joined the talk show circuit, crying and whining about her sorry lot in life and the psychological damage inflicted upon her? No, she'd moved to Texas, made a home for herself here, grown to love the state, the city, as well as her home, which she depended on for her support.

And for what? she sobbed, giving in to the resentment, the bitterness. To have it yanked out from under her and be without a home again.

"Ali?"

She snapped up her head to find Garrett standing in the doorway. She leaped to her feet, embarrassed that he'd caught her hosting a pity party for one. "Sorry," she said, scraping her hands across her face. "Got kind of teary-eyed there for a minute."

"Bad news?"

"Yeah. Seems Mimi never got around to changing her will." She gulped, trying to swallow the tears, but they spilled over her lashes.

"Hey," he said softly and crossed to wrap his arms around her.

The offer of comfort was too unexpected, too needed to refuse. She buried her face against his chest. "It's just not fair," she sobbed. "Mimi wanted me to have the house. She really did."

"I'm sure she did."

"And that dumb son of hers couldn't care less. He's been pressuring her for years to get rid of it. He never understood the sentimental value it held for Mimi, how much of her heart was in that house."

"But you did."

She curled her hand into a fist against his chest. "Of course, I did! It was a wedding present from her first husband. He surprised her with it. Planned to live there with her forever. Raise their children there. Then he died. It's full of their love, the memories they made there together. You only have to walk through a room to feel it, to know how much they loved each other, to know how much losing him cost her."

He held her, rubbing a hand up and down her back to soothe, until she'd cried herself out.

She gulped, swallowed, then turned away, afraid if she continued to let the grief hold her she'd never be able to stop crying. "Sorry. I didn't mean to fall apart like that."

"I'd say you're entitled."

She nodded, swallowed again "Yeah. But I'm done now." To prove it, she turned and forced a smile. "So? Want to raid the refrigerator and see what we can find for dinner?"

Six

Garrett didn't know which was worse. Watching Ali cry or watching her pretend her world wasn't falling apart. Both were heartbreaking to witness.

He sat in the leather overstuffed chair opposite the sofa, his laptop open before him, watching her leaf through a magazine. She wasn't seeing whatever was on the pages. She might be *looking* at them, but her mind was on something else entirely. The tiny furrow of worry between her brows was a dead giveaway that her thoughts weren't focused on the magazine's glossy pages, but on what troubles awaited her in Austin.

"Have you considered buying the property yourself?" he asked.

She glanced up, as if startled by the sound of his voice, then dropped her gaze to the magazine again and flipped a page. "Can't afford it."

"How do you know, when you haven't applied for a loan?"

"Trust me. I know. You've looked for land in the Austin area. You know that property within the city limits of Austin is at premium. What's around Town Lake is like gold."

Frustrated, he set his laptop aside and stood. "Ask for a business loan. Base your ability to make the payments on the bed-and-breakfast's potential income."

She stared up at him a long moment, as if considering, then dropped her gaze again, shaking her head. "Good idea, but it would never fly. They'd want a down payment of some kind, and I have nothing to offer, other than a paltry savings account."

"But you can't know what they'd want until you try," he argued.

She looked up at him and gave him a halfhearted smile. "I appreciate the suggestion, Garrett, as well as your concern, but I have to be realistic. Building false hope would only make the disappointment that much greater when I was turned down for the loan. And they would turn me down," she said firmly. "I may not have your business experience, but I know enough to know I would never qualify for a loan the size needed to buy the Vista."

"But—"

A knock at the door had him spinning around. He swallowed a groan, when he saw Mandy peering at him through the window.

"Is that your friend?" Ali asked from behind him.

"Yeah," he said, and headed for the door, dread knotting his stomach. "That's her."

Before he had a chance to open the door completely, Mandy was breezing inside, wearing a mile-wide smile and carrying a plastic cake carrier.

"Hi, Garrett!" She blew a kiss in his direction, but kept going and didn't stop until she was standing opposite the sofa and Ali.

She set the cake carrier on the coffee table, then stood and extended her hand in greeting. "Hi, I'm Mandy."

Ali unfolded her legs from beneath her and rose, a smile spreading on her face. "Hi, Mandy. I'm Ali."

"I thought y'all might be craving something sweet," Mandy said, then laughed and gave her rounded belly a pat. "Junior always is." She flapped a hand. "Anyway, I was baking a cake, and thought I might as well bake two and bring y'all one. Do you like chocolate?"

"Are you kidding?" Ali said, laughing. "I'm a woman, aren't I?" She scooped up the cake carrier and headed for the kitchen. "I'll cut us all a piece. Would you like a glass of milk with yours, Mandy?" she called over her shoulder.

"Yes, please," Mandy replied, then turned to Garrett and dropped her jaw, mouthing, "She's darling!"

He narrowed his eyes in a look that promised death if she dared spill the beans about who he was or how he and Mandy were related. "Is there any coffee?" he called to Ali.

"Probably enough for a cup."

He gave Mandy a last warning look, then ducked around her and headed for the kitchen. "I'll make a fresh pot."

"I'll make it," Ali offered.

He cut a glance her way, as he pulled the container of coffee grounds from the cupboard. "I better. Looks like you've got your hands full."

Grinning, she licked chocolate from the tips of her fingers. "One of the perks of cutting the cake. I get whatever icing sticks to me." She levered a slice onto a plate, added a fork. "Would you mind getting the milk?" she asked Garrett, as she cut another wedge.

"I will," Mandy said, as she joined them in the kitchen.

"By the way," Ali told her, "thanks for stocking the refrigerator. I was starving when we woke up that first day and was relieved when I discovered a trip to town wasn't going to be required before I could eat."

Mandy set the carton of milk on the counter and flapped a hand. "Glad to do it. It's not often we have the opportunity to entertain f—"

Garrett bumped her arm and gave her a warning look.

"—friends," Mandy finished, then stuck her tongue out at him behind Ali's back. "Do you want milk, Ali?" she asked, as she poured a glass.

"Yes, please."

Mandy poured a second glass and carried them to the table. "This is so cool," she said as she settled in a chair. "It's not often I get to spend the afternoon eating chocolate cake and talking girl talk."

Garrett pulled out a chair, purposely placing himself between Mandy and Ali. "Me, either," he said dryly.

"I would have dropped by for a visit sooner," Mandy said, "but I've had carpenters at the house all week. We're converting the bedroom next to ours into a nursery and I promised Jase I'd keep an eye on them. They're excellent craftsmen," she was quick to add, then chuckled. "It's just that they have a tendency to drag a job out forever, if you don't prod them along."

"Your husband's out of town?" Ali asked curiously.

"He's in Washington, D.C., visiting his mother. But he'll be home tonight," she added. She lifted her fork to her mouth and gave Garrett a mischievous smile over it. "When he heard Garrett was here and had brought a friend to visit, he decided to cut his trip short."

"How nice," Ali said and smiled at Garrett. "You'll get to spend some time with your friend."

"Yeah," Garrett said, that knot of dread twisting tighter in his stomach at the thought of Jase coming home. "Nice."

Ali shifted her gaze from Garrett to Mandy. "How did y'all meet? You and Garrett, I mean."

"College—"

"Mutual friend—"

Garrett and Mandy exchanged a glance as their voices tangled and their explanations clashed. Mandy popped a piece of cake into her mouth and waved her fork at Garrett, indicating for him to explain.

"A mutual friend from college introduced us," he said, praying Ali would leave it at that. He figured the fewer lies he had to tell, the less chance he and Mandy—and later, Jase—would have of getting their stories mixed up.

"Oh," Ali said, seeming satisfied with his explanation, then shifted her attention to Mandy and smiled. "So, when is your baby due?"

That sent the conversation in a whole new direction and left Garrett breathing a sigh of relief.

For the moment.

"Mandy's nice."

Garrett climbed into bed and stretched out beside Ali. "Yeah. She is."

"I can't believe she's so big, and she's only four months along."

"She's big all right."

"I wonder if she's carrying twins," she said thoughtfully.

"The two of you talked about everything else," he said dryly. "I'm surprised you didn't ask."

She laughed softly. "I wanted to, but I was afraid I might hurt her feelings. You know. Like I was saying she was fat or something."

"She is fat."

"She is not," she scolded. "She's pregnant. There's a difference."

He rolled to his side to face her, and plumped his pillow beneath his head. "If you say so."

Smiling, she snuggled close. "What's her husband like?"

"Jase?"

She lifted a brow. "She has more than one?"

He rolled his eyes. "He's a nice guy, I guess."

"Well, that's certainly descriptive."

"He's a cowboy. You know the type. Tall. Lanky. Wears a hat and boots all the time. Walks slow, talks slow."

Growing thoughtful, she brushed a lock of hair from his forehead. "It's hard to imagine you having a friend like that. I mean. Well, you know. You being a zillionaire computer geek and all."

He drew back to look at her. "What is it with this zillionaire tag you keep sticking me with?"

"Millionaire, zillionaire. When you have a bank balance like mine, all those 'aires' are the same."

He snorted. "Believe me, being wealthy isn't what it's cracked up to be."

"Really?" She snuggled closer. "Tell me what it is like."

"A pain, if you want the truth. Overnight, you become everybody's best friend. People you've never even heard of start coming out of the woodwork wanting something from you. A loan. A partner in a new venture. A job." He shook his head. "You learn real quick that it isn't *you* they're interested in. It's your money."

She trailed a finger down his jaw, her lips puckered in sympathy. "Bummer."

"Yeah. Bummer. And everything about your life changes. You live in a fishbowl, your every move watched and speculated on. Your past becomes an open book, with people digging around to find out all your dirty secrets."

She teased him with a smile. "And what skeletons do you have rattling around in your closet, Mr. Miller? How many secrets are you hiding?"

The stab of guilt hit him square between the eyes and without warning. Only one, he thought, and the person who stood to suffer the most from it lay opposite him.

Stretching over her, he switched out the bedside lamp, wanting the shroud of darkness in which to hide his lie. "I don't have any secrets," he said.

"Ah, come on. Everybody has a secret or two they keep hidden from the world."

"You already know mine."

"What? About your dad?"

"Only a select few know what my childhood was like, and I intend to keep it that way."

"I'm not planning on telling anyone, if that has you worried."

Hearing the hurt in her voice, he draped an arm over her and drew her close. "I never thought you would. I imagine, with parents like yours, you'd understand why I'd prefer no one know what it was like."

"Lonely?"

He thought about that for a minute. "Yeah, although it was years before I realized I was lonely."

"When your stepmother came into the picture."

"Before she came along, I didn't realize I was missing anything. Thought everyone's dad was like mine. Went to work every day, stayed in his office at home until all hours of the night. No hugs good-night. No tossing a ball around in the backyard. No contact. No conversation. No nothing."

She laid her fingers against his cheek and something in his chest shifted at the tenderness in the gesture.

"You wanted his love," she said softly, "were starving for it."

He swallowed hard, never having heard anyone express his need so succinctly or accurately.

"Yeah," he said, and shoved back the image of the little boy who'd gone to sleep every night with a teddy bear hugged to his chest, a lousy substitute for the physical contact, the affection he'd wanted, needed from his dad.

The how-come-I-can't-go pitiful look Ali gave Garrett when he drove away from the cabin made Garrett feel about as low as a snake. But he couldn't very well take her with him to visit Mandy and Jase when she was the purpose of the visit. With Jase home now, he didn't want to take a chance on Jase storming the cabin and demanding that Ali meet their mother, which is exactly what Garrett feared Jase would do. The two men might not be related, and Jase might have come into Barbara's life later than Garrett, but they shared a strong protective instinct when it came to Barbara Jordan Miller.

He figured, too, that he had some explaining to do, since Jase would think, as Mandy had, that Garrett had broken his promise to Barbara about contacting Ali.

As it turned out, his fears were well founded.

He'd barely climbed from the rental, when Jase

came barreling out of the house with murder in his eyes.

Garrett held up a hand to stave off a fight. "I can explain," he said.

Jase halted an arm's length away and dropped his hands to his hips, smoke all but coming out his ears. "You damn well better," he said angrily. "We promised Barb we'd leave Ali alone."

"*You* promised," Garrett corrected. "I promised nothing."

Jase opened his mouth, probably intending to call him a liar, then clamped it shut, obviously realizing that Garrett hadn't made the same promise he and his father, Eddie, had. "You were there when we got back from visiting Ali's parents and knew we were told that Ali wanted nothing to do with her birth family. You heard what Barb said, what she asked of us. She said for us to leave Ali alone."

Garrett nodded. "Yes, and I would've honored her wishes, but I saw how much Barbara wanted to meet Ali, how much it hurt her to know that Ali wanted nothing to do with her. Since I'm not related to Ali, I figured she wouldn't feel the same animosity toward me she might feel toward you or Eddie, if you were to go and see her. I thought I could talk to her, reason with her, convince her to meet Barbara. And, if that failed, I thought I could at least convince her to give Barbara the missing piece of the deed."

"And did you?" Jase demanded.

Garrett grimaced, aware that somewhere along the way, he'd allowed his growing attraction for Ali to distract him from his purpose in being in her home.

"Not yet," he added reluctantly. "My intent was to get to know her first so I'd know how best to gain her cooperation."

"And did you?" Jase asked again.

"No, but I have discovered some things about her that make me believe she'd be willing to meet with Barbara. With all of you."

"By God, she'll meet me," Jase said angrily. "She's on my land, in my cabin. I'd like to see her try leaving this ranch *without* meeting me."

"And that's exactly the kind of attitude that will ruin any chance of reuniting Barbara with Ali." Realizing that his anger had spiked to match Jase's, he drew in a breath through his nose and slowly blew it out. "Which is why I'm here," he said more calmly. "We need to talk."

Jase glared at him a full minute, then spun for the house. "Inside. Mandy'll want to be in on this."

"You're saying the Morans lied?" Jase asked doubtfully.

"I can't say for sure," Garrett replied, "since I haven't confronted Ali directly with anything yet, but, yes, I believe they did." Frowning, he turned his coffee cup slowly between his hands. "I wasn't there when you, Eddie and Barbara visited with the Morans, but I don't remember any of you mentioning Ali being estranged from her adoptive parents."

Jase shook his head. "No. They didn't indicate there were any problems at all."

Garrett scowled. "Well, there are. Big ones. And they go back for years. Ali hasn't seen or spoken to her parents since she moved to Texas ten years ago."

"What!" Jase exchanged a look with Mandy, then turned his attention to Garrett again. "The Morans never let on they weren't in contact with Ali."

"I doubt they would, since they all but kicked her out on the street."

Jase sank back in his chair, clearly unaware of that portion of Ali's past. "Maybe you better explain."

Garrett did, sharing the story of Ali's break with her parents, her move to Texas, just as she'd shared it with him, and finished by telling them about Ronald Fleming inheriting the Vista, instead of Ali.

"Damn," Jase murmured, obviously moved by Ali's plight.

"Yeah," Garrett agreed grimly. "Damn. From what she's told me her life with her adoptive parents was anything but pleasant."

"After meeting the Morans," Jase said grimly, "I'd say the fault lies with them, not Ali."

Garrett nodded. "That's my take on it, too."

"So what do we do now?" Mandy asked. "Just tell her the truth about her past? About Jase being her twin and Barbara wanting to meet her?"

Garrett blew out a breath, shook his head. "I don't know what to do. I want to tell her and plan to. It's the when and how I haven't figured out. It's going to be a shock, no matter how it's handled." He looked at Jase. "Think how you reacted when you were told."

Jase snorted a breath. "I was royally pissed, I can tell you that." He glanced at Mandy. Smiling softly, he reached to take her hand. "If not for Mandy, I probably would've never agreed to meet my father. And without Eddie's input, I doubt I would've ever searched for my mother."

He gave Mandy's hand a squeeze, and turned his attention back to Garrett. "You've spent time with Ali, you know her best. How do you think we should handle telling her?"

"I don't know that there is a good way," Garrett said with regret. "In retrospect, I can see that my going to Austin and using my need for property as an excuse to stay at her bed-and-breakfast, rather than being up-front with her and telling her who I was was a mistake. I'm afraid I've complicated things even more by becoming involved with her."

Jase's eyes sharpened. "Involved?"

Realizing his slip, he dropped his gaze. "We've become…friends. Once she realizes I've deceived her…" He dragged a shaky hand down his face, easily able to imagine her reaction. "Well, I doubt she's going to like me very much, which could make things awkward since we have Barbara in common."

Mandy nodded gravely. "Trust factor. It's important to a woman."

"How about this," Jase suggested. "Bring her over here for dinner. Let me get a feel for the situation, get to know her and her me. Maybe this will be easier than we think."

Garrett considered a moment, then nodded reluctantly, unable to come up with a better plan. "Okay, but give me a few more days with her. Maybe I can find a way to tell her my part in this, before we have to tell her about you being her brother. Feed it to her in small bites. Less of a shock that way."

Ali tried not to pout as she made the bed, but it was hard. She didn't see how her going with Garrett to see his friend Jase would have made any difference. It's not like she would have bellied up to the bar with the men, so to speak, and interfered with their "man talk." She had more sense than that. She could've—and would've, given the chance—spent the time chatting with Mandy.

She smiled at the thought of Mandy, thinking how cute the woman looked with her rounded belly. She doubted Mandy was even aware of the loving way she rubbed her stomach when she talked about the baby. But Ali had noticed and had thought it was about the sweetest thing she'd ever seen. Babies were something out of Ali's realm. Not that she didn't want one some day. She did. She just didn't have any friends who had children and didn't have any experience with infants, or pregnant women for that matter.

Taking a pillow from the bed, she stuffed it under her shirt and turned to the mirror to see what she would look like pregnant. She snorted a laugh at the grotesque shape the pillow formed beneath her shirt as she turned to view her profile.

"What man would love that?" she asked herself, chuckling. She propped her arms over the bump as she'd seen Mandy do, and tried to imagine what it would be like to know a baby was growing inside her, what it would feel like when the baby moved. Would it hurt? Tickle?

She turned to face the front again, wondering how a person could carry a baby for nine months, watch it grow, feel its movements, suffer through its birth, then hand it over to strangers as her mother had done. Had her birth mother cried? she wondered. Had she ever regretted giving Ali away?

Sobered by the thought, she dragged the pillow from beneath her shirt and dropped down on the side of the bed, holding the pillow on her lap. What did her mother look like? she wondered as she smoothed a crease from the fabric. Was her hair blond like Ali's, or had Ali inherited her coloring from her father? Was she tall? Short? Funny? Serious? Were she and Ali's father married? What was she doing now? Where did she live? Did she have other children? Was she rich? Poor? Happy? Sad? Smart? Dumb? A housewife? A career-woman?

Ali dropped her head back, with a groan. How many times had she played this game through the years, asked herself these same questions? And with the same results. There was no way she could know the answers to any of the questions that had haunted her for as long as she could remember, nor would there ever be. Whatever tie she had shared with her mother was severed the day her mother had given her up for adoption.

Blowing out a breath, she dropped her chin to stare at the pillow again. Funny, she thought as she traced a finger over the neat stitches along the seam. She and Garrett had different childhoods, yet they had been similar in many ways. Neither of them had been raised by the woman who had given birth to them. And both of them had parents—or a parent in Garrett's case—who were incapable of loving them and giving them affection.

A wistful smile curved her lips as she imagined Garrett as a young boy when confronted with a step-mother who actually paid attention to him, cared about him. She had never had that. She'd seen loving relationships between her friends and their parents, which is how she knew such a thing existed. It was also how she had come to realize the ache in her chest was due to her not receiving the love and care her friends received.

"And isn't that something?" she murmured. It seemed she and Garrett had something in common after all. They'd both, at one point or another in their lives, been denied love.

Intrigued by the realization, she thought back over the time she'd spent with him and the impressions she'd drawn from each. When he'd first arrived at the Vista, she had thought him an arrogant snob, with an overinflated opinion of himself. She'd also thought him sexy as sin. She sputtered a laugh at the contradiction.

Her smile slowly faded as she realized she no longer thought of him as any of those things—except for the sexy as sin part. All it took was a look or a touch from him and her knees turned to rubber.

With a shiver, she hugged the pillow to her chest, remembering the hours they'd made love. The feel of his hands stroking her body. The way his eyes turned dark with passion, sparkled when he laughed. The pressure of his mouth on hers. His taste. The sense of oneness, completeness, she experienced when they were joined.

She broke off the thought, acutely aware of where her mind was carrying her. She was thinking of their relationship becoming permanent and it was impossible that would ever happen. She might have truly come to care for Garrett. And he may have started to care for her. But men like Garrett fell in love with debutantes and heiresses. Women who shared the same social circle, the same lifestyle. Women who moved gracefully and with style in the world of the wealthy. Men like him didn't fall in love with innkeepers. And they sure as heck didn't marry them.

She pressed a hand over her stomach, already dreading him leaving.

"Are you sick?"

She snapped up her head to find Garrett standing in the bedroom doorway, his forehead furrowed in concern. She released a shuddery breath and stood, laying the pillow aside. "I think I ate too much chocolate cake," she lied.

"Do you need to take something for it? There may be bicarbonate in the medicine cabinet."

She shook her head. "I don't need anything. I'll be okay."

He took her by the elbow and ushered her toward the bed. "Lie down for a while," he said as he pulled back the covers she'd straightened only moments ago. "Maybe you'll feel better after you take a nap."

Helpless to do anything else, she let him guide her into bed.

"Garrett?" she asked hesitantly as he pulled the covers over her.

He shifted his gaze to hers. "What?"

"What kind of women do you normally date?"

He frowned in confusion. "I don't know. Why?"

"No reason. I was just curious."

He considered a moment, then shook his head. "I don't know that I date a certain type. Female. I suppose that's my only requirement. And unattached," he added. "But if you want to know the truth, I seldom have time for dates." He dropped a kiss on her forehead. "Rest a while. I'll be in the den if you need anything."

When he turned to leave, she said, "Garrett?"

He stopped, turned. "What?"

"Will you take a nap with me?"

He hesitated a moment, then crossed back to the bed and toed off his shoes. "You know as well as I do, that if I get in this bed with you, neither one of us are going to sleep."

She flipped back the covers and smiled. "Yeah, I know."

Garrett felt Ali's gaze and glanced over to find her looking at him curiously.

"What?" he asked.

Shaking her head, she turned her gaze back to the path they walked. "Nothing really. I was just wondering why you and Jase haven't spent any time together. Did y'all have a fight or something?"

He released a slow, uneasy breath. He'd worried over a lot of things over the last forty-eight hours, but him and Jase not spending time together sure as hell wasn't one of them. He had racked his brain, trying to think of a way to come clean with Ali, tell her who he was and about her birth family without her hating him. But he still hadn't found any.

Hoping to distract her from what was a reasonable question, he teased her with a smile. "What? Are you trying to get rid of me?"

Laughing, she hugged his arm to her side. "Hardly. I just don't want you sticking close to the cabin because of me. He's your friend and I doubt you get to see each other all that much. You should take advantage of the opportunity while you're here."

That she would consider his needs over her own didn't surprise him and was just another trait she shared with his stepmother.

"I'm sure being out of town put him behind in his work," he said vaguely. "He'll drop by or call when he has a chance."

"If you say so," she said doubtfully. "I just didn't want you thinking you had to baby-sit me."

Knowing he couldn't put off taking her to Jase's house much longer, he stopped on the path and turned her to face him. "If you knew something about someone that they didn't know, would you tell them?"

She sputtered a laugh. "I don't know. I suppose. Why? Do you know something about Jase he doesn't know?"

Dropping his gaze, he smoothed a thumb over her knuckles. "No, though Jase plays a part in it." He looked up at her and opened his mouth, intending to tell her about her birth family as he'd promised Jase he'd do. But then he closed his mouth, knowing if he had a hundred years in which to accomplish the task, he'd never be able to find the words to tell her. Not without her hating him.

And he didn't want Ali to hate him.

Shaking his head, he pulled her into his arms and hugged her tight. "Never mind."

She pushed back to look at him. "But if it's bothering you, I'd like to help."

His smile wistful, he shook his head again. "Thanks, but you can't." He slung an arm around her shoulders and began to walk again. "Tell you what. When we get back to the cabin, I'll call Jase, see if he's caught up yet. I think it's time the two of you met."

Garrett didn't see any way the evening could go well. If he could roll back the clock, he would never have deceived Ali. He'd have told her from the first who he was and why he was at her bed-and-breakfast.

Of course, she may have slammed the door in his face, which would have put them all back at square one, with the family only partially reunited and the missing portion of the deed still missing.

But there was no sense wasting time with regrets, he told himself. What was done was done and he was just going to have to accept how Ali felt about him when this was all over.

"You're awfully quiet. Is something wrong?"

He glanced over at Ali, who was looking at him in concern from the passenger seat.

He turned his gaze back to the road, with a shrug. "No. Nothing to say, I guess."

"It's really nice of Mandy and Jase to have us over for dinner."

"Yeah, it is."

"I wish I'd had something to bring. Flowers. Something. I hate to arrive empty-handed."

"They invited us for dinner. We're not expected to contribute to the meal."

"I know. Still. Mandy stocked the refrigerator for us, brought us that yummy chocolate cake. And she's pregnant. I'd like to do something nice for her."

He slanted her a look. "We don't have to go. We can go back to the cabin if you want."

Her eyes rounded in dismay. "Are you crazy? I want to have dinner with your friends."

"Then why all the fretting?"

She flattened her lips and turned to face the windshield. "Men. Not a social grace in your bodies."

He laughed, in spite of his nervousness about the evening. "We may not have any social graces, but I bet we have fewer ulcers."

She sent him a withering look, then faced the front again. "We'll offer to do the dishes," she decided. "That'll be our contribution to the meal."

"Speak for yourself. I don't do dishes."

"Ingrate," she muttered under her breath, making him laugh.

As he drove up to the house, his smile faded.

"Oh, look," she said in excitement. "They're on the porch waiting for us."

Garrett shifted his gaze to the wide veranda-style porch, where Mandy and Jase sat side by side on a wooden swing. Praying the evening passed without a glitch, he parked and switched off the ignition.

As he climbed from the car, Ali hopped out from the opposite side, waving a hand over her head in greeting.

Mandy and Jase rose and met them at the steps.

Before Garrett had a chance to introduce Ali to Jase, Ali climbed the steps, extending a hand in greeting. "Hi, Jase. I'm Ali."

Garrett watched Jase's face as he shook Ali's hand and was surprised by the amount of emotion he detected in the other man's expression.

"Pleased to meet you, Ali." He released her hand

and stepped aside in an invitation for her to join them. "Mandy and I were just about to have a cup of hot spiced cider. Would you like some?"

"I would. Thanks."

Ali slipped her arm through Mandy's. "I want you to know I hate you. I've polished off at least half that cake."

Laughing, Mandy walked with her to a grouping of wicker chairs. "Better thee than me. I've gained so much weight my OB is threatening to wire my mouth shut."

"Come on, Garrett," Jase said, cutting Garrett off before he could join the women. "You can help me with the cider and leave the women to talk calories and babies."

Once inside, Jase stopped and held a hand against the door.

"You okay?" Garrett asked.

Jase nodded, then drew in a bracing breath and straightened. "It's just weird. Knowing that she and I are twins, yet she's a stranger. A complete stranger."

"Yeah, I'd imagine that's hard to grasp."

"It is," Jase agreed as he led the way to the kitchen. "She seems nice, though. Friendly as a young pup. And she looks so much like Mom, it's spooky."

"Yeah. Took me by surprise, too."

Jase stopped in the doorway and met Garrett's gaze. "We're telling her," he said, his tone brooking no argument. "You can pick the time, but she's not leaving this ranch until she knows she has family who wants to meet her."

Garrett nodded gravely, knowing that in giving Ali her family, there was a strong chance he'd lose her. "Yeah. It's only fair."

Ali walked at Mandy's side, while Mandy toured her through Jase's childhood home.

"It's beautiful," Ali said, awed by the tall ceilings and spacious rooms.

"I've always loved this house," Mandy confessed. "When I was in high school, I worked for Jase's mother here in the home office and I'd dream of living here someday with Jase."

"Really?" Ali said in surprise. "Were you and Jase high school sweethearts?"

"Heavens, no!" Mandy said, laughing. "I was more like his pesky kid sister. Jase was my brother's best friend," she went on to explain. "I had this *huge* crush on him, but he never saw me as anything but Bubba's little sister."

"Obviously he doesn't see you that way anymore. How did the two of you get together?"

"It's a long story," Mandy said as she led the way into the den. She gestured toward the overstuffed sofa. "Let's sit down, and I'll give you the *Reader's Digest* version of our romance."

Mandy tucked a foot beneath her and angled herself on the sofa to face Ali. "I moved back to San Saba after my divorce, wanting to be near family and friends while I adjusted to single life. Jase's mother had passed away a couple of months earlier, and he was in desperate need of someone to take over the office end of his family's businesses. Since I'd had experience working with his mother, he thought I'd be perfect for the job."

"Obviously you were perfect for more than just the job," Ali teased.

"I thought so, too, but it took Jase a while to realize I wasn't a kid any longer, I'd grown up. Even then, he wouldn't commit to a relationship with me." She smiled wistfully, remembering. "I knew he loved me, and I thought I'd made it clear that I loved him, but he'd enjoyed the bachelor life and wasn't ready to give it up. He also had this hang-up about marriage.

"He's adopted, you see," Mandy explained. "And it bothered him that he didn't know who his parents were, what kind of people they were. Of course, I never knew that about him. No one did. He kept it all inside. A doctor would ask him about his parents' health history and it would freak him out because he didn't know.

"He adored Mr. and Mrs. Calhoun," she was quick to add. "He never considered them as anything other than his real parents. It was just when he had to address the fact that he was adopted that caused him problems. He felt like he couldn't get married and have children, when he didn't know anything about himself or what kind of genes he might be passing on."

Ali gave Mandy's stomach a pointed look. "Obviously he got over that."

Smiling, Mandy laid a hand over her belly. "Yes and no. Yes, he decided to get married and have babies, and no he didn't get over his concerns." She seemed to hesitate a moment, then said cautiously, "He met his dad. I think once he saw that his father was normal and not some degenerate, it freed him of whatever concerns he had, and he asked me to marry him."

"Are you telling her about that sorry excuse I have for a dad?" Jase teased as he and Garrett entered the den.

Mandy glanced up and, laughing, held out a hand to Jase. "No, I'm telling her what a sweet and adorable father you have."

Jase dropped down at Mandy's feet and brought her fingers to his lips. "Wouldn't have met him, if not for Mandy. She actually met him first. In fact, she's the one who tracked him down. If left up to me, we'd have never gotten together."

"Really?" Ali said in surprise. "I'd think you would've jumped at the chance to meet your birth father. I know I would."

A silence fell over the room and Ali frowned as

she glanced around and found three sets of eyes focused on her. "What?" she said uneasily. "Did I say something wrong?"

Garrett gave her a nudge and she scooted over, making room for him on the sofa beside her.

"What?" she said again, his somber expression concerning her even more.

"How much do you know about the parents who gave you up?" Jase asked.

She turned to peer at him. "I…well, nothing, really. I know I was born in a hospital in North Carolina, but—" She stopped and looked at him in puzzlement. "How did you know I was adopted?" She glanced at Garrett. "I never even told you."

"No," he said quietly. "You didn't."

"Did your adopted parents ever tell you anything about your birth parents?" Jase asked.

She turned to look at the other man. "Not that I remember. Why?"

"My birth mother wrote me a letter. I thought maybe you were given one, too."

She shook her head, her frown deepening at the oddity of the conversation. "No. All I have is a birth certificate, but my parents' names are listed on it as my mother and father. My adoptive parents," she clarified. "The Morans."

"Does your birth certificate state whether yours was a single birth or multiple?"

She laughed uneasily, shifting her gaze from Jase to Mandy to Garrett. "What is this? An inquisition?"

"No," Jase assured her. "I'm just curious."

"Single," she said, although she couldn't imagine why the circumstances of her birth would be important to him.

Jase exchanged a glance with Garrett that Ali couldn't read.

"What's going on?" she asked in confusion. "I feel like all of you know something I don't."

She felt the weight of a hand cover hers and glanced over at Garrett. Her gut clenched at the grimness of his expression. "Garrett," she said uneasily. "Please tell me what is going on."

"Maybe I should be the one to tell her."

She whipped her gaze to Jase who had made the offer. "Tell me *what?*"

"I've met your adoptive parents, Ali."

She looked at him in confusion. "You've met my parents?"

He nodded. "I went to see them."

She couldn't think, couldn't breathe. None of this made sense. Jase had gone to see her parents? "But…why?"

"I'm a twin."

"So? What does that have to do with me and my parents?"

"I'm *your* twin."

She was on her feet, before she even realized she intended to stand. "What?" she cried, then shook her head. "No. This is crazy." She looked at Garrett for help. "Why is he saying these things? I'm not related to him. I was a single birth." She whipped her head around to glare at Jase. *"Single,"* she repeated, her voice rising. "Not a twin."

He pushed himself to his feet to stand before her. "I don't know why your birth certificate says single birth, but you *are* my twin." He pulled a folded piece of paper from his shirt pocket. "My birth certificate," he said and offered it to her.

She snatched it from his hand and opened it.

The date. The state of issue, North Carolina. The name of the hospital. They were all the same as on her birth certificate. The only differences were the names listed as mother and father.

Even with the proof in front of her, she couldn't believe it was true. "No," she whispered, shaking her head. "You're not my brother. You can't be."

He took the certificate from her trembling hands and tucked it back into his shirt pocket. "I know it's hard to believe. But I am."

"I don't understand." She looked at Garrett. "You knew?"

The guilty look on his face was answer enough.

"But how?" she asked him. "Why?"

"My stepmother is your birth mother," Garrett replied.

The blood drained from her face. "No," she said, and backed away, shaking her head in denial. "No." Hiccupping a sob, she spun and ran from the room.

Jase started after her, but Garrett caught his arm, stopping him. "No. Let me talk to her. I'm the one responsible for this."

Though he could see that Jase wanted to refuse, he finally backed down.

"All right," he said, then leveled a finger at Garrett's nose. "But she's not leaving the ranch. Not until she hears it all."

Seven

The drive back to the cabin was pure torture, with Ali sitting with her shoulder hugged against the passenger door, her face turned to the passenger window. Once inside the cabin, she went straight to the bedroom and began packing.

He laid a hand on her arm. "Ali, let me explain."

She whirled to face him. "Yes, please do. I think I deserve an explanation."

He caught her hand. "Let's sit down."

She yanked free. "I don't want to sit down."

He held up his hands. "All right. Fine. We'll stand." He dropped his arms to his sides. "First, let me say I'm sorry. I never intended for this to turn out this way. I never intended to hurt you. No," he said, shaking his head. "That's not true. I *did* want to hurt you."

She flinched as if he'd struck her, and he reached for her.

"Ali, please."

She took a step back. "No. Don't touch me." She gulped back tears. "You knew. All along, you knew about me, my parents, my adoption. You *knew* your stepmother was my mother, that Jase was my brother, and you never said a word. You told me you were in Austin to look for land. Why, Garrett? Why would you lie to me?"

"It wasn't a lie. I *was* looking for land."

"How convenient," she said, her voice sharp with resentment. "You had to be in Austin anyway, so why not drop by and seduce your stepmother's daughter."

"It wasn't like that, and you know it," he said angrily.

Realizing he was shouting, he stopped and drew in a deep breath, searching for calm. Finding it, he continued. "I didn't tell you who I was because I was afraid you'd refuse to talk to me. I thought if I could get to know you, I could figure out a way to persuade you to meet your mother, talk to her."

"Persuade?" she repeated incredulously. "I've wanted to meet my mother my entire life! Dreamed that some day she and my father would realize they'd made a mistake and demand the Morans give me back. You didn't need to *persuade* me. All you had to do was ask."

Groaning, he sank down on the edge of the bed and covered his face with his hands. "I didn't know. None of us did. When Mom and Eddie went to see the Morans in hopes of finding you, they claimed you wanted nothing to do with them. They said you wanted us to leave you alone." He lifted his head to look at her. "I hated you for that. For hurting my stepmother. Eddie and Jase were going to track you down anyway, but Barbara refused to let them. Made them promise they would honor your wishes. That's why I came."

"And you slept with me," she said angrily. "How could you make love with me, and not tell me who you were, what you knew about me? That you knew my parents, my brother?"

He met her gaze in silence, wishing like hell he'd told her from the beginning who he was, why he was there, and knowing there was nothing he could say now that would excuse what he'd done, no words he could offer that would earn him her forgiveness.

She turned away, and began throwing clothes into the bag again. "I'm going home."

"Ali. You can't."

She laughed, the sound so bitter, so filled with futility it nearly broke his heart. "Oh. Right. I don't have a home to go to anymore."

"That's not what I meant," he said in frustration. "It's not safe for you to go there."

"Fine." She slammed the lid down on her bag and zipped it closed. "Then I'll go to Traci's." She grabbed her bag and headed for the door. "I'll be safe at her house. Whoever wants you dead won't know to look for me there. And I'm taking the rental car—it's in my name anyway. You, Mr. Zillionaire, can find your own way back from wherever you came from."

He stood in the bedroom of the cabin and watched her go, knowing he had no right to ask her to stay and knowing there was nothing he could say that would change anything even if he did.

Ali paced around Traci's kitchen, one hand clamped over her mouth to hold back the tears.

Dropping her hand, she whirled to face her friend. "It was all a huge lie! And I fell for it *and* him!"

"But why did he keep his identity from you?" Traci asked in confusion. "Why not just tell you he knew your family?"

"Because he didn't think I wanted to meet my birth parents. None of them did."

"Well, that's just crazy. Why would anyone think a thing like that?"

"Because, my parents, my *adoptive* parents," she clarified, "told them I didn't."

"That still doesn't explain why Garrett didn't tell you who he was."

"He thought if I knew, I'd refuse to talk to him." Tears welled in her eyes. "I slept with him!" she cried. "Can you imagine how that makes me feel? Knowing that meant nothing to him and everything to me?"

Ali dropped down on a chair. "It doesn't matter," she said wearily. "Not anymore." She dragged in a shuddery breath, forcing her thoughts away from Garrett.

"I have a brother, Traci," she said, still unable to believe it herself. "A twin brother." Fresh tears welled. "And I'll probably never see him again."

Traci sank down beside her and draped an arm around her shoulders. "Don't talk like that," she scolded. "You'll see him again."

"You weren't there," Ali said miserably. "It was such a shock. I screamed at him. All of them. Refused to believe him until he showed me his birth certificate."

"Of course you were shocked," Traci soothed. "If the situation were reversed, I'm sure he would've reacted the same way. Give yourself some time. Once you've had a chance to absorb all this, you can call him, meet the rest of your family."

"No, I can't," Ali said tearfully.

Traci gave her a reassuring squeeze. "Sure you can. You're just feeling a bit overwhelmed right now."

"Don't you understand?" Ali cried in frustration. "I can't meet them. Not with Garrett a part of their lives."

"Now that's just plain ridiculous," Traci lectured firmly. "Just because he's your mother's stepson doesn't mean you can't have a relationship with your parents."

"It would mean seeing him, hearing about him." She shook her head. "I couldn't bear it. It would hurt too much."

Traci's eyes slowly rounded. "You're in love with him?"

Ali started to shake her head in denial, then dropped her chin and nodded, tears streaming down her face.

"Oh, Ali," Traci murmured.

They sat in silence a moment, then Traci stood abruptly. "Well, you may be willing to toss away your chance to meet your family, but I'm not letting you. We're calling Jase. You deserve to know the details about your birth, to meet your parents. And if you're worried about bumping into Garrett, Jase can come here. I'll be right here with you. A buffer, if you feel you need one." She leveled a finger at Ali's nose. "But we are calling him. I'm not going to let Garrett Miller rob you of the chance to meet your family. You have as much right to be a part of their lives as he does. Maybe even more."

* * *

Traci bulldozed Ali into making the call to Jase and a meeting was arranged to take place two days later.

Even though Traci knew what time Jase and Mandy were expected to arrive, when the doorbell sounded, she shot off the sofa as if catapulted from it.

"They're here," she said, stating the obvious, then turned and gave Ali a quick hug of reassurance. "Now don't worry," she said nervously. "I'll be right here with you the whole time. If your brother or sister-in-law say or do anything that upsets you, just give me the word, and I'll personally kick them out the door."

Ali forced a smile for Traci's benefit. "Thanks. Hopefully that won't be necessary."

As Traci went to let their visitors in, Ali rose, wiping her damp palms down the sides of her legs.

Mandy entered the living room first and as soon as Ali saw the woman who had been so kind to her, tears surged to her eyes.

"Oh, Ali," Mandy cried, her face crumpling. She rushed across the room to throw her arms around Ali. "I'm so sorry," she said tearfully. "This is all such a mess."

Ali nodded, too choked by emotion for a moment to speak. "Yes, it is."

Mandy withdrew and caught Ali's hands, gave them a squeeze. "We're going to get this all straightened out, I promise." She turned to her husband. "Aren't we, Jase?"

He stepped forward and laid a hand on Ali's shoulder. "I damn sure hope so. I've been without a sister long enough."

After talking with Jase and Mandy for over an hour, Ali had even more questions to wonder about.

"And you say the Morans never gave you a letter from our mother?" Jase asked.

She shook her head. "No. And I would've remembered if they had. I asked about my birth parents a number of times, but they told me it was a private adoption and they knew nothing about them. When I was a teenager, fifteen or sixteen, I think, I tried to find them on my own. All I had to go on was what little information was on the birth certificate. I called the hospital and they told me they couldn't help me, that I would have to contact whatever lawyer was involved." She shrugged. "I had no idea who that was, so I gave up."

"Mom wrote you a letter," Jase assured her. "Same as she did me. She told me so. She even taped a piece of a deed on the back that was given to her by Eddie, our father. I have the other half."

Ali frowned. "Piece of a deed?"

"That's a story all by itself," Mandy interjected. "The night before he left for Vietnam, Eddie was in a bar with a bunch of other soldiers. They had a drink with a rancher and he wrote out a deed to his ranch, tore it into six pieces and gave each of the soldiers a piece, telling them to join the pieces together when they returned from Vietnam, and he would give them his ranch."

Ali's eyebrows shot up. "Are you kidding? He just gave them his ranch?"

"He was a widower," Jase explained, taking up the telling of the story. "His only son was killed in Vietnam. Eddie seems to think the rancher knew they were scared, knew what dangers they were going to face, and he was giving them a reason to survive the war and make it home."

"He gave them his ranch?" Ali said, finding it hard to believe that a complete stranger would do such a thing.

"So it seems," Jase said with a shrug. "All the pieces have been accounted for except Eddie's. He gave his to Mom and asked her to keep it for him until after the war. When she found out she was pregnant, she tried to contact Eddie, but was told he'd died in battle. They gave her the wrong information," he was quick to tell her. "He was injured, not killed. Anyway, with Mom thinking he was dead, when she learned she was carrying twins, she decided to put us up for adoption. I think you can understand her reasoning. A single woman left to raise a set of twins on her own? She was scared, grieving, afraid she wouldn't be able to properly care for us and thought she could insure us a better life if she gave us up.

"She wrote a letter to each of us. All she had of Eddie's was the piece of deed he'd given her, so she tore it in half and taped a piece to each of the letters, wanting us to have something that was his." He opened his hands. "We've already told you how I came to find my piece, as well as our parents."

"You mentioned visiting my parents," Ali began.

"The Doctors Scary?" He shuddered. "Sorry, but those are the coldest, most unfriendly people I've ever had the displeasure to meet."

"Jase!" Mandy cried, horrified that he might have offended Ali.

Hiding a smile, Ali patted Mandy's hand. "It's true. His description is right-on."

Somewhat mollified, Mandy released a breath, but gave Jase a warning look anyway.

"They didn't tell us anything," Jase went on to explain. "At least not how to find you. All they told us was that you wanted nothing to do with your birth family."

"And you believed them," she said, remembering Garrett had told her the same thing.

Jase opened his hands. "Why wouldn't we? We didn't particularly care for the Morans, but we had no reason to think they'd lie." He shook his head sadly. "Mom, she took it real hard. Dad and I were prepared to turn the world upside down until we found you, but Mom put her foot down. Said we had to respect your right for privacy and made us promise we'd leave you alone." He scowled. "Unfortunately she didn't include Garrett in that promise-making."

"He meant well," Mandy said in Garrett's defense. "He's very close to Barbara. Overly protective, at times. It made him mad that you wouldn't agree to meet her."

When Ali opened her mouth to deny her unwillingness, Mandy held up a hand. "That's what he thought, anyway. What we *all* thought." She lifted a shoulder. "Anyway, that's why he decided to play detective." She rolled her eyes. "Not a very smart move on his part, but his heart was in the right place."

Ali released a breath. "If you don't mind," she said, "I'd rather we not talk about him."

Jase and Mandy exchanged a look.

"So?" Jase said, and clapped his hands against his thighs. "When do you want to meet Mom and Dad?"

Ali didn't know how to respond. Jase's and Mandy's expectant and hopeful expressions indicated their desire for her to agree to an immediate date, but a voice inside her cried for caution. What if she agreed to meet her parents and, for whatever reason, they chose not to be a part of her life? She'd had her heart bruised by her adoptive parents so many times in the past, she was hesitant to expose herself to hurt again.

Plus, there was Garrett to consider. Agreeing to meet her parents would surely mean seeing him again, and she wasn't prepared for that. Not yet.

Refusing to be forced into committing to something, she gave an honest, if nonanswer. "I need to think about this. There's more to consider here than just meeting my birth parents."

Jase's disappointment was almost palpable.

Mandy's was just as obvious, but was quickly masked behind a kind smile.

"There's no hurry," she assured Ali. "Barbara and Eddie will understand your hesitation. Take whatever time you need and give us a call when you're ready."

With nothing left for any of them to say, Jase stood. "Thank you for inviting us to come and talk with you," he said to Ali, then turned to Traci. "And you for allowing us the use of your home."

Ali stood, as well. "I—" She stopped, suddenly overcome with emotion, as if she were saying goodbye to them for the last time. "I'm sorry," she said, pressing a finger beneath her nose. "I…this has all been so upsetting."

To her surprise, Jase gathered her up in his arms and gave her a tight tug. "This isn't goodbye," he said as if reading her mind. "We're going to be seeing a lot of each other." He pushed her out to arm's length to smile down at her. "Hell, we're almost neighbors. San Saba's not that far a drive from here."

She stared up at him, realizing this was his way of telling her he'd still be a part of her life, no matter what decision she made about their parents. Tears filled her eyes, joy her heart. "No, San Saba's not far, at all."

Jase reached for Mandy's hand and turned to leave, then snapped his fingers and turned back around. "I almost forgot. Garrett asked me to tell you it's safe for you to go back home."

Ali wasn't sure what she'd expected to feel upon returning to the Vista after staying with Traci a week, but it certainly wasn't the sense of gloom that engulfed her as she walked through rooms that had brought her such joy and comfort for more than ten years.

She blamed her melancholy on the house being sold, on her being forced to move and leave the home she loved behind. But she knew in her heart that wasn't the cause. The root of her sadness was the man who had shared the house with her for a short space of time. Everywhere she looked she saw Garrett. Sitting at the bar in the kitchen eating his breakfast. Sprawled on the sofa in the den, watching *Jeopardy*.

Even her private quarters offered no refuge. The scent of sandalwood she would always associate with Garrett hung in the air, a constant reminder of the night he'd "chosen" her bed to sleep in. And when she curled up in her bed at night to sleep, she envisioned him there, braced above her, as he'd been the night she'd awakened him to tell him about the men she'd seen lurking outside.

She tried telling herself she hadn't fallen in love with him. What she'd felt for him was an infatuation that any woman might have experienced upon finding herself in the company of a man of such wealth and stature. But she knew that wasn't the case. As foolish as it was, she had fallen in love with him. With a man who had as little respect for her feelings and needs as the people who had raised her. A man who had deceived her and withheld information for his own gain.

So she did what she always did in times of strife. She mentally boxed up her sadness and disappointments and filed them away, refusing to give them credence, and went about the task of packing what belongings she'd gathered in the span of ten years.

And if she had to pause and wipe away an occasional tear as she went along, she blamed it on allergies or the dust she was stirring. It certainly wasn't because she was missing Garrett.

Eight

"So he's behind bars?" Garrett asked his security chief, Joe.

"Currently in Switzerland, but the Feds are in negotiations to have him transferred to the United States. Since he committed no crime in their country, the Swiss shouldn't have a problem releasing him to us."

Garrett shook his head, still unable to believe the man who'd made his life a living hell for the last three months was no longer a threat.

"Were you able to talk to him?" he asked Joe.

"Briefly. A more extensive interrogation will take place once we have him back in the States."

"Did he say why he wanted to kill me?"

Joe rolled his ever-present toothpick to the far corner of his mouth and averted his gaze, as if hesitant to share what he knew.

"It was me he wanted dead," Garrett reminded him.

"It was at that," Joe said, and with a sigh, laid out what facts he'd managed to pull from the man. "Jealousy and greed is what it boiled down to," he said in summation. "You had everything, and he wanted it."

"But why me?" Garrett asked in frustration. "There are others with more money who make themselves easier targets."

"But not a one of them went to the same high school you did."

"High school?" Garrett repeated. "He's someone I know?"

Joe shrugged again. "Don't know whether you do or not. The name's Matt Collins."

Garrett frowned, trying to put the name with a face, then shook his head. "Never heard of him."

"He knew you, all right. Had his eye on you for years, the hate building as he watched you get richer and richer. Thought himself smarter than you, deserved what you had. Worked as a tech for the company a couple years back. Got fired for stealing equipment. Since then he's moved from job to job, biding his time, waiting for the opportunity." He pulled the now shredded toothpick from his mouth and tossed it into the leather wastebasket beside the desk. "He walked right into the trap, oblivious to what was going on around him."

"What about the guy who doubled for me? Was he hurt?"

"Not a scratch on him. We sprang the trap before the perp could snatch him."

Garrett wondered how many times he'd been within the man's reach and never known it, then shook off the thought, knowing he couldn't allow himself to think like that and hope to lead any kind of normal life in the future.

He stood and extended a hand across the desk. "I appreciate all you did, Joe. I owe you my life."

Joe rose and clasped his hand, shook. "Just doing my job."

Garrett waited until the door closed behind Joe, then seated himself again behind his desk and reached for the mail he was reviewing when Joe had arrived with his report.

Noticing a padded envelope, he pulled it from the stack, but froze when he saw the familiar logo of the Vista Bed and Breakfast. Noticing his hand had begun to shake, he flexed his fingers a couple of times, before opening the envelope. He peered inside, then pulled out the bundle of photographs enclosed.

A slip of paper clipped to the bundle read: "Souvenir pictures from your trip to Texas, as promised," and was signed with an "A."

He stared at the note a moment, then swore and picked up the phone and punched in the number for the Vista, telling himself it was ridiculous to continue on this way. He listened through four rings before the recorder clicked on.

"You've reached the Vista Bed and Breakfast. I'm sorry I can't take your call right now. Please leave your name and number and I'll call you back as soon as I can."

He held the phone to his ear another moment, just to make sure she didn't pick up, then returned it to its cradle when it became obvious she wasn't going to answer. Scooping up the pictures from his desk, he leaned back in his chair.

How would she categorize this series of shots? he wondered as he thumbed through the pictures. Theme or story? There was only him in each frame, but he didn't recall her saying the number of subjects assigned it to any particular category. He paused at the picture of him standing with one boot braced on the boulder, and chuckled, remembering Ali's instructions.

Give me a forlorn look. You know. Like you've been running from the law for months, and you're missing that pretty little saloon girl you met up in Dodge City.

His smile slowly faded. If she wanted forlorn, she should see him now, he thought. If missing a girl produced the look, he sure as hell qualified, because he missed Ali in the worst sort of way.

Scowling, he sat up and tossed the pictures to the desk. Too bad she didn't feel the same, he thought as he eyed the single line of handwriting on the note clipped to the pictures. No, "Hi, how are you," or, better yet, "Can we hit Rewind?" the phrase she'd used when they'd gotten off to the bad start the day he'd arrived in Austin.

How he'd like to hit Rewind, he thought with regret. If he had it to do over again, he'd do things right.

He tensed, his brain snagging on the idea of a second chance. It was possible, he told himself. He'd agreed to hit Rewind when she'd asked it of him. Shouldn't she be required to do the same?

Losing your temper and deceiving someone doesn't exactly fall into the same "sin" category.

He scowled at his conscience's assessment of the situation. Okay, so she probably wouldn't give him a second chance.

Groaning, he dropped his head to his hands. Dammit, he missed her. Wanted to be with her. And if he was half as smart as people thought him, he would've told her he loved her when he had the chance.

He balled his hands into fists against his desk. There had to be a way to work this out, he thought in frustration. A way to make her understand why he'd done what he'd done, convince her to give him another chance.

The obvious was simply getting his butt back to Texas and asking her for that chance. But he couldn't just show up on her doorstep. What would he say? More, what would *she* say when she saw him? He choked a breath. Hell, that was a no-brainer. She'd slam the door in his face.

No, he had to have a purpose, a reason for going to her house. And he was going to have to come up with one pretty darn quick, because she wouldn't be living at the Vista much longer. Not if Ronald Fleming had his way.

He tensed at the reminder of Ronald Fleming. That's it! he thought, and pushed from his chair.

She couldn't refuse to let Garrett into a house he *owned!*

Throughout the flight home to Austin, Ali kept waiting for a delayed reaction to set in. Anger. Regret. Loss. But she felt nothing. She supposed she shouldn't have expected to feel anything after confronting her adoptive parents with all she'd learned about her birth family. She certainly had no regrets. Those she would reserve for her parents, although she was sure they considered themselves beyond fault. As to loss, how could she mourn something she'd never truly had? Her adoptive parents had never loved her, and whatever feelings she might've had for them they'd frozen out of her years ago.

As she pulled up to the front gate of the Vista and waited for the electronic gate to open, she noticed a bright red Sold banner had been added to the For Sale sign during her absence. The regret and loss she had expected to feel after the ugly confrontation with her parents filled her throat. But she felt no anger. She couldn't be mad at Claire's father for taking something that was never hers to begin with.

Blinking back tears, she drove through the gate and parked in front of the house. Gathering her tote from the passenger seat, she climbed from the car and walked to the front door. Rather than dig for her house key, she punched the code into the keyless entry, turned the knob and stepped into the house she'd thought of as home for more than ten years.

She set her tote on the floor beside the mahogany hall tree, and looked around as she shrugged out of her coat. Open boxes sat on the living room floor, packed with the carefully wrapped treasures she'd collected over the years. White sheets draped the tapestry sofas Mimi had left behind. Gulping back emotion, she hung her coat over one of the hall tree's brass hooks and headed for the den and her stereo, anxious to push back the oppressive silence with the sound of music.

She flipped through her stack of CDs, selected a disc of hits from the sixties, seventies and eighties and slid it into the player. With Mick Jagger and The Rolling Stones grinding out "Ruby Tuesday," she turned for the kitchen.

And jerked to a stop, just managing to squelch the scream that shot to her throat. Garrett stood at the foot of the rear staircase, dressed in the jeans, boots and Western shirt she'd picked out for him. She stared, her heart threatening to break.

That he would have the nerve to enter her home after what he'd done to her, filled her with fury. "What are you doing here?"

"Taking care of some unfinished business."

Which told her absolutely nothing. "How did you get in?"

"Used the code you gave me. Still works."

Silently cursing herself for not thinking to change it, she folded her arms across her chest. "The Vista is closed. You'll have to find someplace else to stay."

"You're here," he said, stating the obvious.

"I *live* here," she reminded him tersely, then remembered the Sold sign out front and added, "for the time being, anyway."

"I paid for a month and stayed here considerably less than that. I'm due a few days."

She dropped her hands into fists at her sides, angry with him for coming here unannounced, for opening a wound she was praying would eventually heal. "Why are you doing this, Garrett? You can afford to stay anywhere you want. Why insist upon staying *here?*"

"I told you," he said, and started toward her. "I'm due a few days yet."

"Fine," she said, and whirled for the writing desk where she kept the books for the Vista. "I'll refund your money." She snatched open the lap drawer, yanked out the checkbook, then dropped down on the chair. "You were here, what? Two weeks? I'll refund half your money."

"I don't want a refund. I want to stay."

She flinched at the nearness of his voice, unaware that he'd moved to stand behind her. Setting her jaw, she pressed the pen to the check and began filling it out. "Well, you're not. The Vista's closed."

"As I recall, it was closed when you agreed to take my reservations for the month of January."

"Yes," she said tersely. "It was always closed in January. That's when I took my vacation."

"What's the difference? Closed is closed, right?"

She slammed the pen down and spun on the chair to look up at him. It was a mistake. But certainly not the first she'd made concerning Garrett Miller.

His brown eyes seemed to grab her, holding her captive. She squeezed her own eyes shut to block whatever power it was he had over her. "I don't want you here."

"Why?"

She flipped open her eyes to glare at him. "Because I don't. Okay?" She spun back around and quickly finished filling out the check, tore it from the book. Pushing to her feet, she thrust it at him. "Take your money and go."

"Could we hit Rewind?"

"What?" she said incredulously.

"Hit Rewind. I seem to have gotten off on the wrong foot with you."

She closed her eyes again, gulped, then opened them to meet his gaze, sure that he was determined to rip her heart right out of her chest. "Don't. Please. Just go."

He lifted a hand and swept her hair back from her face. "Now that doesn't seem quite fair. When you asked me if we could hit Rewind, I didn't refuse you."

The tears welled higher, the pain in her chest so strong she was afraid it would drag her to her knees. "Garrett. Please."

He tucked the lock of hair behind her ear and sidled closer. "Please, what, Ali?"

She gulped, swallowed. "Please, don't hurt me anymore."

"I won't. Not intentionally. I never meant to hurt you before."

"But you did. You lied to me."

He slipped his arms around her waist. "I didn't lie. I just didn't tell you the whole truth."

She pressed her hands against his chest, fighting the urge to melt into his arms, knowing she couldn't resume the relationship they had before, if that's what he wanted. Not when she knew now that she loved him.

"You slept with me," she cried. "Made love with me. How could you do that and know what you knew, and not tell me?" She curled her hands into fists against his chest, the tears a stream of fire streaking down her face. "What was I? A nice diversion for you, while you waited for the perfect opportunity to get what you wanted from me?

"I made love with you because I wanted you, Garrett. *You.* I even fell in love with you. I didn't mean to, and if I had it to do over, I'd do everything within my power to keep from loving you." She swept a frustrated hand over her cheeks, furious with herself for baring her soul to him, letting him see how much he meant to her. "I can't undo what's done. But I *can* protect my heart from any more hurt. I lived my whole life trying to win my parents' love and they couldn't or wouldn't love me back. I won't go through that again. I can't."

"I wouldn't want you to," he said softly. He stroked his fingers along her cheek, watching their movement, before shifting his gaze back to hers. "Feelings don't come easy for me. And I'm not saying that to excuse the way I treated you. I spent the first six years of my life without affection. Never truly experienced anything close to it until my stepmother came into my life. Even then it was hard for me to show my feelings, harder to express them."

He cupped a hand at her cheek. "But I do love you, Ali. As hard as you might find that to believe, I love you with all my heart."

She pressed a hand to her lips, her gaze fixed on his. "Oh, Garrett," she whispered. "I didn't know. I thought—"

He hugged her hard against his chest. "I know. You thought I had used you, deceived you, and I understand why you would feel that way. I handled all this poorly from the beginning. Before coming to Austin I had already made up my mind to dislike you." He drew his head back to look down at her. "I believed you had hurt my stepmother, the one person in my life who cared about me. When I came here, it was for her. I wanted her to be happy, and I knew she wouldn't be until she had the opportunity to see you, talk to you, explain to you why she had given you up." He laid a hand against her cheek. "And maybe I wanted revenge, to hurt you as much as you had hurt her. But that was all before I met you, got to know you. Before I realized you were the victim, not the villain I'd thought you to be."

"Oh, Garrett," she said tearfully. "My parents

should have never told her that. When I read the letter she wrote me—"

"You read the letter?" he said in confusion.

She nodded.

"But I thought you said you'd never gotten a letter?"

"I hadn't. Not until yesterday."

"But…where? How?"

"I flew up to see my parents and asked for it."

He turned her toward the sofa and urged her down, sat beside her. "They had the letter all this time and never gave it to you?"

She dropped her gaze and shook her head. "No. In fact, Mother denied having it until I told her I'd seen Jase's letter and knew that my birth mother had written one to me, too. I asked her about my birth certificate, too. Why it had single birth listed, when Jase's was marked as being a twin." She looked up at him, unable to hide the hurt. "She did it. Mother." She shook her head again, still unable to believe her mother would go to such lengths. "She'd never admit it, but I think she was afraid I'd try to find my birth parents. That's why she never gave me the letter."

"And you read all of it?"

She nodded. "During the flight home." Tears welled in her eyes. "I wish so badly I'd had it years ago. She loved me, Garrett. Even though she gave me up, she loved me. I could feel it in every word she wrote, and I felt her pain. I can't even imagine how hard it was for her to make the decision to give me up for adoption."

"She wanted what was best for you. You and Jase."

She smiled sadly. "I know that now. I just wish I'd known it years ago. Maybe it would've made living with my parents a little easier."

"Would you like to meet her?"

"More than anything. My father, too."

A broad smile spread across his face. "That can be arranged. But first—" He leaned back and dug a hand into his pocket. "This is for you."

She frowned in confusion at the key he offered her. "What's this?"

"The key to the Vista."

She choked a laugh. "Thanks," she said and pushed his hand away. "But I won't be needing a key to the Vista much longer."

He nudged the key against her hand, urging her to take it. "No, it's yours."

"I don't understand."

"It's yours. The Vista. I bought it."

Her jaw sagged. "You bought the Vista?"

"Signed the papers first thing this morning."

"But…why?"

"Since I'm planning on building a satellite location here, I figure we'll need a place to stay when we're in town."

"Garrett," she said, afraid she'd misunderstood. "What are you saying?"

He shook his head sadly. "I guess I've handled this as poorly as I did reuniting you with your mother." He closed his hand around hers. "I want you to marry me, Ali. I know how much you love this house, and I'd never ask you to give it up. We can split our time between D.C. and Austin. Or, if you'd prefer, this can be our permanent residence, and I'll keep my house in D.C. for when I need to be there on business."

"Wait," she said weakly. "Back up to that part about you wanting to marry me."

Laughing, he wrapped his arms around her and hugged her tight. "That's one of the things I love most about you, Ali. You don't have a clue how irresistible I find you."

She clung to him, as if he were a mirage that would disappear if she dared let go. "I can't believe this. Me, Ali Moran, marrying a zillionaire."

"I'd worry if I thought it was my money you were after."

She jerked back to look at him in alarm. "I swear it's you I love, not your money."

Smiling, he drew her back into his arms. "And that's another thing I like about you. You'd be as happy poor as you would be rich."

"Uh, Garrett." She pulled back to look at him. "That's not exactly true. I've been broke before, and I really don't want to ever be that way again."

"And you won't be," he assured her. "I'll always take care of you. Always."

Tears filled her eyes at his promise, and she leaned to press her lips to his. "And I'll always take care of you."

"Ah, Ali," he said, hugging her tight. "I love you so much."

"And I love you."

He set her aside. "Now about meeting your mother," he said and stood.

She sputtered a laugh. "What are you going to do? Make me sign a pledge, or something?"

"No, I'm going to get her." He turned toward the rear staircase. "Mom? Eddie? You can come down now."

Ali's eyes went as round as saucers as she heard the pounding of feet overhead. "They're here?" she said in disbelief.

Smiling proudly, he nodded. "Just waiting for me to pop the question before they came down to meet you."

She shot to her feet. "Now?" she cried, and began scrubbing at her cheeks and finger-combing her hair. "But look at me. I'm a mess!"

Garrett caught her hands and brought them to his lips. "No, you're not. You're beautiful."

"Oh, you're just saying that," she chided, then froze, her eyes going wide, as a man and woman appeared at the foot of the staircase.

The woman spoke first, her voice, as well as her posture hesitant. "Ali?"

Ali couldn't speak. The resemblance to herself

was so strong, she knew she was looking at her mother. She placed a hand at her throat, nodded. "Y-yes. I'm Ali." She took a tentative step, another, then was running across the room and throwing her arms around her mother.

"Well, I'll be a son-of-a-gun," Eddie said, swiping a tear from his eye. "She looks just like you, Barbara."

Barbara pushed Ali back to hold at arm's length, so that she could look at her. "Oh, no, Eddie," she said softly. "She's beautiful. Our daughter is absolutely beautiful."

She reached for Garrett's hand and drew him to join the circle, she, her husband Eddie and their daughter formed.

"My family is complete now," she said, her smile radiant. "Eddie, the babies we lost so many years ago, and the son of my heart, Garrett."

Turning her face up to Garrett, she gave his hand a squeeze. "If I'd been given the charge of choosing a wife for you, or choosing a husband for my daughter, I couldn't have found a more perfect match for either of you, or one I could love any more than I do the two of you."

Late that same night, Ali lay in her bed, unable to sleep for thinking about all that happened that day. In the span of a few short hours, she'd become engaged, had the key to the Vista presented to her and met her birth parents. It was a wonder she wasn't doing cartwheels down the street!

She heard the squeak of her bedroom door opening and sat up. "Garrett?" she whispered uncertainly.

"Who were you expecting?" he teased as he climbed into bed with her.

She shot a nervous glance up at the ceiling. "What if Barbara and Eddie heard you?"

"Don't worry. I was quiet as a mouse."

Smothering a laugh, she cuddled up next to him. "I feel like a teenager sneaking around behind her parents' back."

He slipped a hand beneath her pajama top and cupped her breast. "Kind of adds an element of excitement, doesn't it?"

"I'm not sure I can take much more excitement," she said breathlessly.

Smiling, he pressed his lips to hers. "I love you, Ali."

She laid a hand against his cheek. "I'll never get tired of hearing you say that." She slipped her arms around his neck. "Make love with me, Garrett," she whispered.

"What if Barbara or Eddie get up for a drink of water or something and hear us?"

She nipped at his ear. "I think they'll understand, don't you?"

Epilogue

Two years later....

Ali drew in a deep breath, savoring the scent of wild honeysuckle that filled the air.

"You okay?"

She glanced up to find Garrett looking at her, his brow furrowed in concern. Smiling, she hugged his arm to her side. "I'm fine. Just enjoying the fresh air. It's beautiful here, isn't it? So quiet and peaceful."

Garrett looked around at the tranquil setting they stood in, then turned his gaze to the memorial they'd come to unveil. "That was the hope when this was designed."

"Do you think they know?" she asked. "The soldiers, I mean. Do you think they somehow know the rancher honored his promise to them?"

"One of them does," he said, and tipped his head toward Eddie, who stood on the fringe of the group gathered, his gaze on the statue of the six soldiers. "Your dad."

She blinked back tears, still finding it hard to believe that after all these years, her dream of being united with her birth family had become a reality.

"I can't imagine how he must feel," she said, "knowing he's the only one of the soldiers to make it to this day."

"I imagine he's experiencing a lot of different emotions at the moment. Pride. Sadness. Joy."

She looked at him curiously. "Joy?"

"Think about it. For over thirty years, Eddie lived a solitary life, thinking he'd lost the woman he loved and unaware he'd fathered a set of twins. Now he and Barbara are married, and he not only has a son and a daughter, but a son- and daughter-in-law, as well."

A toddler waddled up and stretched up her hands to Garrett. "Hol' me."

"And grandchildren, too," he added, chuckling, then reached down and swung his niece up into his arms. She immediately laid her head on his shoulder and popped her thumb into her mouth. "Hey, sunshine," he said. "Are you sleepy?"

"Uh-uh," she said, even as her eyes shuttered close. "Molly no take nap."

Hiding a smile, Ali slipped her arm around Garrett's waist. "You're going to make a wonderful father."

He lifted a brow. "You think so?"

"I know so. Molly's a hard-sell and she thinks you're fabulous."

"That's because she has me wrapped around her finger. All she has to do is bat those pretty blue eyes at me, and I'll do whatever she wants."

Ali laid a hand over her swollen stomach. "If you're that big a sucker for little girls, let's hope we have boys."

Garrett released a shuddery breath. "Twins. I'm still having a hard time wrapping my mind around the idea of us having two babies, instead of just one."

"Better get used to it," she warned. "They'll be here sooner than you think. Oh, look," she said, spotting a couple making their way up the path to the memorial. "There's Stephanie and Wade Parker."

"The lady responsible for starting all this. That's Wade's daughter with them, isn't it?" he said, straining to see who was following the couple.

"Yes, that's Heather." Ali laughed softly. "And

that's their son Clayton Heather's pulling in the wagon. Isn't he a doll?"

"Better not let Wade hear you refer to his son as a 'doll,'" Garrett warned. "Men are funny like that. Always worrying women are going to turn their sons into sissies."

"And women are afraid men are going to spoil their daughters and turn them into prima donnas."

Smiling, Garrett pressed a kiss to Molly's cheek. "Hard not to spoil someone who's so darn cute."

"Have you seen Leah Forrester?" she asked, as she searched the crowd.

"Is she the one who's married to the Special Forces guy?"

"Yes. Sam. Though he's no longer in the military."

"I saw them a minute ago over by the pavilion, checking on the arrangements for the dinner we're having later."

"That woman is an organizational wonder. I can't imagine organizing an affair for a group of this size."

Out of the corner of her eye she saw her father, Eddie, begin to make his way toward the podium, and eased closer to Garrett. "I think the service is about to start," she whispered.

As Eddie stepped onto the flatbed trailer that was serving as their dais, quiet settled over the crowd.

Emotion swelled in Ali's throat, as she watched him walk toward the podium, his head up, his shoulders square, knowing he was concentrating hard on his gait, to hide the limp the war had left him with. When he reached the podium, Ali laced her fingers through Garrett's and squeezed.

"My name is Eddie Davis," he said into the microphone. He turned to look behind him at the statue of the six soldiers. "And I'd like to introduce you to some of my friends." He lifted a hand. "That guy in the middle there," he said, pointing. "That's Poncho. He's the only one of the six who doesn't have family representing him here today. Poncho chose a different road to travel, but he was a good soldier and a good friend.

"The guy to the left of Poncho is Preacher. A kinder person, or one with a more generous heart, you'll never meet." He gestured again. "And next to Preacher is T.J. For years, T.J. was listed as Missing in Action, but thanks to the work of Sam Forrester and his team of Special Forces, T.J.'s classification was recently changed to Killed in Action, which allowed his family to finally lay him to rest.

"If you'll look to the right of Poncho, that's Romeo." He laughed softly. "Now, Romeo knew how to romance a woman, no doubt about it, which is how he came by the nickname. But Romeo had a natural friendliness and spirit of fun that surpassed gender and made him a favorite with everyone he met.

"That ugly devil to the right of Romeo—" he

chuckled "—well, that's me." His smile faded, and he blew out a shuddery breath. "And I'm here to tell you, it feels mighty strange to be looking at a memorial statue of myself and still be standing here breathing."

Laughter rippled through the crowd. When it subsided, Eddie gestured again, pointing to the statue on the far right. "And that tall, lanky man is Pops. If you'll notice, the artist who created the memorial placed Pops' statue where it appears he's walking a half-step or so behind the others, his eyes cut to the right, as if he's keeping an eye on the others."

He paused a moment, gulped, then turned to face the audience. "There's a reason for that. Pops trained us, looked after us, kept us in line. Kicked our tails, when he thought we needed it. Most importantly he loved us." He paused again, to drag the back of his hand across his eyes. "Pops tried his damnedest to take care of us, get us all home alive." He shook his head sadly. "But some things just weren't meant to be."

He glanced back at the statues. "Each of these six men represents thousands of other soldiers just like him. Men, who were willing to put their lives on the line for their country in the fight for freedom."

He held up a hand, as if staving off an argument. "Now I know there are those who hate war and are constantly protesting for peace. And there are those who think we shouldn't be honoring soldiers who, in their eyes, are the same as murderers. But you know what? Not a one of these six men started that war. They did what was asked of them, what was expected of them. For some, it meant making the ultimate sacrifice. Their lives. For others, like me, it meant losing a foot, or a limb."

He gripped his hands on the sides of the podium and leaned forward, his gaze intense. "There was one man who appreciated the sacrifices our soldiers were asked to make and that was Walt Webber. In a bar more than thirty years ago, Mr. Webber wrote out a deed and gave each of us soldiers portrayed here a piece of that paper, telling us to join those pieces when we returned and take ownership of his ranch.

"Some say Mr. Webber was crazy, that the loss of his own son in Vietnam had driven him over the edge. There are others who say he never intended to give his ranch to a bunch of strangers. Whether there is any truth in that statement, I don't know, but I do know this. When Walt Webber looked into the faces of those six soldiers that night, he saw youth and he saw fear. He'd lost a son in the same war we were going to fight, and like any father, he wanted to do something to alleviate that fear. He wanted to give us a reason to stay alive, to make it home. So he signed his ranch over to us and gave each of us a piece of the deed to keep."

Eddie dug into his pocket, pulled out the faded

piece of paper and held it up for all to see. "This is the piece that Walt Webber gave to me that night. To some of you, it may look like nothing more than a scrap of trash, but to me, it represented hope, one man's belief that I'd make it home one day."

He laid the piece of paper on the podium, then lifted his gaze to the audience again. "I'm proud of you," he said, speaking directly to the children of the soldiers. "I'm proud of what you've done to make this day possible. You believed when others doubted. You persisted when others would've given up. You persevered when faced with seemingly insurmountable problems. As a group, you made the decision to take Walt Webber's ranch and turn it into a sanctuary and retreat for *all* veterans, not just the ones it was originally given to. In creating this place, you honor not only the memory of the soldiers memorialized here, but the memory of Mr. Webber and his son, as well."

He braced a hand on the podium and turned to look at the statues. "T.J. Preacher. Poncho. Romeo. Pops. I've never forgotten a one of you boys." He dragged an arm across his eyes, clearing the moisture from them. "And I never will."

* * * * *

THE GREEK TYCOON'S
SECRET HEIR

by
Katherine Garbera

Dear Reader,

The Greek Tycoon's Secret Heir was inspired by two things. The first was my cousin Patty Ann's descriptions of Greece when she visited there just after college. Her stories were lush and vivid. I think I fell in love with the country at that very moment. Years later I still haven't visited, but in my imagination I've been there many times. And I always have a strong, handsome Greek man at my side…well, that's the fantasy, isn't it?

The second thing to inspire me was actually my hero, Christos. I was thinking about how our life sometimes changes unexpectedly, and we find ourselves thrust into a role that we had never anticipated. In Christos's case, he was the second son of a powerful man. The spare, not the heir, and he partied hard, did whatever felt good and in general lived only for himself. To become the man he was meant to be, I knew that he was going to have to face a challenge. For Christos, the change comes when his brother is killed in a plane crash. Suddenly, Christos isn't the second son any more… he's the only son.

Ava Monroe is a woman who once defined herself with lies. She grew up poor and was embarrassed by that poverty, so she created a fantasy background for herself. When she met Christos, she wasn't mature enough to realise that lies have a way of coming back to haunt you. Five years later she is much more mature, when Christos comes back into her life.

Please enjoy this story and look for *The Wealthy Frenchman's Proposition* next month.

Happy reading!

Katherine Garbera

KATHERINE GARBERA

is a strong believer in happily ever after. She's written more than thirty-five books and has been nominated for *Romantic Times BOOKreviews* career achievement awards in Series Fantasy and Series Adventure. Her books have appeared on several bestseller lists. Visit Katherine on the web at www.katherinegarbera.com.

This book is dedicated to Patty Ann Souder and
her men Bill, Neil and Ian. Thank you, Patty,
for being the big sister I never had.

Acknowledgements
Special thanks to Aleka Nakis who helped me
with my Greek words. Any mistakes are my own.

One

"There's a man waiting for you in the principal's office," Laurette Jones said as she came into Ava Monroe's classroom. "I'll take care of your class until you come back."

"Is everything okay with Theo?" Ava asked. Her son was enrolled in pre-kindergarten at the exclusive Florida boarding school where she taught second grade. It was rare for her to be called away from her class in the middle of the day. The relative quiet of the warm February afternoon suddenly seemed ominous.

"I don't know. Karin asked me to come and get you." Laurette worked for principal Karin Andrews in the administration offices.

"Thanks, Laurette," Ava said, hurrying down the hallway, fighting the urge to run. She knew she was borrowing trouble, but Theo had asthma and they'd yet to find any medicine to get it under control. Just the thought that he might be having a breathing episode made her palms sweat.

She stopped by the nurse's office on her way and learned that Theo wasn't there. Relief swamped her. She hoped that Theo hadn't gotten into trouble in class. He wasn't a hellion but he was lively, and his teacher was pretty understanding most days.

She rounded the corner leading to the administration offices and heard a deep voice speaking in a heavy accent. She froze in her tracks. She'd never forgotten that voice, because she still heard it in her dreams. Christos Theakis. Her heart beat faster as she tried to tell herself she was imagining things. But she knew she wasn't. She rapped on the frame of the open door that led to Karin Andrews's office.

"Come in, Ava, we've been waiting for you."

She stepped into the office. And there he was. Christos leaned against Karin's desk, but straightened to his full height when she entered. He was about six feet tall and dressed in that cool European style that was both casual and sophisticated.

She brushed her hands down the sides of her floral-print skirt and told herself she wasn't still the small-town girl he'd once seduced. But she felt as though she was.

"Hello, Christos. I am so sorry about your recent loss."

He nodded his head solemnly at her offer of condolences. She saw grief and sorrow in his eyes, but he quickly controlled the emotions.

She'd had Christos and the entire Theakis family on the brain since they'd been in the news over the past month. His older brother, Stavros, sister-in-law, Nikki, and two nieces had been killed when their private jet had crashed minutes after take-off from Athens, Greece.

Ava, who had once been nanny to the girls, had burst into tears when the reporter had revealed the names. Things hadn't ended well with her employment with the Theakis family, but she'd adored those children.

Her son had been confused about why she was crying and had consoled her as only a four-year-old could, with his favorite stuffed animal, Monkeyman, and lots of hugs.

But the sting of knowing that the little girls she'd played with and cared for were deceased was still with her.

"We need to talk."

Christos's terse words snapped her back to the present. Such arrogance. She used to find it attractive. Ah, who was she kidding, she still did. There was something appealing about a man who knew what he wanted and made no bones about it. So different from the wishy-washy men in her circle, who struggled even to decide where they should eat dinner on a Friday night.

"Yes, we do," she said, trying to project a little arrogance of her own.

Christos arched an eyebrow at her and turned away. "May we use your office, Ms. Andrews?"

Karin flushed under Christos's gaze, something Ava had rarely seen the ultraprofessional woman do. She gave Christos a warm smile as she stood and walked toward the door. "Of course. And please, call me Karin."

The walnut-paneled door closed behind the principal with a distinctive thud. Christos said nothing and the silence built around them. Ava tried to figure out what to say but all the words running around in her head sounded banal.

Finally she glanced up at him and found he hadn't moved from his position against the desk. "So...why are you here?"

"To claim the Theakis heir."

Ava was exactly as he remembered her. The strawberry-blond hair, the delicate features and those wide blue eyes that were more mysterious than the deepest fathoms of the ocean. She had been unique to him. An anomaly in a world filled with people who wanted to be near him because of his money, his connections or his pedigree, she'd wanted to be with him in spite of all that. Or so he'd thought. She'd seemed fresh and innocent, and he knew that was a large part of the reason he'd been so attracted to her.

He would have bet his vast fortune that Ava was incapable of lying. And he knew now that he would have lost. He let the silence grow between them, watching her, knowing it made her uncomfortable. He still wanted her. Damn her for that. Even knowing she'd given birth to his brother's child...

Ava deserved the discomfort, he thought. She'd slept with him *and* his brother, and now he needed the child. His brother's son. God, what a mess.

Christos was the playboy of the family, the jetsetter who, for the most part, had always been more interested in his own pleasures than anything else. But for a few brief months during that summer when Ava had been in Greece...forget it, he wasn't going to rehash that.

He'd cast her out of his life, but everything had changed with Stavros's death. God, he missed his older brother and his nieces. He didn't miss his sister-in-law as much, but then Nikki had never been the kind of woman who'd wanted to be friends with him. He'd always been the second son to her. Not the heir.

His own temper was legendary, as was Stavros's, and the fight they'd had over Ava...well, it had taken on mythic proportions. And the part that stabbed him in the gut was that he'd thought they had years to work it out. Instead he'd never share a quiet moment with his brother again.

He knew what his father wanted from him. Take over the business, marry and produce more Greek babies. Ensure that the Theakis line continued. His father had sent him to Ava to claim the boy whom Stavros had paid her to keep quiet about.

He even knew what Stavros would say to him if he

had been able to see into the future…he would advise Christos to marry Ava and claim the boy as his own. Move them back to Greece where the boy could be raised to inherit the shipping empire that had been in their family for generations. His father's advice had been the same, but then Stavros and Ari were cut from the same cloth.

"I'm surprised you're here. I didn't think I'd ever see you again," Ava said at last.

He couldn't deal with the circumstances that had brought him here and he wouldn't talk about them with her. Not now. Tristan, one of his best friends, assured him that grief lessened over time, but Christos couldn't imagine this pain fading. "What does the boy know about his father?"

"The boy? His name is Theo. And I…I told him that you were an important Greek businessman whose interests kept him busy."

That he *was an important Greek businessman.* God, he couldn't believe she was still clinging to the lie that he was the father. He'd been careful every time they'd come together. Only slipping up once, he thought. But even then he'd pulled out as soon as he realized what he'd done. And Stavros…well, his brother had always been blunt when it came to sex and condoms—he didn't use them.

"A lie."

"You are a businessman. And you're always busy, at least, according to *Hello!* magazine. I don't see how

Stavros's death changes anything. You made your choice a long time ago."

He shrugged that aside. He wasn't going to get into the paternity issue again. That boy was a Theakis and he was returning to his family. They had the legal document she'd signed when she'd taken the money Stavros had offered.

He tried not to think about those long-ago days in Greece. As soon as he'd seen her with his brother he'd left, returning to a life of endless traveling and parties that he used to blur memories of their time together. He'd gone back to his old lifestyle with a vengeance. Being the second son meant his life was full of frivolity and socializing. No one expected anything of the second son. He had focused on his business interests during the day, but he'd partied all night.

"Where's the boy?" he asked.

Ava tucked a strand of hair behind her ear, eyeing him warily. Crossing her arms over her chest, she glanced out the window. "What do you mean, the heir? You told me…" Her voice quivered.

"I know what I told you but times have changed. I need you to be the woman I once thought you were."

That was nothing less than the truth. He needed something from Ava that even she couldn't have predicted. He needed her to be the kind of mother his had been. The kind of mother who could raise a boy to handle a world of privilege and expectation—because he wouldn't have enough time to do that.

"What woman was that?"

"One I could trust. My father's health is failing and he misses his grandchildren."

"Theo is nothing like the girls. He can't replace them," she warned.

"What do you mean?"

"He's American, Christos. He knows a little of your background and heritage, but he's not Greek."

"I'll teach him what he needs to know."

Still she shook her head. "Ari hates me."

"My father will love your son."

"I don't know. I'm not the naive young girl I was," she said.

"You're still young," he said. She was twelve years younger than he was, which he'd once thought excused some of the lies she'd told him. But he wouldn't be as forgiving this time.

"Being a mother has matured me in a way nothing else could have."

"Then you know that keeping your son from the Theakis family is not something that I can allow to continue."

She nodded. "When I saw the news about Stavros and his family, I thought about contacting you."

"Why didn't you?"

"I was afraid to deal with you."

"I can understand that," he said. He'd treated her almost cruelly when she'd come to him with the news of her pregnancy. But then, he hadn't been interested in cleaning up his brother's mess. So he'd turned her away.

After his father's heart attack, he'd hired a private investigator to find her. When the old man had seemed so fragile and Christos had made promises he wasn't exactly sure he could keep. Find the Theakis heir and bring him home.

He'd never forgotten Ava, despite the way things had ended between them. He'd come here to claim Theo as the Theakis heir, but watching the way the light played over her hair made him realize he wanted to claim the woman, too.

"I want to know the boy."

"Oh, okay. When?" she asked.

She was nervous; he read that easily in her stance and the way she was stammering to answer his questions. He told himself to lighten up—except, he couldn't. What he felt about her and the boy was too intense. She'd lied to him and he wanted to see her squirm a little now.

"Today, Ava. I think we can work this out on our own without involving my attorneys."

"Of course," she said. "I wasn't saying you couldn't see him. Just asking when you wanted to."

"Does he have our family name?"

"No."

"Was that in the agreement with Stavros?"

She crossed her arms under her breasts and arched one eyebrow at him. The show of temper made him hotter than he'd have thought it could.

"Why do you care? You said you wanted nothing to do with my child."

"But that has changed," he said. "Theo *is* a Theakis and I need him."

"As I just said, he shares *my* last name."

"That will be the first thing I change. I'll have my attorneys start the paperwork."

"Uh, isn't that moving fast? Why—"

"It isn't fast. Not after we've missed so much of his young life."

She flushed—with anger, he imagined—and nodded toward him. "I'm sure that Theo will be pleased to meet you. He knows your name."

"Very good."

She didn't respond to the last but he caught another glimpse of her temper in her eyes before she turned away.

"I'll have Karin call him out of class. He's a little afraid of the principal's office. Maybe you should wait in the gardens. I'll bring him to you."

Theo chattered as she walked him down the hall toward the gardens, asking her specific questions about Christos. But she really didn't know what to say. Finally they stepped out into the Florida sun and he slipped his little hand in hers, quieting as he looked at the tall man standing with his back toward them.

She knelt down next to her son and hugged him close. "He's very excited to meet you."

"Are you sure?"

"Yes, she is," Christos said, coming over to them. "Theo, I'm Christos Theakis."

Theo took Christos's hand and shook it. "Hello, Father."

Christos drew back and looked up at her sharply. She couldn't read his look.

"The Greek word for father is *baba*, Theo," Ava said.

Christos drew Theo into his arms and Ava turned away. It had been easy to believe that she was doing the right thing for her son by keeping him from Christos. Christos had been very angry during their last encounter, when he'd accused her of sleeping with both Theakis brothers. And she'd been unable to defend herself against that anger.

He'd wanted her to take a DNA test to prove paternity, but she'd refused, wanting him to trust her. She knew that she'd lied to him about other things, and had acknowledged those lies, but on this matter, she had needed him to believe her. Because, before the situation with his brother had blown up, he'd told her they'd moved past her falsehoods. And she'd needed that to be true for the relationship to survive.

She'd seen the proof that he'd moved on with his life in the pages of the tabloids and society magazines. But here in this quiet garden as he hugged Theo, she wondered if she'd made a mistake.

She edged away from them. Tried to remind herself of all the reasons she was no longer in love with Christos. Why she'd never really been in love with him in the first place. But, watching him, those reasons seemed flimsy. And her heart, which had been dormant during the five years they'd been apart, started beating again.

She was *so* not going there. Christos was the man who'd changed the entire course of her life, and she finally had it back on track. She wasn't getting involved with him again. Except—she'd have to, if he was going to act as Theo's father. She couldn't keep Theo from him now that he was reaching out to his son. The Theakis family was a close one, something her own wasn't, and she wanted that for Theo.

Karin stopped by to return Theo to class, leaving Ava alone with Christos. He stared after his son. Her throat tightened as she watched the cocktail of emotions rushing across his face. She'd always suspected there was more to Christos than the playboy image he presented to the world. She'd caught glimpses of the real man during the intense time they'd spent together. Enough to make her fall hard.

But this was only the second time she'd seen any overt evidence. The other time…well, that didn't bear thinking about right now.

"You've done a good job with him."

"Thanks. I…I'm not always sure what I'm doing. But he's a good kid."

"Yes, he is." Pushing his hands into his pockets, he walked closer to her.

"Why did you tell him I was his father?" Christos asked.

"You still don't believe me about that?"

He shook his head. "I gave you a chance to prove yourself to me, Ava. To prove that Theo is really my son, and you denied me."

"Because I wanted your trust."

"Once a liar."

"That's not fair, I apologized for those lies. I was young and thought you wouldn't want a girl from my background."

"Your very poor background," he said. "What better way to make sure you never had to go back to that trailer park than to bear the son of a Theakis."

She shook her head, trembling all the way to her soul from his words. "It wasn't like that."

"You can explain it to me another time. Right now you have two choices, Ava."

She still liked the way her name sounded on his tongue. Which really ticked her off, because she wanted to slug him for being a jerk about the past. She'd made mistakes, yes, but what was it about this stubborn Greek that wouldn't let him look beyond them? "What are they?"

"You can relinquish your rights to Theo and give him over to me to be raised as a Theakis."

"Why would I do that?" He had to be crazy if he thought she was going to give up her son.

"It is his right to be raised in our family. And you have had him to yourself for the last four years."

"You gave those years away," she said, and the past flashed through her mind. She knew the exact moment when she'd become pregnant. Remembered with clarity the way Christos's face had tightened with a mixture of lust and anger when she'd declined to stay in Greece and become his mistress.

He'd kissed her hard and soon anger had melted to lust and they'd made love in his study. The encounter hadn't been a sweet seduction; they'd both been so hungry for each other, knowing it was the last time they'd be in each other's arms.

She'd clung to his shoulders and he'd held her so tightly. He'd cradled her on his lap, and she'd realized that they'd forgotten to use protection. That he'd pulled out at the last moment.

He hadn't said anything and neither had she. Then a few days later everything had fallen apart with Nikki's accusations about her and Stavros. And Christos had sided with his sister-in-law.

"Maybe. But not anymore. I want Theo. I've taken over Theakis Shipping," he said, turning away from her and looking out over the lushly landscaped gardens of the school. "I'm becoming the heir I never had to be and I must look to future generations."

"Now you need an heir," she said. She was saddened to think that that was the only reason he was here. Not because he'd finally wanted to acknowledge he had a son and had been desperate to see him.

Oh, God, she couldn't let Christos hurt Theo. Wouldn't let Theo come to love a man who had ice in his veins. A man who could make love to a woman and hold her so close, as if he'd never let her go, then calmly accuse her of infidelity.

"The Theakis family needs Theo," he said.

This isn't about you, she reminded herself. But it was.

"You mentioned two choices."

"Yes, I did. If you are interested in remaining in your son's life, then I'm willing to marry you."

Two

The house he'd rented overlooking the Atlantic Ocean was large and lush but empty. Even with the staff of five he'd hired, it still felt so empty. Christos leaned deeper into the leather office chair, snagging the phone as it rang.

"How'd it go today?" Tristan Sabina asked.

Tristan was one of Christos's two best friends. The other was Guillermo de la Cruz. They'd formed an odd little triad of mischief makers and playboys for more than half their lives. They'd met at an exclusive boarding school in Switzerland and had bonded through their troublemaking antics.

The three of them had been tabloid fodder for longer

than he could remember, moving through life as if the world was their oyster. They'd started a business together in their twenties, a string of nightclubs located in posh hotspots all over the globe. The exclusive clubs, called Seconds, were the place to see and be seen the world over, and every night the bouncers turned away more celebrities, wannabes and hangers-on than they let in.

And Tristan, Gui and Christos were the kings of the kingdom they'd built.

Christos settled the phone between his ear and his shoulder and knocked back a shot of tequila. "Who knows? I thought she was going to hit me when I told her I was willing to marry her."

"You Greeks have no way with women," Tristan said. "You should have pulled her into your arms and kissed her senseless, then told her you were marrying her."

"It's not about her," Christos said, struggling not to get angry at his friend.

"It sounds as if it is," Gui said calmly, always the voice of reason, as he joined the three-way conference call. "You've never talked about what happened."

"Nor do I intend to."

"How was the boy?" Tristan asked.

"The boy was…he seemed…"

"What, Christos?" Gui asked. The three-way call was a little cumbersome, but it was the best way to keep in touch now that they all had other legitimate business concerns.

"He has Stavros's nose."

"You have the same one. It's the Theakis features. They bred true," Tristan said.

"Did you ask her again if Stavros was the father?" Guillermo asked.

"No. She lied before. Why wouldn't she again?"

Tristan cursed under his breath. "Do you want company in Florida?"

"No. I'm going to wrap up the legal arrangements for the boy and then fly back to Greece next week."

"What about the woman?" Guillermo asked.

"She's thinking it over."

"What exactly is she thinking over?"

"If she's going to marry me." Christos didn't want to think too much about Ava or his marriage offer. He could still remember the last time they'd discussed the subject, and hadn't that been a kick in the pants.

"Marriage? Is that the only solution?" Tristan asked.

"It is for me. I…"

"You still want her and you think that will keep it under control?" Gui asked.

"I'm not exactly thinking."

"True," Tristan said. "I'm scheduled back in Paris in three weeks, on the thirtieth. I can be at your place on Mykonos on the twenty-third."

An electronic beeping noise came through the line. "Me, too."

"You don't have to—"

"We know," Gui said. "I want to meet her for myself."

"Gui, she's not like—"

"I'm not saying she is. I just want a chance to see what kind of woman is the mother of the Theakis heir."

"So do I," Tristan said. "You and Stavros are so different."

"*Were* so different...hell, I guess we still are," Christos said.

Emptiness buzzed on the line. "Are you sure you don't need us?"

"Yes," he said, and tossed back another shot of tequila.

There was a rap on the library door. "I must go." He hung up the phone. "Enter."

"Sir, there is a Ms. Ava Monroe to see you." Antonio Montoyo was his butler and traveled with Christos wherever he went. Though Antonio was only fifteen years older than Christos, their relationship was closer to father and son than the one he shared with Ari Theakis.

"Is she alone, Antonio?"

"Ah, no. She brought along the boy, Theo."

And there was the rub. No matter what the truth was, the world was going to believe that Theo was his son. Nikki, his sister-in-law, had done too good a job of hiding all of Stavros's affairs.

"Send them back."

"Ah, sir?"

"Yes, Antonio?"

"You aren't dressed for receiving."

He arched one eyebrow. He'd just come in from swimming in the sea and was dressed in trunks and no shirt. Granted, it was winter in Florida, but the daytime temperature still wasn't cold. And he'd be damned if he'd change for Ava. He couldn't explain his feelings for her, hell, wouldn't even try, but she held a lot of cards with that small boy of hers and he wasn't going to give an inch otherwise.

"I'm fine. Better that she see me as I really am now."

"And that is, sir?"

"A playboy masquerading as the head of a Greek shipping line, a man of the sea like my father and brother."

"I've known you a long time, Christos, and you are nothing like either of those men."

"Enough," he said.

Antonio left the room with a small nod of his head. The butler's disapproval was something he'd deal with later. He respected Antonio. Despite Antonio's insistence on keeping up appearances, Christos knew he wouldn't fail to drop him some advice.

The doors opened a few seconds later and Ava stepped into the room. She'd changed. Dammit. She now wore a pair of faded old jeans that clung to the slim length of her legs and a cashmere sweater that matched the blue of her eyes. Her hair hung loose around her shoulders.

Theo stood next to her dressed in a pair of baggy navy sweat pants and a matching fleece top. They both thanked Antonio as the older man left.

"Have a seat," Christos said.

"Thank you for seeing us," Ava said.

"I was expecting you," he said. True, not this soon, but he'd figured she'd come to him with her answer.

"I know," she said, quietly.

She glanced at her son and then back up at him and he saw a hint of protectiveness in her gaze along with that other emotion he could never identify.

She cleared her throat. "I was discussing your proposal with Theo and he has a few questions."

He was surprised. But in a good way. Theo would one day run a multibillion dollar corporation. Learning to weigh options and make decisions was an important step to learn.

"What are your questions, Theo?"

"I want to know about Greece, *Baba.*"

Baba. He hated hearing that from the little boy. He was Theo's uncle, not his father. He needed to talk to Ava and deal with this. But not in front of Theo. "Perfectly understandable. Come over here and I'll show you some pictures of our home."

The boy hesitated and Ava bent over to pick him up. "Ava, put him down."

She set him on his feet.

"Are you afraid of me?" he asked Theo.

The boy shrugged, his eyes the dark obsidian that Christos saw every morning in the mirror. He didn't want the boy to fear him. But, to be honest, he had no idea what to do.

He glanced at Ava and she straightened. "Come on, Theo. I'm curious about how the Theakis household has changed since I was last there."

They crossed the room together. And though he knew he held all the cards in this situation, he felt like an outsider.

"Does this mean that you've decided to accept my offer?" Christos asked.

"We've been talking it over. I want to make sure that Theo will be happy." Ava tried to keep her voice cordial. She'd spent the entire afternoon on the treadmill in her bedroom, running off the anger that had sprouted deep inside when he'd said he was *willing* to marry her.

She'd wanted to tell him to take a flying leap into the ocean and swim back to Greece, but Theo was enthralled by Christos. He'd spent all afternoon asking her questions about him. And then finally asked if he was going to have a father. And Ava's heart had broken. She did the best she could for her son, but she couldn't be a father.

Christos nodded at her in a way that revealed nothing of what he felt. Ava didn't know what she wanted from this meeting with Christos, but him sitting, aloof, behind that large walnut desk wasn't it.

He thought he held all the cards, she knew that. She could tell from the way he was staying seated in his position of power. She'd come to him. The problem was she was drawn to that arrogance. To the utter confidence that he exuded.

His chest was bare and she struggled to keep her gaze from it. From that gold medallion nestled in his chest hair.

He'd always been in good shape and he certainly hadn't let himself go in the five years since she'd seen him.

Too bad, because it would be so much easier to resist him if he'd developed a beer gut like many of her other male friends. Some sign of emotion from Christos would also make things easier on her but he was still the iceman when it came to feelings. The only time he'd ever revealed any fire had been when they'd made love. And, of course, when she'd seen the hard side of his temper.

Theo's hand trembled a little in hers. He wasn't afraid of Christos exactly, but his exposure to men had been limited. At the school most of the staff were women. Her best friend Laurette was engaged, but her fiancé, Paul, traveled a lot, so even he wasn't around much. Though he did make a fuss over Theo when he came to her house.

"The Theakis family compound is on an island in the Aegean," Ava said. They didn't just live on the island, they practically owned it. They had properties all over Europe and the world, but Mykonos was their base of operations.

Christos reached out and lifted Theo onto his lap. Her son looked so small against the thick muscles of Christos's chest and arms. He reached around Theo to hit a button on his computer and images started flashing up on the screen.

He leaned in low and for a moment brushed his nose over her son's head, inhaling deeply. Then Christos looked up at her and she saw a yearning in his eyes. But what did it mean? Did he want Theo, or wish that Theo was his son?

She regretted not taking the paternity test years ago, but a part of her still stood by her conviction. The man she'd made love to should have known she'd never lie about something as important as intimacy. The other lies she'd told…they were little ones.

She blinked back a few tears. She was looking for some sign that he wanted Theo for more than continuing his line.

Images from a past that she'd locked away flashed on the computer screen. Mykonos had changed little in five years. Why should it? The island dated back to the very beginning of recorded time and the few short years since she'd been there…

She realized she wasn't ready to take a trip down memory lane, not even to ease her son about his upcoming move to the Greek island. And she knew that Christos hadn't been kidding about taking Theo.

"Will you excuse me for a minute?" she said.

Both males looked up. "Where are you going?"

"I need to use the bathroom."

Christos nodded. "It's down the hall to the left."

She left the room as quickly as possible and stopped in the hallway. She heard the deep rumble of Christos's voice as he spoke to Theo, telling him about his heritage.

She realized that this situation was out of her control and she had absolutely no idea how to get it back. She'd dreamed of a time when Christos would return and claim Theo. Claim *her.* Yeah, that was the rub, wasn't it?

That she'd been waiting five years for him to realize he'd been wrong when he'd accused her of infidelity. And now he was here, offering her something she'd always wanted. The one thing she'd dreamed of when they'd first begun their affair. Yet she knew that saying yes to Christos's proposal wasn't going to make everything into that mythical happy ever after.

"Are you okay?"

She glanced up at Antonio. She wondered if he remembered her, or if the stream of women through Christos's life had made him forget.

"I'm fine, Antonio. I just needed a minute to myself."

"Of course. Why don't you go out to the gardens? I'll let Mr. Theakis know where you are."

"Thank you," she said, and followed Antonio's directions. She stepped out into the cool February evening. The smell of the ocean and the lush shrubbery surrounded her.

She followed a path to the center of the garden and found a bench that overlooked a small fountain of a triton—half man, half fish with a large, dragon-like tail. It was lit from the base and she watched the water spill out.

"Ava?"

"Over here," she called.

Christos came around the corner. He'd put on a fleece pullover and a pair of deck shoes. His hair was thick and black, rumpled as if he'd run his fingers through it.

"Where's Theo?"

"I sent him to the kitchen for something sweet."

Theo had a sweet tooth like nobody's business. Well, to be honest, that was one of the things they shared, so she limited any kind of junk food in their house. "Why?"

"We need to talk."

Christos sat down on the bench next to her. His body heat reached her in waves and she fought the urge to scoot closer to him.

"What have you decided?"

She shrugged, not ready to tell him yet. Not really sure if she was going to say yes to him and change her life for this man. At one time she'd been ready, but she wasn't sure she could risk her heart again.

Theo was smart and funny and concerned about what moving would do to his mother. In a candid moment he'd revealed that Ava's family had cut her off completely when she'd returned from Greece pregnant. Of course, the little boy hadn't put it in those exact terms, but Christos could read between the lines of Theo's simple words…*it's just Mommy and me.*

He hadn't wanted to personalize his relationship with Ava or her son too much yet, but it was too late for that. The little boy was slowly, shyly winding his way into Christos's cold heart, and Ava…hell she'd always been his Achilles' heel, hadn't she? He wanted her. Why the hell hadn't that changed?

Here in the moonlight she looked too fragile, too vulnerable to have done all the things he knew she had. And despite the fact that she'd played him for a fool, he had never wanted her to lose her family and their support.

What a damned mess this was.

"I have questions," she said, turning to face him.

Her eyes were big and wide, forthright and honest. He knew the honesty was mostly a mirage. But in this moment, with the soft trickle of the water in the fountain, surrounded by the lush scents of hibiscus and the fragrance of her perfume, it didn't feel like a mirage.

It felt too damn real. He hated that this woman made him vulnerable. With anyone else he would have swooped in, taken the boy and left. But not with Ava.

"About?" he asked her.

"When are you planning to leave?" she asked.

"Next week. I'm waiting for the paperwork—and your decision, of course. The lawyers think they can have the papers to officially make Theo the Theakis heir done on my timetable."

"I don't think I can leave next week. I can't leave the school in a bind."

"Does that mean you're coming with me?" he asked. The breeze stirred her hair and a strand blew across her face. She tucked it back behind her ear only to have it blow forward again.

He reached out and captured it, wrapping the strand around his finger. It was fine and soft like the sea mist when he was on his speed boat racing across the Aegean.

"Yes. I...I don't want Theo raised the way you were, Christos."

He liked the sound of his name on her lips. Always had. He dropped his hand from her hair and leaned forward, facing the fountain. The pounding of his heart and the racing of his blood through his veins made a mockery of his lauded self-control. How the hell could he still be so affected by her?

He stood up to give himself the position of power. She was just a girl, he thought, looking down at her. And he'd slept with many more sophisticated than she was. Why then was she the one he longed to hold again?

"How do you mean?" he asked. He'd had a great childhood, once he'd adjusted to living away from home. And it *had* been an adjustment, coming on the heels of his mother's death. But Tristan and Gui had been there from the beginning and he'd found a home away from home in their friendships.

"In boarding schools, away from home all the time. I know that's what the Theakis family does with their children."

Yes, she was intimately acquainted with how Stavros had raised his daughters, having been the Theakis nanny that summer long ago. He felt the quick burn of anger in his gut. "I won't discuss my brother with you."

"I wasn't talking about Stavros, but his daughters."

Remembered little-girl giggles made him turn away from her as tears burned his eyes. Little Vennie had always hugged him so tightly whenever she'd seen him. And Althea, ah, her kisses had been so sweet. God, he missed those two. Despite the feud with Stavros, he'd still seen his nieces once a month and they'd been close.

"I will of course consider your opinion in the matters of Theo's schooling, but the ultimate decision will be mine."

"Don't do this."

"Do what?"

"Be that arrogant Greek male."

"That's who I am. Get used to it."

She shook her head. "I can make it more difficult for you to leave."

"You are welcome to try. I'm sure that your *pro bono* lawyers will have some ideas as to how to help you, but they'll be playing out of their league. I've hired the best family law attorneys available here in the States. And I do have that agreement you signed for Stavros."

"What makes you think I can't afford a lawyer?" she asked.

"You're a teacher, living off your weekly paycheck," he said, stating the simple facts he'd read in the report his detectives had made.

"Stavros sent me some money when Theo was born," she said. "That was part of the agreement I signed."

"Are you going to use my brother's money to fight me on this issue?"

It made him feel like the worst sort of bully when she shrank back. Dammit, what was it about Ava that made him act like…an arrogant Greek male. He'd spent a good portion of his life trying to distance himself from that part, but she brought out his primal instincts.

"Maybe I will. I think there are a lot of benefits to Theo and I moving to Greece with you, but if you act like a jerk, I'm going to make it difficult for you."

"A *jerk*?"

"Yes, a jerk. You do know what that word means, don't you?"

"Yes, Ava, I'm familiar with it. I'm not sure why you are calling me one."

"You just asked if I'd use your brother's money to fight you. It's my money now, Christos. Mine and Theo's. I accepted it for his sake."

"Touché. I'll stop saying it's Stavros's. What else makes me a jerk?"

"Acting as if Theo is a commodity…calling him 'the Theakis heir.' He's a boy. I love my son. I don't want him to be banished to a sleep-away school," she said. There was a wealth of love in the way she spoke of Theo.

"Going to school will enable him to form bonds with future leaders. It's far more than just getting kids out of their parents' hair."

"He can do that in other ways. I want—"

"This isn't about your wants, Ava." She glared at him and he held back a smile. She tried to hide all of the fiery passion and temper underneath such a serene surface. But it was always there, waiting to break through.

"I'm afraid it is, Christos. This isn't going to be one of your dictates. I don't work for you or any of the

Theakis family anymore. And when it comes to Theo, I'm the final authority."

His gut instinct was to take the boy to the private airport where his jet was waiting and just leave. Once he was back on Mykonos with Theo, she'd have a difficult time seeing the boy again. He'd be charged with kidnapping the boy, but he paid his lawyers a lot of money and they'd figure a way to resolve that.

"You are not the *final authority* when it comes to Theo," he said.

"Yes, I am. There's no father listed on the birth certificate."

"Yes, but I have proof that Theo is a Theakis." He hated that piece of paper that he'd found in Stavros's private office four days after his brother's death. The legal document promised Ava an annuity in return for not making a claim of paternity against Stavros. The very money she'd just mentioned. But the paper did acknowledge that the baby was a Theakis.

"You may have that paper I signed, but that doesn't mean I'm going to just lie down for this," she said.

"I don't need threats. Just understand that Theo and I are leaving for Mykonos in less than ten days."

"I have one more question," she said.

He looked at her in the moonlight and tried to be objective. She wasn't *that* attractive. She was pretty, yes, but he couldn't explain the bone-deep desire he had for her. It went beyond looks. "Yes?"

"Why are you offering marriage?"

Three

It was tempting to just let Christos make all of the decisions and say he was forcing her into marriage, but she had to be strong for Theo. She wanted to be the kind of parent that hers never had been and that meant standing up for herself now.

"Marriage will legitimize Theo's birth," he said, his voice low and husky in the darkening light.

Whenever he spoke of Theo she felt as though she was missing something. "I didn't think there was still a stigma to that."

"Maybe here in America there isn't, but in my father's eyes there is. And with his legitimate heirs gone…"

Her heart broke at the thought of the deaths of Vennie

and Althea. And the fact that Theo would never know his cousins. But she also felt angry that Theo was an afterthought. "If that's all Theo is to you then I'm afraid we're done here."

"He's not only an heir."

She crossed her arms over her chest. "He's not?"

"What do you want from me?"

"I want to know what you really feel toward Theo."

"I like him. I see Stavros in him and I miss my brother."

She dropped her arms and felt her heart melt a little. She heard the truth in his words. "Okay, so all of that's why you want Theo. But why are you willing to marry me? I thought you could only marry a Greek woman."

A hard laugh escaped him. "Times have changed."

She walked toward him on the cobblestones stopping when only a breath separated them. She wanted...wanted to hear him say that he was offering marriage because he'd finally realized she was the one woman he couldn't live without. Looking into his obsidian eyes and seeing how guarded he was, she knew that was a fantasy.

"I'm not going to let you keep these barriers between us," she said, knowing she couldn't be the kind of wife that Nikki had been. Nikki had let Stavros push her to the background of his life, a place where Nikki was forced to watch her husband carouse with other women. Ava refused to blend quietly into the background as she might have five years ago when she hadn't been as sure of herself. Before she'd had Theo she might have compromised herself, but not now.

He took a deep breath, the warm exhalation brushing along her cheek. His hands fell on her hips and he drew her to him. "Then by all means come closer, my dear."

She brought her hands up, putting them on his chest to keep some space there. Why had she thought she could take control of the situation and Christos?

"This isn't what I meant," she said, but there was a rightness to his hands on her. She wanted to lean forward and put her head on his chest. To feel his arms around her once again. Oh, man, this had *bad idea* written all over it, but she didn't want to move away.

"This was always right between us," he said, the words uttered under his breath.

Yes, she thought. Yes, it was. She tipped her head back to meet his gaze. His lips were firm and full and so close to hers. She remembered the way he'd kissed her, and she sucked her lower lip between her teeth, biting down on it before she did something really stupid like lean forward and touch her lips to his.

Someone cleared his throat and Christos held her firmly against him when she would have jerked away.

"Yes, Antonio?"

"Master Theo is wheezing," Antonio said.

"He has asthma," Ava said, pulling away from Christos and running back toward the house. She had left her purse in the study and she hurried to find it. She grabbed her bag and found Antonio and Christos in the hallway. "Where is he?"

"Kitchen."

She ran down the hall in the direction that Antonio had pointed. She skidded to a halt, seeing her little boy sitting on the chair, his little chest going in and out as he struggled to breathe.

"Hey, baby," she said, sinking to her knees next to his chair.

"I'm fine," he said, the words breathy and not at all in his normal tone.

"No, you're not."

He shook his head. "Mama, I don't want to use the inhaler."

She didn't argue with him. She struggled with Theo and his asthma all the time. He hated the weakness and refused to acknowledge when he needed the medicine. "I know, baby."

She pulled out the inhaler and the long chamber that attached to it. She shook the inhaler. She was dimly aware of Christos standing quietly in the doorway, but she paid him no mind.

Theo glanced over his shoulder at Christos and then leaned into her shoulder. "I don't want *Baba* to see."

"It's okay," she said.

Theo shook his head.

She turned to ask Christos to leave but he'd come further into the room, leaning back against the table. "Mind your mother, Theo, we'll talk about this after you've had your treatment."

She lifted the inhaler toward Theo and he took it into

his mouth. She dispensed the medicine, counting quietly and watching him the entire time.

Christos put a hand on Theo's shoulder and when they were done, she looked up at him and saw a shadow of the same worry she felt for her son. It was a moment that brought them closer together after the nonsense on the patio.

Well, it hadn't been nonsense, she thought, but when faced with something like their sick child, it seemed silly. She wanted to marry him. It was all she'd ever wanted, so even though she wanted to know what had changed his mind about being her husband, she wasn't going to ask any more questions.

Theo needed the stability that having two parents would bring him. She saw the seeds of caring in Christos's eyes when he looked at Theo and she wanted that directed at her again.

She wanted to find a path back to the passionate couple they'd been that long-ago summer, and, without the outside influences of Stavros and Nikki Theakis, they might just have a chance.

"Tell me what's up, *paidi mou*?" Christos said.

Theo shrugged in that little-boy way of his. Ava put her arm around her son, struggling not to pull him tight against her chest because his breathing was easier now.

"I want you to like me," Theo said.

"Why wouldn't I?"

"Because I'm not perfect," Theo said.

"Yes, you are," Ava said.

"Your mother is right. To us you are perfect as you are. Don't try to hide something that's a part of you, especially if it can hurt you."

Theo nodded and Christos lifted the boy into his arms. Ava stood next to them, feeling the bond starting to form between father and son. She felt a rekindling of the love she'd always felt for Christos, only this time it was a little deeper than before.

Christos insisted on driving Ava and Theo back to their house, Antonio following with Ava's car. Antonio waited with Christos's vehicle, and Christos joined Ava as she settled the boy into bed. Their house was small, but very comfortable and welcoming. The living room was dominated by bookcases along one wall and a large chair that had a colorful blanket draped over the back of it and a large overstuffed pillow on it.

The walls were covered in pictures of Theo from birth until, if he wasn't mistaken, a few weeks ago. There were Christmases chronicled with visits to Santa.

He walked slowly down the hall looking at the pictures of the boy's life. He felt cheated by his own hand. Theo was his nephew; he should have stayed involved with him. He should have been there at the boy's christening, which was documented by photos and a certificate on the wall.

Of course, she'd had the boy baptized in the Roman Catholic Church instead of Greek Orthodox. His father would have a fit.

"Thanks for seeing us home," Ava said as she came into the hallway and partially closed the door to Theo's room.

"You're welcome. How bad is the asthma?"

"They don't know. He might outgrow it."

"I have it."

"What?"

"I know, shocking, isn't it? It runs in the family. My mother's side." His condition wasn't something he advertised and thanks to medication he kept it under control, but when he'd been a child it hadn't made his life easier. Hard to believe it now, but he'd been a pudgy, wheezing kid.

"Yes," she said. "I had no idea. You seem so fit."

"Fit?"

"You know what I mean."

"Strangely enough, I do. Swimming is good for the lungs. I'll show him some of the things I do to control it."

She nibbled on her lower lip, which brought to focus another reason he'd come back to her place. He wanted her. The arousal that had burned through him earlier in his gardens was back.

"Theo's afraid of water."

"What? The Theakis are of the sea."

She shrugged. Somehow she doubted that was going to make Theo realize that he should love water. "I don't know. I've tried to get him into the pool here, and in the ocean, and he won't do it."

"I'll take care of that," Christos said.

As they walked down her hall of memories, he felt

more the outsider than he had before. But that was nothing new. His entire life he'd been out of step with the rest of the world. Well, the world that his father had created.

"Do you have anything to drink?" he asked.

"Sure, come on in the kitchen," she said, leading the way into the bright room. There was a booster seat on one ladderback chair. He glanced around and saw the life she'd created for herself and Theo.

This was what he'd always imagined her life to be. This cozy, homey little place. And he knew he didn't fit in with it. He didn't want to. He had long ago made his peace with the life he had.

Right. Even with Stavros gone and him stepping up at Theakis Shipping, he still felt like an outsider. Like the spare heir that he'd always been to his father.

He rubbed the back of his neck, feeling the expectations of everyone weighing on him.

"I've got a bottle of pinot grigio that might be a little old, or soda, or light beer."

He shook his head. "Beer. Thank you."

She got him a drink and then sat down next to him with a can of diet soda in front of her. "We have a lot of details to iron out. I'll let them know at work that I'm leaving. I really don't think they'll be able to find a replacement by next week. Could you delay your departure until the following week?"

He could, but he didn't want to. He needed to get out of this place and back to his world. Back to the place where he was in control. But Ava had asked him for little else and he'd seen tonight how necessary she was to integrating Theo into his life. "Yes, I can do that. Tomorrow we'll make arrangements for you and Theo to move into my house."

"Can't we stay here?"

"I think Theo will be more comfortable with you, but if you decide to stay here that's fine."

She stood up and paced around the kitchen. "You can't be a dictator about this. Theo and I can move into your place over the weekend. The school week is just too hard."

He pushed to his feet, coming over to cage her body between his and the counter. "I'm not a dictator, Ava."

"You act like one. I'm not ready to sign over all decision-making rights to you."

"I'm not asking that."

She smelled so damned good, he thought. He couldn't resist lowering his head and inhaling. Wrapping himself in the sweet scent that was Ava.

She shook her head. "You are too used to getting your way."

"Not true," he said. He did like to get his way, but his life had changed and now he was living up to others' expectations. It was true that with Ava he liked to feel in control. It made the entire situation more palatable.

"Liar."

"That's not very nice, Ava."

"You don't think I'm nice," she said softly.

He wasn't getting into that. "You feel nice, *moro mou*."

He lowered his head and pressed his mouth against

hers. Her lips parted and he tasted the saccharine sweetness of the cola she'd drunk. He brushed his tongue over the seam between her lips, keeping the contact light to prove to himself that he was still in control. But he wasn't.

In his mind, he lifted her up on the countertop and pushed her legs apart so he could stand between them. In his mind, he slipped his hand under her sweater and palmed the soft weight of her breasts. In his mind, he was a man who didn't care about the past and was free to give in to the passion that she called from him as effortlessly as the sirens lured sailors.

Ava wasn't sure this was the best idea, but being in Christos's arms was the one thing she couldn't resist. The last few years had been hard as she'd struggled to find her place in the world with Theo. But she was happy with who she was and didn't know whether taking this leap—going to Greece with the one man who'd broken her heart—was the right thing to do.

His warm breath brushed her cheek, helping her believe this was right. Exactly what she needed. And then his mouth moved over hers and she stopped thinking. His lips parted and his tongue thrust past the barrier of her teeth, tasting her with long languid strokes.

She slid her hands up over his shoulders, clinging to him as his mouth moved over hers. She remembered this of Greece and Christos: the warmth of his skin, the possessiveness of his hands on her body.

His hands swept down her back, clutching at her hips

and lifting her up against him. Off-balance, she clung to him as his mouth moved over hers. He lifted her up onto the countertop and stepped between her legs, spreading them farther apart with his hips.

The movement reminded her of where they were and that she didn't exactly trust Christos. She lifted her head, stared down at him in the revealing illumination of the recessed fluorescent lights.

"I…I'm not ready for this," she said, carefully trying to calm the flush of arousal running through her veins. She couldn't resist running her fingers through his thick silky hair.

"You feel ready," he said. He ran one finger down the line of her jaw to her neck, sweeping slowly down to rest on the pulse beating frantically at the base.

"That's a chemical reaction," she said, gathering her wits a little bit at a time.

"So?"

"Christos—"

He rubbed his other thumb over her lips. "I've missed the sound of my name on your lips."

She shuddered and leaned into him. She rested her head on his shoulder, because she didn't want to see his eyes and maybe glimpse the truth—that this was just a line to get her into his bed, except, when had he ever had to lure her there? She'd wanted him from the first moment she'd stepped off the private plane on Mykonos and seen him.

Even Nikki had noticed and warned her away from

her brother-in-law. Reminded her in that forceful way of hers that Ava's responsibility was to Nikki's children.

She stiffened in Christos's arms and pushed away. "Are you really going to marry me or is that just a ploy to get me to cooperate?" she asked.

Christos kept his hands on her waist holding her steady even though she tried to draw away. "You'll just have to wait and see, won't you?"

"Christos—"

"Don't question me, Ava. You'll have to trust what I've told you. There is nothing you can say that will make me change my mind."

"I *can* make this difficult for you," she said, after a long moment. She hated that this issue of trust was between them. There could never be peace between them until he acknowledged he'd been wrong five years ago.

"You're welcome to try, but I fight hard and always win."

"Funny. I would have said our first match-up ended in a draw. Did pushing me out of your life and accusing me of infidelity feel like a win to you?"

He cursed. Then leaned down so close that their noses touched. "Don't bring up the past or I'll take Theo out of here and never look back."

She felt a frisson of fear and tears stung her eyes. The thought of losing her son was more than she could bear.

Christos cursed again and drew her back into his arms. "Sorry."

"For?"

"Being a bastard. I don't want to talk about the past with you. I can't forgive what you did or how things ended between us."

His arms were gentle around her and she wondered at the contradiction of this man. She was afraid to trust and at the same time afraid not to. Despite the fact that he had that icy control over his emotions, she could feel the fire beneath the surface.

She blinked to try to stop the tears that were burning in her eyes, but they fell anyway, flowing down her cheeks.

"I'm not going to take your son away," he said.

"We could have a DNA test," she said at last. She'd resisted having one originally, because she'd gone to Christos a virgin; he should have understood that she would never give her body so easily to another. And she wanted his trust. What woman in love didn't want her man to trust her?

"That's not necessary. Theo is of Theakis blood, that is enough."

She nodded against his shoulder, suddenly very tired. Christos tipped her head up and thumbed away the tracks of her tears.

Then he brushed his lips over hers. "Let's start anew."

She nodded. Yes, starting anew sounded good to her. Christos left a short while later and she tried to tell herself that they'd resolved the past, but a part of her knew they hadn't. She hoped leaving it be would be enough, but experience had taught her that incidents from the past always came back to haunt her.

Four

The muted sounds coming from the nursery enticed Christos out of his office. The singing was off-key and the words undistinguishable, but the joy…he could hear it all the way downstairs.

He was tempted to leave the work he really didn't want to do and go upstairs and join them—the boy he'd claimed as his heir and the woman…the woman he wanted to claim as his own.

Ten days shouldn't change a man's life, he thought, yet that was exactly what had happened. It was ten days since he'd seen *her* again. Since he'd met Theo for the first time and wished for things he'd never wanted.

His mobile phone rang. The last thing he wanted to

do was talk to anyone. When he glanced at the caller ID screen and saw it was his father, he was tempted to let it go to voice mail, but the old man would simply call Antonio and force Christos to take the call.

"Hello, *patera*."

"Why haven't you called?" Ari Theakis asked. Straight to business. The old man wasn't exactly known for his emotional outbursts. That might be why Christos had given in when his father, lying in a hospital bed, had begged him to take over where Stavros had left off.

"Was I supposed to?"

"Yes. Have you seen my grandson?"

"Yes. He's living with me." Living with Theo and Ava was different than he'd expected it to be. Now that they were here, he'd realized how empty his homes had always been. Unlike the servants and paid staff that usually inhabited his residences, Theo and Ava didn't leave him alone. One or the other was always popping into his office and inviting him to do something—watch TV, read a book, play with Rescue Heroes.

"Good. When will you be bringing him home?"

"Soon," he said. The timetable for their departure had been delayed by Ava's replacement, who needed another week before she could take over the class and Ava had told him she didn't want to make her class go through an adjustment twice, which they would have to do if a substitute was brought in now.

He'd had to respect that request. So they were still

in Florida. "We need a legal heir now. I don't like the thought of the Theakis line ending with you."

"Believe me, *patera*, I'm well aware of that," Christos said. Theo had to be declared Christos's heir before the annual board meeting in the fall. Otherwise another branch of the Theakis extended family could take control of the shipping line if anything happened to Christos, something his father didn't want and even Christos agreed would be a bad thing. His Uncle Tony didn't have the best head for business. But then, he'd been a second son, just like Christos.

"What about the girl?"

"Ava?" The last thing he wanted to do was talk about her with his father.

"Yes."

"What about her?"

"Don't play with me, boy. I'm still the head of this family."

"She'll be coming home with me. She refused to relinquish her rights to the boy." He was glad about that. Reveled in the fact that Ava was a really good mother. He had a hard time reconciling what he knew about her with the person she was today. Maybe she had changed when she became a mother, as she'd said.

"Is that wise? We don't trust her."

"*Patera*, you asked me to take over and to bring home an heir before the board of directors held their emergency meeting. I'm doing it and I'll do it my way. If you don't like it, I'm happy to go back to my other business interests."

Actually, that solution would be for the best. Ava and Theo could go back to their lives, and he could return to the world he knew. No more long hours running a shipping line and feeling his brother's presence each time he entered the office.

There was silence on the line and Christos had no doubt his father was wishing that Stavros hadn't died in that plane crash. Who knew, maybe he was even thinking that a swap would have been better. Christos in Stavros's place. But even Ari didn't have control over life and death and Christos was now the only Theakis brother.

"I have to go. I'll have Antonio send our travel plans once they are in place."

"Are you marrying the girl?"

"Yes, I am."

"Good. The boy will need siblings."

"*Patera…*"

"The wedding should take place here on Mykonos. I'll have Maria see to the arrangements," Ari continued, making plans to rule Christos's life.

"Have her call Ava. I'll give Antonio those numbers."

He hung up. Suddenly the library felt too small. He walked out onto the patio and stood there in the shadows of the early evening. His father always made him feel as if…as if he wasn't good enough. Even now, when he was doing Ari's bidding, there was a part of him that knew he was always second-best. The son least likely to become what his father wanted.

"Christos?"

He glanced over his shoulder. Ava stood in the doorway to the living room. She wore a pair of black leggings that made her legs look a mile long. She had a long-sleeved T-shirt on, and she looked so comfortable and approachable. She was relaxed in his home, and he wasn't.

"Yes?"

"Do you want to join us for story time?"

Story time? This was what his life was becoming. If Gui and Tristan could see him, they'd never let him live it down. But his friends weren't here. Only Ava and Theo and the house staff.

The thing was, he wanted to join them. He wanted to go up those stairs and sit on the pile of pillows that Ava had stacked in the corner and listen to her sweet voice telling tales where parents didn't have expectations that could never be met. And brothers didn't die. And princesses were really pretty and sweet and true.

"You okay?"

"Yes. I have a lot of work to do."

"Oh. Um…okay."

But it didn't seem okay to him.

"What is it?"

"Theo wanted to hear the ending of the tale you were telling him when he fell asleep last night. The one about some sea monster."

Ava'd had an obligation to attend a function at her school and he'd found himself alone with the boy. "Let me tie up a few details down here and then I'll be up."

She nodded and turned away, but then came back. "Thanks for all you're doing with Theo."

He smiled. He liked the boy. As much as Theo looked like a Theakis, it was obvious to Christos that he had Ava's personality. He was very curious about everything, but cautious at the same time. Christos rubbed his hand over his eyes and looked up at the sky, seeking the familiar pattern of the stars. But it didn't sooth him.

He wanted Ava. That was the cause of the restlessness in him. Not the long hours spent working at Theakis Shipping or the fact that he had a new heir he was getting to know.

There was a restless yearning in him for her, and having her in his home but not in his bed was winding him too tight.

Ava tried to relax into the cushions but this close to Christos, she couldn't. Theo was tucked up between the two of them with Christos's arm draped over them both. His earthy cologne filled each breath she took.

His profile was sculptured and classical. One look at him and there was no doubt that he was Greek. His thick ebony hair and dark olive skin…

"Ava?"

"Hmm?"

"You're staring at me," he said.

She flushed. "Just thinking how much you look like Theo."

He arched one eyebrow at her, clearly letting her know that he wasn't buying her somewhat flimsy excuse. She shrugged.

He continued the story he was telling. She loved the deep cadence of his voice. She leaned back against the pillows, closing her eyes for just a minute, and drifted to sleep without realizing it, waking only when she heard the soft sounds of Theo's whisper.

"She can sleep with me, *Baba.*"

"Should I carry her to your bed?"

Ava forced her eyes open. "Did I miss the end of the story?"

"Yes," Theo said. "I've already brushed my teeth."

Ava glanced up at Christos, who shrugged his shoulders. "We didn't want to wake you."

"Thanks for helping him with his nighttime routine."

"No problem," he said, rubbing his hand over Theo's head. "Let's get you tucked in."

Ava braced one hand on the floor to get up. Christos offered his hand and tugged her to her feet. The strength behind his tug knocked her off balance, and she fell against his hard chest. He wrapped an arm around her waist for a second before letting her go.

God, she wanted this man. She wished that life were simpler. That she was more sure of herself and the decision she'd made to go to Greece. Then she'd be unafraid of taking a chance on acting on the passion between them.

"Come on, Mama. Prayer time."

They tucked Theo in and she and Christos left the room together. The moment was surreal in that she'd spent so many years imagining what it would be like to have Christos in their lives, and here he was. But she knew they were both just playacting for the sake of their son.

She closed the door leading to the hallway, leaving it open a crack the way she always did. It was early, and too soon to retreat to her suite of rooms just yet. Now that she'd had her little power nap, she needed...wanted to get to know Christos.

Their summer affair had been full of hidden rendezvous and secret embraces. As nanny to Stavros and Nikki's daughters, she'd been part of the staff, and Christos...well he'd been busy away from Mykonos during the week, flying in on the weekends and sweeping her off to his yacht the minute her shift with the girls ended. Feeding her exotic foods, telling her tales of the sea and making love to her.

She followed him down the stairs into the formal living room. He went to the wet bar and poured two fingers of Scotch into a glass.

"We need to talk," Christos said.

"About?"

"Theo's religion. We're all Greek Orthodox. I'd like you both to convert."

"Ah... I'll think about it," she said, religion having not

been on her mind. "I was hoping we could spend some time together tonight and get to know each other better."

"Doing what?"

She wasn't sure. She'd been sneaking around to see Christos during their torrid affair and she had no idea what he usually did with his free time. On Mykonos he'd talked of little besides the passion that flowed so powerfully between them.

"I don't know. Watch a game, or talk, or whatever it is that you like to do."

"Come over here, Ava," he said.

She took a few steps into the room and then realized that she wasn't being herself. She was still stuck in the past when it came to Christos. She wasn't as shy as he always made her feel. Pushing aside the doubts that had been brought on by the way things had ended between them, she sank down onto the white leather couch. "You come here."

He arched one eyebrow at her in that totally arrogant way of his.

He poured himself another drink and came over to her side. Sprawling out on the couch, stretching his free arm along the back, he took a sip of his drink and just watched her.

"Now what?"

She thought about it. Somehow she had the idea that telling him to take off his shirt wasn't going to really help her quest to know more about the man he'd become. But it would satisfy her curiosity.

"Ava, you're staring again."

"I can't help it. There's a part of me that can't believe you're really here."

She realized she'd surprised him when he stiffened on the couch.

"Staring at me helps?"

"No. I stare at you because…" She took a deep breath. "Because you're incredibly attractive and I've always liked looking at you."

He leaned forward, putting his glass on the coffee table. "That's good."

"Is it?"

"We're going to be married," he said.

"Is this going to be a real marriage?" she asked.

He pushed to his feet. "I'm not interested in being married to an unfaithful woman."

"I'm not interested in any man but you, Christos. I never have been."

He looked at her. "If you even look at another man…"

The jealousy she remembered. And she had no way to combat it. He had to trust her. And she had to show him that he could. "I'm only looking at you."

"Prove it."

"How?"

"Come to me," he said, holding his hand out to her.

Ava was the only woman in the world who evoked such deep feelings in him. Feelings that made him volatile. And he hated that.

"I don't see what that will prove," she said, nervously tucking a strand of hair behind her ear.

He just kept his hand extended toward her and waited. It was time to set the boundaries of the relationship and to let her know in no uncertain terms exactly who was in charge.

Finally she pushed to her feet and took a few steps toward him. He loved the way she moved. There was something distinctly feminine in the way her hips swayed with each step she took.

"I'm here, now what?"

He shook his head and waited for her to close the gap between them. She placed her hand in his and he drew her closer until their chests brushed.

"Now tip your head back," he said.

He wished he could say that he was in complete control but he wasn't. He wanted this woman with the kind of passion that shouldn't have been possible because he didn't trust her. Yet a part of him did. He trusted this reaction from her.

Her head fell back and their eyes met. He forgot about games and proving anything when he saw that look in her eyes. He lowered his head to hers, intending to stake a claim with his kiss, but when her lips parted under his, he forgot about plans and games.

"Excuse me, sir."

Christos didn't take his eyes off Ava. "Not now, Antonio."

"Mr. Sabina is on the phone and he said it was urgent."

Damn. He dropped his arms and stepped away from Ava. "I'll take the call in my study."

Antonio nodded and left the room. Ava had one arm wrapped around her waist. The fingers of her other hand moved slowly over her lips. "May I come with you?"

He started to say no but then just shrugged. "It's business so it might be boring."

"That's okay. I want to know what you do, try to understand it."

He couldn't imagine why that would be something she'd be interested in. He was very aware of her presence behind him as they walked down the hall to his study. She sat in one of the large brown leather guest chairs as he went behind the desk. He picked up the phone.

"What's up, Tristan?"

"Vincent Perez has been embezzling. I realize that it's late at night where you are, but we're going to need to deal with this in the morning."

"Do you need me back in London?" he asked. The corporate offices for Seconds nightclubs were located there. And maybe some distance and time away from Ava would help him get his head back in the game and away from how tempting she was.

"No. Gui is taking care of pressing charges. He was the closest. But we're going to have to look at the rest of the finance staff and find a suitable replacement for Vincent. Are you available at nine your time tomorrow?"

Christos palmed his BlackBerry from his pocket and checked his calendar. "Yes."

"How are things going with the woman?" Tristan asked.

"Good."

"Good?"

"We're almost ready to return to Greece, and then I think all the details will straighten out."

"Ah, is she there with you?"

"Yes."

"Did I interrupt anything?"

"*Au revoir,* Tris."

"I did," Tristan said, still laughing as Christos disconnected the call.

Ava watched him with those wide blue eyes of hers. "What's in London?"

He didn't want to talk business with her, but maybe it was better than the alternative—lifting her out of that chair and into his arms.

"A business venture I have with a couple of friends." When they'd started Seconds, they'd been twenty and defiant, each refusing to follow in the predestined path his family had outlined for him. Tristan's family was in publishing on a big scale. And Guillermo—well, Gui's family were royal and they didn't approve of owning something so base as a chain of provocative nightclubs.

"I don't know any of your friends," she said, quietly.

"Why would you?"

"We were intimate with each other, Christos, shouldn't we know at least a few of the people who are important in each other's life?"

He rubbed the back of his neck, wondering if that was why she'd turned to Stavros. Was it because he'd insulated her from everyone else? He didn't want to dwell on the need he'd had to make her completely his, to become her entire world.

"We were lovers, Ava, little more."

"Now we are parents and you want us to marry."

"I believe you want that, too," he said, unsure where she was going with this. He tried not to think about what she'd said about Theo. He let the boy call him *Baba*, because to tell him not to would have been awkward, but he didn't believe he was the boy's father.

"I can't be married to a stranger. Not even for Theo's sake."

"What do you want from me?"

She pursed her lips as she thought. Always so cautious, this one was. "I want a chance to become friends with you. I don't know a lot of happily married couples, but the ones I do know…well, they are friends with each other. I think Theo deserves that from us."

He nodded. It was one of the reasons he'd offered to marry her instead of just taking Theo back to Greece. "That's amicable to me."

"You have to stop trying to make everything between us sound like business."

"Why do I have to do that?"

"Because it makes me want to slap you when you do it."

"I didn't realize you have violent tendencies."

"Only with you, Christos," she said.

He walked around his desk and leaned against it so that only a few feet of space separated them. "Business is the only way I know how to manage this."

"Manage what?"

The way he felt about her, but he couldn't say that. "Marriage."

"This is a marriage of convenience?"

"It is convenient for both of us," he said.

She rolled her eyes. "I think we should try to be friends."

"How do you propose we do this?"

"Have dinner with some of my friends tomorrow night," she said.

He glanced at his calendar. "I can do an earlier dinner. Perhaps around seven?"

"That's fine."

"Who will we be dining with?" he asked, wanting to run a background check on them to ensure they were the right type of people for Ava to be associating with.

"Laurette Jones and her fiancé, Paul Briscoe." She stared up at him.

"You're staring again."

She flushed. "Will we be lovers?"

"We will be married."

"I can't be intimate with someone who doesn't trust me."

"You were before."

"I'm different now."

Yes, she was. There was an inner strength and core to her that the girl she'd been hadn't had. Before, she'd been a kitten who'd come when called. Now she was a tigress who might come when he called or might turn on him with her claws bared.

And he'd had no idea that the differences in her would make him want her more than ever.

Five

Mykonos was exactly as she'd remembered it. Bright, whitewashed buildings seemed to sparkle from the hills over the deep blue Aegean Sea. Theo's little hand in hers gave her the strength to step off the plane when she saw Ari Theakis waiting for them. Christos's father had never liked her and the situation with Stavros and Christos hadn't exactly helped.

To be honest, she'd been intimidated by the man from the first moment she'd met him. He carried himself with the kind of arrogance that could only be honed in confidence and self-security. Even confined to a wheel-chair, now, he still exuded that arrogance and power.

That utter self-confidence was something she wanted

for Theo, and even if she wasn't still attracted to Christos she would have accepted his offer of marriage in the hopes that living in his presence and the presence of Ari would somehow rub off on Theo and give him that.

"Come on, Mama."

"Be careful going down the stairs," she said.

"I'm not a baby," he reminded her, bounding down the stairs and stopping in front of Ari.

"What are you waiting for?" Christos asked from behind her.

"Your father doesn't like me."

"He doesn't like many people, it's not personal."

"You know what I mean," she said.

Christos put his hand on her shoulder. "You can't change his mind about the past, but you can influence how he sees you in the future."

"You think so?"

"Yes. And he will be grateful to you for giving him a grandson."

She glanced back at Ari in his wheelchair, an attendant close behind him. Theo was standing in front of him, shuffling his feet around and looking a little nervous.

Ava hurried down the stairs to her son's side but before she reached him, Ari reached out to Theo and pulled him into his arms.

She stopped for a moment, seeing what Christos had meant just moments ago—the intense love this man had for her son. He hugged Theo tightly to him and buried his face in Theo's thick black hair.

Ava was touched and turned away to give Ari the privacy he needed to deal with his feelings. Christos slipped his arm around her shoulders. "You okay?"

"Yeah. I forgot Ari was human."

"What did you think he was?"

"Some kind of demigod," she said, only half in jest.

"He just thinks he is."

"It's about time you got here." The husky voice had them turning back toward Ari and Theo.

"*Patera*, it's good to see you, too," Christos said, dropping his arm and walking over to his father. Theo stepped back from Ari and came to her side. She glanced at the three males, unable to miss the striking resemblance between them.

"Mr. Theakis, it's good to see you again."

"Ms. Monroe, I see you are back."

She tried to smile, but that wasn't exactly a *Welcome to Mykonos*. "Yes I am. Theo and I are very excited to be here."

"It is good that you brought the boy. He needs to learn to be a proper Theakis."

He turned his wheelchair around before she could respond and headed toward the limo, attendant hurrying in his wake. Clearly he wasn't interested in developing any kind of friendship with her. In the past he'd treated her as a servant...which, as the nanny for Althea and Venni, she had been. But she'd hoped...ah, who cared what a cantankerous old man thought.

"Mama, Grandfather said he's prepared a special room just for me to play in."

"That will be nice, won't it?" Ava asked her son, wondering if she was going to find herself, like Nikki Theakis, relegated to the status of an observer in her own child's life. She shook her head, vowing not to let that happen.

"Yes." Theo curled his hand around hers, holding it tightly in his grip.

As Christos and his father talked next to the waiting limo, she stooped so she was on Theo's level. "What's up?"

"He held me really tight, Mama."

"He's just happy to see you."

"That's what he said. I'm glad he likes me."

"Of course he likes you. Everyone likes you."

"Is everything okay?" Christos asked, striding back from Ari.

"Yes," she said, standing up.

"Please, come. I have a meeting at the office in a little over an hour. You can ride back to the house with my father."

"You're not coming with us?"

"Not right now. I'll see you both later."

Ava tried not to feel that she was being abandoned, which was a silly feeling anyway. But she didn't really know Ari and he didn't seem to be looking forward to getting to know her better.

Christos lifted Theo in his arms, said something that only the two of them could hear and gave him a hug and kiss. When he set Theo on his feet her son ran over to the limo and climbed into the long black car.

"I'll see you at dinner."

She nodded.

He turned to walk away then paused. "Are you sure you're okay?"

"I will be. It's just…"

"What?"

"I don't have many fond memories of my last glimpse of this airport. It's like…" She shook her head. She wasn't going to tell him that everything was coming back to her. The overwhelming anger and fear. She had been so afraid when she'd realized she was pregnant and on her own.

"Everything's different this time," Christos said.

"You're right. I'm being silly. I think I'm tired from all the traveling."

"I expect you are," Christos said. "You have my mobile number?"

"Yes."

"Call me if you need anything," he said.

"But your meeting…" she said.

"Today I can make time for you. If I'd planned our arrival better I would have saved the day for you and Theo."

The chaotic feelings from the past started to melt away as she realized that things really were different this time and Christos was going to be by her side. She'd been alone for so long; it was hard to accept that she wasn't anymore, especially when what she usually saw of Christos was his back as he walked away.

The room that Ari had prepared for Theo was every child's dream. It was actually a suite of three rooms, the sleeping quarters sumptuously painted so that it seemed you were in the middle of the Aegean Sea with the bed a big sailboat in the middle. The mural on the wall started with the sunrise, continued around the room to the big bay windows that overlooked the lushly land-scaped back garden and then, on the other side of the window, night fell and stars filled the sky.

"This room is…"

"Fitting for the Theakis heir," Ari said from the doorway.

"Yes it is. Thank you for doing so much for my son."

"I didn't do it for *your* son, Ms. Monroe, I did it for my heir."

"Mr. Theakis…"

He went to the adjacent room before she could say anything else. Damn. She hated the way he kept dis-missing her.

She followed him into the playroom, which was almost bigger than her entire little house in Florida. Theo stood in the middle of the room just staring at everything. He couldn't tell where to start first in his play. Finally he just sat down in the middle of the room and looked up at her.

"Mama? Where's my Rescue Heroes?"

"I'll get them."

"While your mother goes to get those things, let me show you this area, Theo. I had a state-of-the-art plasma-screen TV installed for you. Each morning you will watch your lessons in Greek history and the history of the Theakis family."

Ava paused in the doorway. "Mr. Theakis, we need to talk before you plan out Theo's days."

"I'm not planning his days, Ms. Monroe, I'm teaching him to be a proper Theakis. Unfortunately those lessons are ones he's been lacking."

Ava glared at the older man. She wanted to say, *Whose fault is that*, but couldn't, not in front of Theo.

"We can discuss this later."

"Check with my secretary and have him put you on my schedule," Ari said and left the room.

Ava grabbed a pillow off the couch in front of the TV and threw it against the wall. Theo grabbed one and did the same, laughing. She started laughing with her son, feeling some of the tension ease out of her.

"Do you want to watch Greek lessons?"

He shrugged. "I do want to be a good Theakis."

"You can't be anything else. You *are* a Theakis."

Theo nodded.

But as the afternoon wore on, she noticed that her son's playing was different. Each time he did anything, he'd stop and ask her if it was proper Theakis behavior, which made her crazy. She left him playing to try to find Ari, but the older man's secretary told her that Ari was unavailable…for the next few weeks.

She'd vowed to fight Ari, to ensure that she was in charge of Theo's upbringing, but how could she when he wouldn't talk to her? She was stymied, unsure how to deal with Christos's father.

She didn't have to, she thought. She and Christos shared responsibility for Theo. She'd give it a few days and if Ari didn't come around, she go to Christos with her concerns.

Christos rubbed the back of his neck and glanced at the clock. Damn, nine o'clock. Time had slipped away from him as he'd been in meeting after meeting. The last week had been completely crazy with meetings and catching up. Theakis Shipping wasn't an easy conglomerate to run and Christos's time was at a premium. He'd called Theo to talk to him before he went to bed but had been unable to get back to the house for dinner.

Theakis Shipping was suffering, thanks to his ignoring it for as long as he had. Everyone seemed to have stopped making decisions when Stavros had died and had been waiting for him to step in. Christos was willing to do just that, but not all in one week.

"We'll finish this in the morning," he declared, and the staff nodded and left the conference room. He left the office without glancing back, fighting the urge to get in his Ferrari and drive to the dock where he kept his yacht and then leave Mykonos and Theakis Shipping far behind.

The house was quiet when he entered it. He paused at the landing on the second floor, glancing to the wing on the left where he knew his father had assigned rooms to Theo and Ava. He needed to turn right and go to his quarters.

He scrubbed his hand over his face and forced himself to his rooms. The door leading to his balcony was open and a cool breeze flowed in. He dropped his briefcase on one of the chairs in the sitting area.

As soon as he stepped out onto the balcony he knew that he wasn't alone.

"Good evening, Ava."

She turned from the railing. She wore a long, flowing skirt that shifted around her legs with the breeze and a thin summer sweater that hugged the curves of her breasts. "I've been waiting for you."

"Why?" he asked, trying to fight the urge to scoop her up in his arms and carry her into his bedroom.

"I wanted to talk to you."

"Can it wait until morning?" he asked.

"It could if I thought I'd see you at breakfast."

He'd been out of the house before dawn every morning since they'd arrived on Mykonos. "My schedule is demanding."

"I know," she said. "That's why I'm here."

"What's up?"

"It's about Theo and your father."

"Is he too sharp with Theo?"

"No, nothing like that."

"Then what?"

"He's just so Greek. He's trying to make Theo into a miniature version of him. I don't like it, but he won't listen to me."

Christos could well imagine what Ari was teaching his grandson. "Being a Theakis is an important part of Theo's upbringing. *Patera* is probably just trying to catch him up on everything he's missed in the last few years."

She shook her head. "It's more than that. Every time Theo does something now, he asks me if he's living up to the Theakis name. He's four, Christos. He should be playing, having fun and enjoying life, not worrying about keeping up your family image."

"It will be your family, too, in a few weeks."

"I can understand that, but he's still just a little boy."

"I'll talk to my father and tell him to back off."

"No. I don't want you to do that."

"What do you want then?" he asked.

"Some advice on how I can deal with your father. He keeps telling me that I'm not Greek so I can't understand, and his secretary won't give me any time on his calendar."

She sounded so upset and so earnest that he wanted to fix this for her. But he knew the old man wasn't going to soften in his attitude toward Ava. Even if she'd been a Greek woman, he'd treat her the same way.

"It's just his way. Don't let it bother you."

"I can't help it. All day long he watches me and

everything I do. Then when Theo's out of the room he tells me all the things I'm doing wrong."

Christos walked over to her and pulled her into his arms. She nestled against him as though she belonged there. And for the first time that day, he felt a measure of peace. This was what he'd been missing during the long hours at the Theakis Shipping office. And he knew this was a false promise. Ava wasn't waiting here for him. She'd been waiting for advice. He should drop his arms and move away…except he was wound so tight from wanting her that he'd take whatever he could get.

"That's his way. Just tell him to mind his own business."

She pulled back and glanced up at him. "That might work for you. You get to leave this house."

"Is that what this is all about?"

She shrugged and drew back. "I'm not sure what my life is going to be like as your wife."

"Taking care of Theo and socializing with me in the evenings."

"Oh. I'm just…"

"What, Ava?"

"I don't know. I feel so isolated from everything. I don't want to crowd Theo, but there's no one else here who likes me."

"I like you," he said.

"Really?" she asked.

"Yes, really."

He had the feeling he was getting closer to whatever

was upsetting her. "I…I don't have anyone I can ask to be my attendants in the wedding. I'd like to invite Laurette to be my maid of honor, but she can't afford to fly from Florida. And that still leaves three openings…I know you have three groomsmen, right? Antonio, and then Tristan and Guillermo?"

"I'll arrange it all. I like Laurette and you should have your friends with you. Is there anyone else we should bring over from the States?"

She shook her head.

"Don't worry. I'll have Guillermo and Tristan each draft a woman to bring down the aisle."

"That's not the point," she said.

"What is the point?"

"I'm…not sure I can live here."

He rubbed the back of his neck. "We're to be married in less than two weeks."

"I know. That's why I'm bringing this up now. This last week has given me a glimpse of what my life will be. I need something more to do."

He understood what she meant; even he didn't really like living in the Theakis compound, but certain concessions had to be made. He ran through the job openings they had at Theakis and couldn't think of one thing that was suitable for the mother of the Theakis heir to fill. But then he remembered that Nikki had served on their family's foundation board.

"I've got a few ideas that I'll investigate tomorrow."

"Do you have time for that?"

"No, but I'll make time for you. I want you to be happy here."

Ava knew she needed to leave Christos alone to let him have some rest. He was working very hard; she saw the signs of stress in his eyes and in the way he carried himself. "This probably isn't the best time for you to marry me."

"Is that what this is all about, Ava? You want to back out of the wedding?"

"No," she said. "I definitely don't want that. I just don't like seeing you so tense all the time."

He quirked one eyebrow at her. "Why don't we go back into my bedroom and you can help me relax?"

"Sex with you was never relaxing," she said, trying to play off the desire she had to do just that.

"Was it relaxing with my brother?" he asked, with a bit of bite to his words.

She blanched. She'd forgotten he still believed she'd slept with his brother. Stavros had promised her he'd make everything right when she'd signed that agreement years ago, but he never had.

"I told you I never slept with Stavros," she said.

"So you said." He was so Greek at the moment. The fire and passion in him burned beneath that arrogance.

"Christos, you still don't believe me?" She should let this go, but he'd asked her to marry him. How were they going to have a life together if he didn't trust her?

"I don't want to talk about it. I'm not interested in the other lovers you've had."

"There haven't *been* any other lovers," she said. *Only you*. There'd only ever been Christos for her.

She walked over to him and stopped when barely an inch of space separated them. She put her hands on his shoulders and went up on her tiptoes so that she could stare into his obsidian eyes.

"I'm not going to marry you until we resolve this issue."

He shook his head. "Then you may return to the States."

"Christos, stop being impossible. How can I prove to you that Stavros and I were never intimate?"

"You can't," he said.

She turned away so he wouldn't see the tears burning in her eyes. "We have to have trust between us. If we had the DNA test done on Theo…would that convince you that I'm not lying?"

"Ava…you would do that? I thought you wanted me to trust your word on Theo."

"I do. But I can't see how we're ever going to live together as man and wife if I don't prove myself to you."

"You don't have to prove yourself. I'm a jealous man, you know that, right?"

"Yes. But I've never done anything to make you jealous," she said.

"Just seeing you walk into a room and be noticed by another man makes me jealous," he said, putting his hands on her shoulders.

"I only see you," she admitted, tipping her head back on his shoulder.

"*Moro mou,*" he said drawing her back into his arms.

Ava stopped thinking the minute her lips touched Christos's. The cool breeze stirred her hair and she burrowed closer to his warmth.

She'd told herself she was here only because of her contentious relationship with his father, no other reason. But as his lips moved over hers, she knew she was a liar.

She was here with Christos because she wanted the man and he'd…he'd been gone too often since they'd arrived in Mykonos. And she'd had second thoughts. Fears that their life together would be like this, this distance always between them. But here was the fire she remembered.

It was hard not to fall for Christos.

He took a halfstep back from her and watched her through half-lidded eyes. He held her wrists loosely in his hands, his gaze moving over her, making her hyper-aware of him and at the same time of her body.

She didn't need to protect herself from the past tonight. She was here with Christos. The man she'd been thinking about too much of the time lately. And damned if she wasn't going to enjoy him.

"Come," he said, drawing her toward the shadowed bedroom.

He was confident, sure of himself, and with plenty of cause. He lowered his head and she held her breath. Brushing his lips over her cheek, he held her close but with that tenderness no one had shown toward her before him.

His long fingers caressed her neck, slow sweeps up and down, until she shivered in his arms. She needed more from him. She grabbed his shoulders and brought her mouth to his.

He sighed her name and took over the kiss. Sliding his arms down her back, he edged her toward the bed. It hit the back of her legs and she sat down. He followed her, never breaking their kiss.

His tongue moved easily with hers, tempting her further, tasting her deeper and making her long for him. Her skin felt too tight. Her breasts were heavy, craving his touch. Between her legs she was moistening for him, ready for him.

Squirming, she shifted around until she was on his lap, her legs straddling him. She lifted her head to look down at him. His skin was flushed, his lips wet from their kisses. She flexed her fingers against his shoulders. He really was solid muscle.

"Do you remember what we used to do?" he asked.

She wanted to laugh at his playfulness. She'd never forgotten the wicked, sexy games they'd often played together. "Mmm, I'm not sure, it's still a little foggy."

"What can I do to remind you?"

She reached for the bedside table and turned on the lamp. In the soft glow of the light she saw that Christos was turned on.

"Could you...take your shirt off?" she said. She'd

been longing to touch his chest since the night he'd lifted her onto her kitchen counter and stepped between her legs.

"Do you think it will help?" he asked, pulling off his tie and tossing it on the comforter of his king-sized bed.

"Definitely," she said.

He reached between them, the backs of his fingers brushing her breasts as he unbuttoned his shirt. She shook from the brief contact and bit her lip to keep from asking for more.

The fabric parted to reveal the tanned skin below. That small gold medallion still hung around his neck. She touched the gold charm. "This I remember."

"Good, I'm glad to know it's coming back to you."

She leaned down and pressed her lips to his chest. He tasted of some male essence that was uniquely Christos. And she hadn't realized how hungry she'd been for him until this moment. She'd been ignoring the fact that she was still a woman and not just Theo's mother for too long.

With Christos, she wanted to revel in her femininity again. She slid her lips over his warm skin. He tunneled his fingers into her hair, directing her head toward his nipple. She knew that he liked to feel the edge of her teeth against that sensitive skin.

To tease them both she let him only have the soft brush of her tongue. "Is this what you want?"

"Ava…"

She made a wondering sound against him, drawing his hard nipple into her mouth. She held him between her teeth and sucked on him. He groaned her name, his hips surging up between her legs.

He was hot and hard and she was ready for him. Maybe because it had been a long time since she'd made love…and of course, her last time had been with him.

Gently, he pulled her head away from his body and lifted her over him. He pushed the sweater she wore out of his way. She had no bra on and the air in the room combined with the heat of his gaze made her nipples bead.

He ran his finger down the center of her body, over her sternum and between her ribs, lingering on her belly button and then stopping at the waistband of her skirt.

He slowly traced the same path upward again. This time his fingers feathered under the full globes of her breasts, coming very close to touching her nipples. A shaft of desire pierced Ava, shaking her.

She needed more. She wanted more. Her heart beat so swiftly and loudly she was sure he could hear it. She scraped her fingernails lightly down his chest. He groaned, the sound rumbling from his chest. He leaned back and braced himself on his elbows.

His muscles jumped under her touch. She circled his nipple then scraped her nail down the center line of his body, following the fine dusting of hair that narrowed and disappeared into the waistband of his pants.

His stomach was rock-hard and rippled when he sat up. He pulled her closer, until the tips of her breasts brushed his chest.

"Ava." He said her name like a prayer, holding her against him.

His hard sex nudged her center and she shifted on him, trying to find a better contact. It was impossible with the layers of cloth between them.

He kissed his way down her neck and bit lightly at the base. She shuddered, clutching at his shoulders, grinding her body harder against him.

His big hands cupped her buttocks and urged her to ride him faster. Guiding her motions against him, he bent his head and his tongue stroked her nipple. Then he suckled her.

Everything in her body clenched. She clutched at Christos's shoulders, rubbing harder and faster against his erection as her climax washed over her. She collapsed against his chest. He held her close.

Ava hugged him to her and closed her eyes, reminding herself that this was just sex. He'd walked away from this once before, leaving her shattered and broken. But, right now, with his strong arms around her, it felt as though she'd found her home.

Six

Ava reached down, stroking Christos through his pants. He was so hard he could feel his pulse between his legs. He was close to losing it all. Not exactly the suave playboy image he liked to maintain, but with Ava all bets were off. They always had been. She was a fire that he'd never been able to control.

He lifted her chin and captured her lips with his. She sighed and wrapped her arms around him. When he looked down at her, tears were visible in her pretty blue eyes.

"What's the matter?"

She shook her head. "Nothing. It's just…I've dreamed of this for so long."

"Making love with me?" he asked. "*Moro mou*, you are easy to please."

"I guess I am," she said. "When it comes to you and Theo, I think I have everything a woman could want."

He felt a twinge of something close to anger at her mention of Theo. Not directed at the boy, but directed at Ava, because he still couldn't accept her insistence that he was the boy's father. And at his brother, because Stavros had known how much Christos was into Ava that summer, and he should have stayed away from her.

"What is it? Why does your face get all tight when I mention Theo?"

"I hate the fact that…"

"That you don't believe that you're his father?"

He lifted her off his body and set her on the bed, no longer in the mood to linger there with her. He reached for his shirt and drew it on as he paced across the room to the wet bar.

"Christos."

"Yes?"

"You must be coming to believe me, right? Why else would you marry me?"

He shook his head. Even he knew better than to tell her that he was marrying her for the Theakis heir and, well, hell, for the sex that had always been incredible between them.

"What will it take to convince you?" she asked at last.

He glanced over his shoulder, noting that she'd drawn her sweater back on. She had her hands on her hips and he knew she was angry with him.

Too damn bad.

He was angry, too. Things had been going well between them. "What the hell difference does it make? Theo is here, I've claimed him and you and I are to be married."

"It makes all the difference in the world. Even *you* must be able to see that. Do you really want to marry a woman who you think is capable of sleeping with you and another man? Your own *brother*?"

"Hell, no. Our prenuptial agreement is specific about what will happen if you do that again."

"Again? I never did it before."

"It's past, Ava, let it go."

"How can I, when you won't?"

"I'm not going to argue this with you."

"You can't walk away from this. I'm not going to let you. If you want me to marry you, if you want Theo to stay here on Mykonos, we need to finish this now."

"How?"

"I guess trusting me is out," she said, nibbling on her lower lip in that sexy way she always did.

"You lied to me," he said. She had lied about several things. Things like who her family was and where she'd come from.

"That was different. My family is nothing like yours. I thought you'd prefer a woman who came from a similar background."

He understood that. Would have forgiven her the tales about her family back in the States if she'd come to him and told him the truth. But instead he'd had to find out about it from Nikki. His sister-in-law had been concerned when she'd learned of his and Ava's affair and had revealed Ava's background check to him. Everything in it suggested that Ava was a poor girl hoping to bag a wealthy husband. Her lies had only confirmed that.

"I was young and I told you the truth eventually."

But it had been too late. He could never believe that she hadn't overheard him and Nikki talking that morning on the terrace.

"It's inconsequential."

"It's *not*. That's the reason you believe I'd sleep with Stavros."

He set down his whiskey glass before he threw it across the room. He hated those images in his head. The ones of Ava and his brother that he'd never been able to erase.

"Enough. Leave this room."

"No."

"No?"

"I'm sure that's a word you don't hear very often but I think you know what it means."

"Ava—"

"Christos, I'm prepared to be very stubborn about this. I want us to have a real marriage, to have a real family with Theo, and we can't if you don't believe me."

"Fine, we'll have a paternity test."

"Now you'd believe a test over my word?" she asked, there was something broken in her voice and though he wanted to pretend it didn't affect him, it did.

"Ava…"

"Forget it. We're not taking a paternity test. I no

longer want to do that. I'm going to convince you that you're wrong."

"How will you do that? Stavros is dead. I can never ask my brother about what happened between the two of you."

"You never talked to him about it?"

"No. And he never denied it when we fought over you." He'd told Stavros they were dead to each other and had left Mykonos and Greece, spending the majority of his time traveling to his various businesses and staying so busy he never had time to feel the gaping wound that had been left by that action.

"Oh, Christos."

He hated that she might pity him. "How do you mean to convince me?"

"By letting you see the woman I am. I could never betray you and I will stop at nothing to prove that to you."

Ava hadn't realized how much Christos had lost after she'd returned to America. They'd both had their lives shattered by the lies that Stavros had told, first to Nikki and then, when Nikki had gone to Christos, to his own brother.

Christos had seen her alone with Stavros on more than one occasion. She'd been providing a cover for her boss and his mistress, another lie that she'd contributed to that at the time had seemed…well, not exactly harmless, but necessary.

Convincing Christos to trust her was going to be difficult, she didn't kid herself. Not only because of the seeds of the past but because she was realizing she still didn't really like who she was at the most basic level. She'd spent her entire life pretending to be someone she wasn't, pretending that the small, run-down trailer she'd grown up in was a large ranch house, for starters.

She'd lied about so much of where she'd come from that she didn't want to face the truth. But it was past time for that. Theo had never met his maternal grandparents and never would. Her father had kicked her out of the trailer when she'd come home pregnant and jobless.

"I don't like where I came from," she said into the quietness. "And I would never have met you if I hadn't created a different background for myself, so I'm not going to apologize for that. Perhaps it would have been better just to keep silent about my family."

"I wouldn't have judged you by your family. But lying about where you came from…I don't understand that. Hell, half the time I'm hoping no one is judging me by my *patera*. He makes me crazy."

She shook her head, allowing a small smile to touch her lips. "That's because all the Theakis men have to have their own way."

"True. But that's not what you were running from."

"No. I grew up in a run-down trailer that sits in the middle of nowhere. We never had any money."

"Money's not important," he said.

"If you have it. If you don't, it's all anyone ever talks about."

"I don't see what this has to do with my trusting you," he said.

She took a deep breath. Of course he wouldn't. She realized in this moment that she had a choice. She could continue to avoid talking about how she'd grown up and never gain Christos's trust, or she could slowly tear down those barriers.

And was there really a choice? She'd had a glimpse of real happiness in Christos's arms when he'd held her and Theo. Taking a deep breath, she said, "I hate that part of my past. It's the root of every lie I ever told, not just to you, but also to myself."

He reached for the whiskey glass on the wet bar countertop and poured himself another drink. He picked it up and swallowed it quickly. "You lie to yourself?"

"Don't you?"

He shook his head. "No. I face all my failings constantly. They are at times a running litany in my mind."

"What failings?"

He shrugged. "Let's keep this about you."

"We can't have a relationship if I'm the only one who talks."

"We can start with you. Once you've...how did you put it? Ah, yes, once you've let me see the woman you are, then we can delve into my psyche."

"You can be an arrogant jerk," she said.

"So I've been told."

"I don't have many things that mean much to me," she said. "Only my son and then this glimpse of a real relationship with you..."

She had no idea what else to say. She wanted to be

witty and funny and charm him out of his arrogance but she suspected she'd never be able to do that.

She heard him set down his glass, then his footsteps echoed on the tiled floor as he walked toward her. She couldn't believe they'd just shared an explosive sexual encounter on the bed and now they were immersed in this conversation, embroiled in a past that, no matter how fast she ran or how many twists and turns she forced her life to take, still held her trapped.

He stopped in front of her, and she had a glimpse of his bare chest under the shirt that he'd not rebuttoned. She wished she'd just stayed there in his arms.

"Look at me," he said.

She glanced up, surprised to see a very serious look in his eyes. "What?"

"I'm only arrogant when someone really strikes a chord deep inside me. I don't know how to deal with genuine emotion, and you have always made me feel more than I'm comfortable with."

She had no response to that.

He cupped her cheek and she stood very still, afraid she was going to say something that would drive him back across the room.

"I think the reason I felt so betrayed by you is enmeshed in that. If it had been any other woman, I would have just moved on, but you...you have always made me feel like I'm really alive."

Tears burned her eyes and she knew she was right to push for this trust between them. "Me, too."

He dropped his hand and stepped back. "So how do you see this working?"

She blinked her eyes to clear the tears away. "We should spend time together, and not just to talk about the past. Get to know each other again."

"I think we made a start tonight," he said, nodding to the bed behind her.

She nibbled on her lower lip. "Uh, I think we should stay out of bed until we're married. We know we're sexually compatible and I think that just complicates things."

"Sex never complicates things."

"For you, maybe. For me, it makes me want to just curl up in your arms and say to hell with the rest of the world, and that's not any way to solve problems."

Christos poured himself another drink. "Fine. No sex until we're married."

"Do you think you'll trust me by then?"

"I have no idea, but being married does grant me the privilege of your bed and I don't intend to deny myself."

Two weeks, she thought. Could she change his mind in that time?

Theo woke Ava by running into her bedroom and jumping on the bed. His little voice was loud and filled with joy. She'd never really been a cheerful morning-person, but when faced with Theo's grin she couldn't help but smile back at him.

"What are you so excited about?" she asked him. He

was dressed and had on a pair of sandals that Ari had given him when they'd arrived. The shoes were traditional Greek ones that even Ari wore.

"*Baba*. He's going to take us out on his boat today."

"He is?" she asked. She hoped that Christos knew what he was doing. Promising to make time for Theo was one thing; actually promising to take him out on the boat was something else. She didn't want to see Theo disappointed if Christos had to stay late at the office.

"Yes. As soon as you get up. I've been awake for a long time now."

"I'm sorry, sweetheart. Give me a minute to wash my face and I'll be downstairs for my coffee and we can talk about this."

"You don't have to do that. *Baba* is bringing you your coffee."

"He is?" She didn't want to see Christos until she had a chance to comb her hair and brush her teeth. She was about to toss back the covers and make a run for the bathroom.

"I told him…" Theo trailed off. She could guess what her chatty little son had said. Something about Mommy being cranky until she had her first cup of coffee.

She ruffled his hair and drew him close for a hug. "Did you tell him I need coffee first thing?"

Theo nodded against her neck, hugging her back.

"Yes, he did."

She glanced up at Christos, who stood in the doorway holding a mug of coffee in each hand. He wore a pair of casual white trousers and a black T-shirt. He looked as if he'd had a good night's sleep, something she envied him.

He came into her room and handed her one of the mugs. She tried to pat down her hair, which was probably flat on one side and sticking straight out on the other. She took a sip of the coffee and tried to play it cool.

"What's this about a boat?"

Christos leaned against the dresser in the corner and sipped his coffee. "After our conversation last night, I decided to take the day off and invite you both to join me on my yacht."

"I thought we were going on a boat," Theo said.

"A yacht is a name for a big boat."

"Oh. How big?"

"Big enough," Christos said. "Would you like to join us, Ava?"

"Yes. I'd like that."

"Good. We'll get out of your hair and wait for you downstairs."

Theo gave her a sloppy kiss and a hug and ran out the door. Christos paused in the doorway.

"Are you sure about this? Taking a day off work?"

"You said something last night that made sense."

"Only one thing?" she asked. Actually she was surprised anything she'd said made sense. She'd been flying blind, driven by emotion, and that never boded well for making sense.

"Well, the not-sleeping-together thing is insane."

She flushed. "Depends on your point of view."

"I'm going to change yours on that topic. But I was referring to when you said that you couldn't build a relationship by yourself."

"I'm glad you were listening," she said.

He put his coffee mug down on the dresser and walked back to the bed. He sat down next to her, his lean hip pressing against her body.

"I always listen," he said.

"I hope so," she said. She'd pinned her hopes for a happy future on the fact that one day he'd really hear her say that she hadn't betrayed him and believe her.

He traced his finger along the line of the sheet where she had it clutched to her chest. "What are you sleeping in?"

She shook her head. "I think we'll leave that to your imagination."

He fingered the cap sleeve of her shirt. "I think we shouldn't. I'm picturing you naked."

"Clearly I'm not."

"Pity."

"Sometimes Theo gets scared at night and sleeps with me."

He ran his finger down the edge of the scoop neck of her pajama top. "What scares him?"

She struggled to keep focused on the conversation and not the feel of his finger moving over her skin. "Different things. He can't always recall."

"Do you always soothe him?"

"Yes. We pray and I sing to him."

"That's one of the things I admire about you," he said.

"What?"

"The way you mother Theo. You're very good with him."

When he'd first been born, she'd been surprised at how much she loved her son. Having him had added a dimension to her life that she'd never realized was missing. He gave her someone to love and on whom to pour all the caring she'd hidden away for years.

"He's easy to love."

"Yes, he is," Christos said. He leaned toward her and she lifted herself up to him. "Are you sure about this no-sex rule?"

She shook her head.

"*Baba*, come on. She'll take all day to get ready if you don't leave her room."

Christos dropped a quick kiss on her lips and stood, picking up his coffee mug on the way out of the room. As the door closed behind the two Theakis males, Ava pulled the covers over her head and tried not to let her heart believe that today was the start of a new life with Christos and Theo.

Seven

Christos eyed his father as the old man maneuvered his wheelchair down the stone ramp leading to the garages. Theo, dancing around him with all that energy, gave Christos something to focus on, but he couldn't turn his mind away from the fact that his father was heading his way. Absently he noted the watergun in Theo's hand.

The conversation last night with Ava still played in his mind. Hell, everything from last night was vivid, especially the way she'd moved against him. The way her soft skin had felt pressed to his.

"Baba?"

"Yes, Theo."

"Is Grandfather coming with us?"

"I didn't invite him," Christos said under his breath, but then his father wasn't really one to wait to be asked. "Why don't you go ask him?" Christos suggested.

Theo ran toward Ari, and Christos went back to packing the things they'd need for a day on the boat. He'd slept little the night before. Once Ava had left his rooms he'd gone to the study and worked all night so that taking the day off wouldn't be a problem.

He didn't exactly hate his new life, but he wasn't sure it was his yet. And Ava's conversation last night had driven home to him the fact that it was past time for him to start figuring out what this new life was going to be.

"You have a call at the main house," Ari said as he came into the garage.

"From whom?"

"Tristan. He said he needed to speak to you this morning. He's on his mobile."

Theo was standing at the back of Ari's wheelchair. He held his water gun in one hand at the ready and scanned the lawn. Christos knew that the boy was pretending to be a bodyguard. He'd played this game with Theo a few days ago.

"Is it safe for you to leave your grandfather and come to the house with me?"

"No, sir. I'd better stay here."

Christos ruffled the boy's hair as he strode past him back toward the main house. Antonio was waiting in the foyer with Christos's BlackBerry.

"Your father insisted on going after you."

"No problem. Did you have a chance to talk to Tristan?"

"No. But he left you a voice mail and a fax is coming through in the study. Do you want me to call Captain Platakis and tell him that you will be delayed?"

"Not yet," Christos said. He didn't want to break his plans with Theo and Ava.

Christos went down the hall into his study and glanced at the fax coming through. More embezzlement business. He dialed Tristan's number.

"Sabina here."

"Tris, it's me."

"Sorry. I'm a bit distracted. We're on a charter flight to Mykonos."

"Why?"

"Need your signature on a few documents."

"The ones that you faxed?"

"Yes. They are the formal charges we're filing against Vincent. I've also sent you the résumés of the three candidates we're considering promoting."

Christos pulled the pages from the machine and started scanning them. "You and Gui make the choice."

"So it's started."

"What?"

"You're not going to be an active partner in Seconds now that you're running the shipping line."

"Don't be ridiculous. I have plans for the day that I can't set aside. If this can wait until evening…"

"What plans?"

"Plans."

"The kind that involve a woman?"

He didn't answer, but that didn't stop Tris.

"From your silence, it sounds serious. Which is why we are coming to you."

"Tristan, I don't interfere in your love life," Christos said.

"I don't have one that lasts more than one night."

"Exactly. Leave me be."

"We just want to meet her. You knew we were coming."

"I'm not going to be on the island today," Christos said.

"We'll find you."

"Somehow I thought you would. I'll leave Antonio at the Theakis compound, he'll prepare your regular quarters."

"Where does Ava stay?"

"In the main house with Theo."

"How is the boy? Is he your son?"

Christos was starting to wonder if Theo was really his son. Christos knew he should just ignore Ava's wishes and have the DNA test conducted, but he wanted…he wanted a chance at something more than the kind of marriage of convenience most of his colleagues had.

Tristan had married for love and against his family's wishes, and for a few brief years had been the happiest man that Christos had ever known. Then his wife had passed away, a victim of cancer.

"What was it like?" he asked.

"What was what like?"

"Being married to Cecile."

Tristan cleared his throat and didn't answer for a moment. "Heaven. Is that what you're searching for?"

"I don't know that I am, but I want a chance at that."

Tristan cleared his throat again. "I hope you find it. With Ava and Theo. You deserve that kind of happiness."

Christos recognized sadness and resignation in Tristan's voice. "You can have it again."

"No, I can't. It was a once-in-a-lifetime love. The kind that makes your soul burn brightly."

Tristan rang off and Christos sank down in the leather executive chair, thinking of the tears in Ava's eyes last night, tears that made him believe that she, too, wanted that kind of once-in-a-lifetime happiness with him.

Ava wasn't sure what to expect when she got downstairs, but seeing her son playing with Ari wasn't it. Theo jumped off Ari's wheelchair when he saw her and ran to the open trunk of a Jaguar convertible, one of Christos's many cars. He'd given her the keys to a Rolls-Royce.

Theo grabbed a second water gun and brought it to her. She pushed her sunglasses up on top of her head. She hoped that Theo would suggest she be the bad guy. She certainly wouldn't mind dousing Ari with water.

"You can be the back-up detail."

"Thanks, sweetie," she said, dropping a kiss on Theo's head and accepting the weapon from him. "Where's your *baba*?"

"He had to take a call up at the main house," Ari said, giving her outfit the once over. "Are you sure that's what you should be wearing?"

She glanced down at her shorts and halter-style tank top. "We're going out on a boat."

"I know, but Christos may see some associates at the marina for lunch. You don't want to look like a tacky American."

She'd bought this outfit at Ann Taylor, the epitome of conservative American dress. She knew she didn't look tacky, but Ari made her want to defend her clothing. And she wasn't going to, because she'd learned the hard way that winning any argument with Ari was next to impossible.

"*Baba* isn't working today," Theo said.

"Business always comes first with Theakis men."

Ava smiled sweetly at the older man. "One of the things I've always liked about Christos is that he makes his own decisions."

"My son is stubborn, but also very loyal."

That was true. Christos's loyalty to Stavros had been one of the things that had driven the two of them apart. "He wants to be a good father to Theo."

"Mama, I think you need to stand behind that tree over there. The bad guys will be coming up from the garden."

She tossed her bag in the front seat of the convertible and got into position. Ari got to her as no one else could. She suspected it was partly because she didn't feel that she was good enough for Christos. Living here at the

Theakis compound brought home how different her life had been from Christos's.

"Mama?"

"Yes?"

"I hear someone coming."

She did, too. The footfalls were heavy on the stone walkway. She hoped it wasn't Antonio. The poor man had been doused with water a lot in the past week.

She heard the whirring of the motor on Ari's wheelchair and then Theo's small hand on her back. "When I give you the signal, we'll attack."

She nodded at her son. A shadow of a man was visible around the side of the large tree trunk and Theo nudged her with his elbow. She jumped out on one side while Theo covered their target from the other. They both fired at the same time, dousing not Antonio, but Christos.

"*Baba*, we got you!"

Christos grabbed his chest and staggered backward. Water dripped from his torso and face. Theo raced forward and pulled a piece of rope from his pocket. He took Christos's wrists in his hands.

"Mama, help me," he said.

Ava dropped her weapon and reached for Christos's wrists, which was when everything got a little crazy. Christos bent and picked up her gun with one hand and brought the other arm around her waist, holding her to his body. He held up the water gun to her face.

"Back away or the hostage gets it."

Theo put up his hands, still holding his gun and took

two steps back before he dropped into position and fired at Christos. Christos doused her with a shot of water to the face before turning his attention to Theo. Both of them raced down the path toward the garage and Ava stood there chuckling.

"I don't know what's gotten into him," Ari said.

"He's having fun."

"Fun has never been his problem."

"What *is* his problem?" she asked.

Ari shrugged and pulled a pair of sunglasses from his pocket. He turned the wheelchair toward the house and she realized that he was going to just roll away as if they weren't having a conversation.

"For someone who places so much emphasis on manners, you are very rude."

He stopped his chair and glanced over his shoulder at her. "Are you talking to me?"

"Do you see anyone else?"

"I don't like your American attitude."

She could name several things about Ari she didn't like. "I don't care for your Greek-male arrogance."

"Good."

He started back toward the house and she shook her head, watching him go. This was what she'd been trying to explain to Christos last night. The disdain that his father held for her made her days long and difficult. To his credit, Ari did seem to adore Theo and gave the boy a lot of attention.

She walked back toward the garage, noticing that

both Christos and Theo had disappeared. She had a feeling that she was going to get attacked guerilla-warfare style. And she needed that distraction, because she felt out of her element here. Something that Ari always induced in her.

She'd given birth to his grandchild, but apparently that wasn't enough for the older man to cut her any slack. She wondered if he knew the truth of what had happened in the past or just the tabloid version of everything that had transpired between her and Christos and Stavros. As observant as Ari was, she couldn't imagine he would have missed the fact that Stavros had been having an affair and that it wasn't with her.

She heard a rustling behind her a split second before she was hit in the back with an icy spray of water. She turned on her assailants, scooping her son up in her arms and wresting the squirt gun from him. She hit Christos in the face with the spray and then turned and ran for the car.

Theo's laughter filled the air and she felt something ease in her soul. No matter how much Ari might disapprove of her, this was exactly where she belonged. Christos captured them both, wrapping his arms around her from behind. She felt his warm body press against her. She tipped her head back on his shoulder.

"What did my father say to you?" he asked.

"Nothing important. Can you still take us out on your yacht?"

"Yes," he said. She could tell he wanted to ask her more questions, but she shook her head and set Theo down.

"Let's go!" Theo said, climbing into the car and fastening his seatbelt.

Christos tried to keep his mind on driving to the marina and off the wet shirt that clung to Ava's curves but it was hard…and that wasn't the only thing in that condition.

His mobile phone rang and he ignored it. He'd had it with his interfering father, friends and business associates. He needed this clear, bright, sunshiny day for himself and his family. Ava wrapped her arm around her waist and shivered a little as the breeze blew through the car. Keeping his eyes on the road, Christos reached behind him into the bag she'd stowed in the back seat and pulled out her sweater.

"Thanks," she said when he handed it to her. "Did you take care of all your business this morning?"

"Business?" he asked, wondering how she knew about it.

She shrugged. "Ari said you had a call. And last night you mentioned that there was a lot of stuff on your plate at work."

"Stuff? Is that what you think I do?" he teased. He didn't want to talk about business today or think about the heavy load he'd have to deal with tomorrow. Each day there was a new complication at the office. For just today, he wanted to feel…free. The way he used to when Stavros was still the one charged with carrying on the Theakis traditions.

"Meetings, conference calls, I don't know. What do you do?"

"Stuff," he said, unable to stop smiling over at her.

She playfully punched him in the arm. "You're in a good mood today."

"Am I not usually?" he asked, not wanting to assign too much significance to the fact that he was happy just to spend time with Theo and Ava. That wasn't like him. He didn't like to depend too heavily on someone else for his happiness. That was a road that led straight to disaster.

"Sometimes you are. You look very tense when you get home."

He turned into the parking lot at the marina and saw that Captain Platakis had his yacht ready to go. "Transition periods are always difficult in a business situation."

"In a personal one, too," Ava added.

"Indeed. Too bad that I can't map out a plan for our relationship the way I can for Theakis Shipping."

"Am I complicating your life?"

"In ways you can't even fathom."

"Oh, I think I can."

"What does *fathom* mean?" Theo asked from the back seat, reminding Christos that the boy was listening in on their conversation.

"Understand," Ava said.

"Oh. Why can't you understand?" Theo asked.

Christos reached around and ruffled the boy's hair. He

was way too young to have to learn that women had secrets a man could never unravel. "It's a man-woman thing."

"A love thing?"

Ava flushed. "Probably, sweetie. Are you ready to go out on the boat?"

"Wait a minute," Christos said, putting his hand on Ava's thigh to keep her from opening her door. He turned to Theo. "What's a love thing?"

"You know, *Baba,* when a man and a woman start to love each other."

Theo undid his seatbelt and climbed into the front seat, sitting on Ava's lap. She stroked her son's hair. "He asked a lot of questions about why you and I weren't together."

Christos wasn't sure what that meant. Did she think she had loved him?

He opened his door and climbed out of the car, needing distance. The happiness he'd felt earlier dimmed a little. What exactly was happening between him and Ava? Lust he could handle. Love…he didn't believe it existed. Sure, he cared for his father and Theo and couldn't even think of what he'd felt for Stavros. But love? Romantic love? He'd never experienced anything that made him believe it was real.

Not even with Ava.

"Christos?"

"Hmm?"

"Are you okay?"

"Sure. Why wouldn't I be?"

"You're glaring at the car."

"The sun's in my eyes," he said. "Theo, please run down to Captain Platakis and tell him we'll be ready in five minutes."

The boy hesitated and glanced at Ava. She stepped in front of him and turned toward Christos.

"He's afraid of water."

"What?"

She gave him a look that said she wasn't repeating it. He'd forgotten she'd mentioned that the boy didn't like water. "Theo, come here. Ava, will you go tell the captain we're here?"

She hesitated. And he gave her a hard look. He was to be Theo's father by marriage if not biologically, and that meant he had rights where the boy was concerned. Meant there were times when Ava was going to have to let go.

She sighed and he wondered a little more about the love thing she'd talked to Theo about. He was glad to have this very real problem to solve for his son. Fear of water he could help the boy get over. Understanding women…not so much.

Eight

Ava didn't feel comfortable on the platform in the middle of the room with Maria and the dress designer, Dorothea Festa, staring at her. She felt foolish standing there in a slip while they measured her and talked in Italian behind her back. Never had she felt more out of place than this moment.

Not even two days ago, when they'd returned from the boat trip to find that Christos's friends had arrived. Tristan and Guillermo had started bonding with her son, doing male things that had excluded her. But seeing Theo bloom under the male attention had soothed any jealousy she felt. Now she was in here, being fitted for a wedding dress worthy of a Theakis bride, while Theo was out near the pool with Tristan and Gui.

Christos was at the office, unable to take another day off even with his friends here. Her relationship with him had grown a little closer over the last few days, since their boat outing, but it was more the bond of parenting. Christos had backed her up against Ari when he had tried to have a nanny and private tutor brought in for Theo. He'd worked with Theo on basic Greek, and Theo had soaked up enough that he was now attending a day school in the village with other local children. Ava had volunteered to work in the classroom during the day. Her own rusty Greek was improving rapidly.

But their intimate relationship was at a standstill. She knew she was responsible for that by saying they shouldn't have sex until they were married. Or maybe Christos had just lost interest in her. He was busy at work and stayed out late at night with his friends. Perhaps she was assigning too much importance to herself and the impact she wished she had on him.

"Ms. Monroe, please hold your arms out."

Ava did as she was asked. The designer's assistant put the tape measure around her chest and then her waist and hips. She glanced down at her body dispassionately. She'd lost all the weight she'd put on when she'd been pregnant with Theo, but her body would never be the same.

Even the designer seemed to notice this as she patted that little bit of a belly Ava hadn't been able to get rid of.

"We can cover this with a full skirt," Dorothea said.

"I don't really want a full skirt," Ava said.

"I'll see what I can do. Will you be wearing a support garment underneath?" Dorothea asked.

"If I have to. Did you see the picture I cut out?" she asked.

"Yes. But that dress is too…common. I have some ideas that Mr. Theakis has approved."

"Christos shouldn't see the dress."

"Mr. Ari Theakis," Dorothea said turning back to Maria.

"Dorothea."

The woman glanced back at her. "Yes?"

"I'm not wearing anything that Ari suggested. If you don't think the dress I want is acceptable, I'm open to suggestions, but I will be making the final decision on the dress."

She bit her lower lip. "Of course, Ms. Monroe. Let me go get my design book. I'll be right back."

"Don't go to Ari," Ava said.

But Dorothea ignored her as she walked out of the room. Ava glanced at Maria, who refused to look over at her. She knew that the other woman wasn't going to side with her; she had her paycheck to think of. Dorthea's assistant busied herself with papers, perhaps writing down Ava's measurements.

Ava put on her robe and walked out of the second-floor sitting room where they were having the fitting. She wasn't sure what to do. Was she really going to let Ari intimidate her into wearing a dress she didn't want?

Someone cleared their throat behind her and she turned around. Guillermo. Gui. He was tall with a leonine mane of thick brown hair. His features weren't classically handsome but his face wasn't one you'd forget. He was tan with sunlines around his eyes and was a bit taller than Christos.

"Yes?"

"We're ready to have lunch and Theo wondered if you'd have time to join us."

She nodded. "Of course. Let me change and then I'll join you—on the terrace?"

"Yes," Gui said, but didn't leave. "Is everything okay?"

She shrugged, not wanting to lie to the man; she'd made a promise to Christos and to herself to stop pretending about things that made her uncomfortable.

"Do you want to talk about it? I have three sisters and two sisters-in-law…"

She laughed a little at the way he said it. One of his sisters-in-law was the Infanta of Spain—the royal princess and heir to the Spanish throne. "So you're used to listening to women's secrets?"

"Yes, I am. And if my sisters are to be believed I'm very good at helping with problems."

She was tempted. For the longest time she'd been on her own, handling her problems by herself. But she had no idea how to handle Ari. Standing up to him just made him more belligerent. Backing down made him gloat.

"Thanks for the offer, but this is something I think I should handle on my own."

Gui nodded. "If you change your mind, the offer is open."

"Thank you. I hope that Christos knows what a good friend you are."

"I remind him of it often," he said in that teasing way of his, but she was sure that he didn't have to.

The bond between the three men was closer than one between blood brothers. "How long have you known Christos?"

"Since we were ten."

"That long?"

"Yes. We met at school."

"Boarding school, right?"

Gui nodded. She took a deep breath, aware that she wasn't fooling him by talking about the past. She sat down on the loveseat under the window that looked over the sparkling blue water of the Aegean. "I don't know how to make Ari accept me."

Gui sat down next to her, putting his arm along the back of the loveseat. "Why would you want to?"

She looked into his diamond-hard eyes and tried to find the words to tell him how out of place she felt here on Mykonos and with Christos. But this strong, confident man would never be able to comprehend that, and she felt even less worthy of being a Theakis bride.

Christos wasn't having the best day. Two of the ships that they used to import goods from Asia were in quarantine and he couldn't find one official who would take a call from him to tell him what was going on. Hector, the man who was supposed to be in charge of these types of crises, was at the hospital with his wife, who was giving birth to their first child.

A text message from Theo had come in via Tristan's phone just minutes after he was told that he wouldn't be able to get an answer on the quarantine for another hour. So lunch with Theo and his friends was about the only thing he could do.

He pulled the Ferrari into the circle drive in front of the main house and got out. Antonio was waiting for him in the foyer with a drink and a look that said there was trouble brewing.

"Do I even want to know what's going on?"

"Probably not," Antonio said. "Your father is in conference with the designer he hired to make Ava's wedding dress. From what Maria told me, Ava wants a dress that is nothing like what your father ordered."

"Tell the designer to give Ava what she asked for."

"Your father is refusing to pay for it."

"I'll take care of it. In fact, let's get the old man out of the planning process. Please tell Ava that she is in charge of the wedding."

"Yes, sir."

"Where is she?"

"Upstairs. Master Theo is on the terrace with Tristan."

"Good. Tell them I'll join them in a few minutes."

"Yes, sir."

Antonio walked away and Christos went upstairs to

find Ava. The sitting room was empty so he went to her suite and knocked on the door. He heard the rumble of Gui's voice.

He wasn't going to jump to any conclusions. Yeah, right. What the hell was Gui doing in Ava's rooms?

Christos opened the door to the room and walked in as if he owned the place. Ava and Gui both stood up as he entered. He spared a hard glare for his friend and wrapped his arm around Ava's waist, pulling her into his body.

He took her mouth in a kiss that wasn't meant to be sweet or romantic. It was meant to stake a claim. But holding Ava in his arms always led him to one reaction.

God, he wanted her. He softened the kiss, sliding his hands down her back to her hips and wrapping one arm around her waist to anchor her to him.

The thin fabric of her robe wasn't much of a barrier.

"I'll be going now."

Christos took his time lifting his head, keeping one arm wrapped around Ava's waist. "What were you two discussing?"

"Your father," Gui said. "Women like to tell me their troubles."

"You always were a sucker for a damsel in distress."

"I'm not in distress. Thanks for listening," Ava said. She pulled out of Christos's arms. "Are you home for lunch?"

"Yes. Theo invited me. Tristan put him up to it."

"I'll see you all downstairs in a few minutes," she said, walking out of the room.

They both watched her leave.

"I've never seen you so possessive before," Gui said.

Christos rubbed the back of his neck. He couldn't explain it to anyone, wasn't even going to try. He only knew that Ava was his and it was important that Gui and the rest of the world know it.

"What upset her?" he asked his friend.

"She's worried that you'll be embarrassed in front of society if the wedding isn't perfect."

Christos cursed under his breath. "I don't give a crap about that."

"I told her. But she's still concerned. Your father has her convinced that the Theakis set the style, not follow it."

"Ari couldn't care less about fashion," Christos said more to himself than Gui.

"He's making things difficult for Ava."

"Why?"

Gui shrugged. "Perhaps to make sure she'll stay. She did run away before."

"The paparazzi were all over her."

"I saw the coverage. That can be a lot to handle for a young woman."

"Yes," Christos said, not enlightening his friend that Ava had been driven away by more than the tabloids—Theakis Nanny Snags Both Brothers, one headline had screamed. His anger hadn't helped.

Gui walked toward the stairs. "Aren't you coming?"

"In a minute. I want to talk to Ava alone."

There had been nothing untoward between Gui and Ava when he'd walked in. Ava was reserved around his friends, and he was coming to realize that that was her way around most men.

This time he wasn't as caught up in the white-hot passion that blazed between them. It was still there, but he had more breathing room to make sensible decisions. Like branding her with his kiss? Yeah, well, he was still possessive where she was concerned.

Gui left and Christos looked around the sitting room while he waited for her. It wasn't sophisticated and cool the way his rooms were. She'd left her mark on the place. Pictures of Theo were mounted on the wall, along with little sayings that she was fond of. Nestled in one corner were the big story-time pillows and against the wall a rolling laptop caddy, which he knew she'd had brought in for Theo.

Ava was adjusting to living in his home just as she'd hoped she would.

When she exited her bedroom, Ava was surprised to find Christos waiting for her. He sat in the nest of pillows where she usually read Theo his bedtime story.

"Come here," he said.

She walked over and sat down next to him on the pillows. He drew her into his arms, gently rubbing his thumb over her lower lip.

Her mouth was a little swollen from the powerful kiss he'd given her. "I'm sorry if I hurt you."

"You didn't," she said. "It made me think I'd made a mistake asking you to wait until we were married…."

She didn't want to tell him how she'd stood in front of Maria and Dorothea and that snooty assistant and felt like the dirty little girl from the trailer park, someone who'd never be able to win his attention, much less keep it. That feeling harkened back to something that Stavros had said to her when he'd made a pass at her years ago: *Christos will never see you as anything more than some cheap American tail.*

Certainly Christos hadn't come after her when she'd left Mykonos and Greece to return to the States. But she'd always hoped that it had been anger and not a lack of caring that had made him let her go.

"Nothing was happening between Gui and myself. We were just talking."

"What about?"

"He was giving me advice about dealing with your father."

"Really? What did he suggest?"

She nibbled her lower lip. "Telling him to go to hell. But somehow I don't think I can do that."

Christos smiled at that. "I can't see you doing that either. I've left word with Antonio that you are in charge of our wedding. Don't let anyone bully you into anything."

"That's harder than it sounds. I'm not at all sure I can make the right choices."

"I'm sure you can. You're not the same young woman you were five years ago. Don't forget that."

"Does that mean you believe I've changed? That kiss you gave me when you came in…" Bringing it up might not be the wisest idea but nothing ventured, nothing gained. "It was a real claim-staking kind of kiss."

"Yes, it was."

"Nothing happened between Gui and myself," she said again.

"I know."

"You trust me?" she asked.

"I trust that nothing happened between the two of you."

She swallowed hard, wanting to let it go.

"Because you trust your friend."

"What does it matter?"

"It matters to me."

"Why? We're here together. We are getting married."

That was exactly why it mattered so much to her. And she was so afraid that she was making Christos out to be this great love of her life in her mind. When the reality was…just another lie that she was telling herself.

"Because we *are* getting married."

He tucked her head closer to him, resting his chin on top of her head. "Ava, you are so complicated."

"So are you," she said. She had no idea what he really wanted from her.

"Why are you home?" she asked at last. She missed him during the day, although she was really trying to find a way to stand on her own. But right now she just closed her eyes and sank deeper into his arms.

"Theo asked me to come," he said, stroking her back.

"He misses you when you're gone."

"I miss him, too."

She tipped her head back and saw the sincerity in his obsidian eyes. "Even though you aren't sure he's your son."

"He's a Theakis and I do love him."

Though she'd wanted to hear him say that he believed Theo was his son, she didn't push. "I'm glad for that. I couldn't stay here if you didn't treat him right."

"Yet you'll stay here and let my father treat you poorly?"

"That's not fair. Your father is hard to deal with."

"I know. Do you want to live somewhere else?"

"What do you mean, not at the compound?"

He shrugged. "I've taken you away from the life you knew. I want this place to be your home."

Though it wasn't yet home, a physical place that she felt comfortable in, she didn't want to disrupt Theo's life with another move so soon. "I don't mind living here. Your father and I just have to sort things out. And I've talked to Theo's school about volunteering there. I think I can make this work…."

"Don't let him run you off," Christos said, and she had a feeling he was talking about way more than the wedding.

"I won't. I'm not going to let you do that to me, either."

"Good."

She smiled. "We'd better head down to lunch. Theo's probably already eaten but he'll expect to see you."

She tried to rise but he tugged her back into his arms.

"Yes?"

"I know you wouldn't betray me with Gui."

She caught her breath as the words sank in. Was he saying he trusted her? Or was this just an olive branch? A tentative offering that they could use to build a life together.

She leaned down and kissed him. She wanted to tell him with words all she felt about him, but words were something that Christos didn't trust from her. Actions, on the other hand, might be just what she needed to convince him that she was a woman worthy of being a Theakis bride.

Nine

His wedding day dawned cloudy and rainy. Not exactly a good omen, but then he'd never put much stock in things like fate. He controlled what happened around him with an iron fist and his own stubborn determination. Besides, the ceremony wasn't until dusk and after a lifetime of watching the seas he knew that the skies would clear long before the ceremony started.

Too bad women weren't easier to predict. Or, to be more specific, Ava. His focus had narrowed completely to her. His body was whacked out from wanting her so much. His emotions were a mess and he was caught somewhere between wanting to disappear into a job that could consume his life and walking away from being a Theakis to take Theo and Ava to some unnamed island.

He adjusted the tie at his throat, trying not to look at his reflection in the mirror. Ava had made a million and one small changes to her own life and he was well aware that he'd made none. He'd stood above her, superior in the knowledge that she'd betrayed him and should make amends. But now, coming to know her as he was, he suspected...

"Ready for the big day?" Tristan said, entering the room. He had a bottle of champagne in one hand and three glasses in the other. Gui was right behind him with a small digital camera.

"Ready as I'll ever be," Christos said. "I never thought I'd marry."

"It's not too late to change your mind," Guillermo said. Gui was a confirmed bachelor who'd even tried to talk Tristan out of marrying his long-time love, Cecile.

"Yes, it is," Tristan added. He put the glasses on the small table in the corner of the room and then opened the champagne. "You should know better than to suggest he could cancel, Gui. Ava would be devastated and I think that Ari would probably have a heart attack."

"Better never to get married than to have to end it later," Gui said. "You have to agree with that, Tris. Did you have doubts before you married Cecile?"

Tristan turned away and in his posture Christos saw the lingering pain of emptiness left by Cecile's death.

"No. I didn't have any doubts. I knew that she was the one woman for me."

Christos put his hand on his friend's shoulder and squeezed. He wished sometimes that his emotions were as powerful as Tristan's had been. But since Ava had come back into his life he'd been struggling to contain his emotions, working on not letting the possessiveness and jealousy that were always near the surface swamp him.

Gui raised one eyebrow at him. "What about you?"

He had no idea what he felt for Ava, only knew that she was his and he wanted the world to know it. "I'm not backing out. I've given my word."

"And the word of a Theakis is unbreakable," Theo said dancing into the room. He looked so cute in his tuxedo, like a Mini Me, Christos thought. Looking at the boy, he realized that this was his chance to make up for all the things he'd screwed up. With Theo he could make himself a better person.

"That's right, Theo."

"*Baba*, you look very handsome, just like Mama thought you would."

"How do you know that?"

"I heard her tell Maria."

Gui laughed. "You shouldn't eavesdrop, Theo. That's not polite."

"I didn't mean to."

Christos ruffled the boy's hair as Antonio entered the room carrying more champagne glasses. Antonio was dressed in a tuxedo and would also be serving as one of Christos's groomsmen.

"I think that this time it was okay," Christos said to Theo.

"I'm sure it was," Tristan said. "Let's have a toast to your *baba*, Theo."

Tristan poured champagne into each of the glasses. Ari entered in time to claim a glass. Seeing his formerly robust father in the wheelchair suddenly gave Christos pause. He struggled to see past the chair and most days was successful—the old man was so cantankerous that it was hard to pity him—but, today, when Stavros's absence was so palpable, it was harder.

Tristan made some kind of toast and Christos raised his glass and took a sip, but he couldn't stop looking at his father. He felt Theo's small hand in his grip and glanced down.

"I don't like this. Can I have something else to toast with?"

"It's not a proper toast if you don't do it with champagne," Tristan said. Being a Frenchman he had always believed that wine in all its forms was the only thing one should drink. "It's an acquired taste, Theo. All true gentleman enjoy it."

"It took me a while to get used to the taste as well."

"I will get some sparkling water for Theo." Antonio left the room.

"When did you get used to it, *Baba*?"

He shrugged. "Over time I think. Not being born French it may have taken me longer than Tristan."

"Touché," Tristan said with a mocking nod in his direction.

"Your father was born something better than French," Ari said.

"Greek?" Theo asked.

"No, a Theakis," Ari said. Christos met his father's gaze and for this one moment they were on the same page.

He glanced at Theo and wondered if he'd be happier knowing that the boy was really his son. The doubts were still there, but didn't change the way he felt for Theo. And today, he was happy to be a Theakis groom going to his bride. Happy to be the son of Ari. Happy that for once he and his father both wanted the same thing.

He pushed his doubts about Ava's past fidelity out of his mind, just for today.

Ava had never been one of those girls who'd had big dreams of her wedding day, mainly because she'd always known her father wouldn't pay for her to marry any man. But this was something out of a fantasy.

Once Christos had told her to take control of the wedding, she'd decided to do just that. She'd combed the society pages for wedding details so she'd have an idea of what the Theakis family were used to and then used her two weeks to plan an event that wouldn't embarrass them.

The end result was a ceremony and reception that she felt confident people would be talking about for a long time to come. But *she* still felt like a fraud. She felt as though the entire ceremony was one big lie. She put her head down in her hands.

"Don't do that, Ava, you'll smear your makeup," Laurette said. As promised, Christos had flown her and Paul in from Florida to help Ava prepare for the wedding, and Laurette was serving as her maid of honor.

"What am I doing?" she asked.

"Getting married to your very handsome Prince Charming," Sheri Donnelly said. Sheri worked for Tristan and had agreed to be in the wedding party as a favor to him. Guillermo's youngest sister, Augustina, was also serving as a bridesmaid. Augustina was sixteen and so beautiful that Ava had a hard time looking at her. She was also sweet and very shy.

"Prince Charming? Only if Prince Charming was arrogant and bossy," Ava said. Christos was definitely the only man for her, but she had to wonder sometimes why she'd fallen for such an opinionated man.

"There's no accounting for taste," Laurette said, fluffing her short blond hair. Laurette was the one woman in the world whom Ava actually felt comfortable with.

"Very funny," Ava said, finally smiling.

Sheri shook her head. "I'm in the same boat. In love with a guy I shouldn't be in love with."

"Tristan?" Ava asked. Though Sheri was dressed in a gown the same as the other bridesmaids' she still looked…well, plain. She blended into the background and was easy to ignore. But she was spunky, and Ava had noticed that the other woman was different when she was around Tristan.

Sheri flushed and looked away. "God, please tell me it isn't that obvious."

So glad to have someone else's problems to deal with instead of her own, Ava walked over to Sheri, putting her arm around the other woman's shoulders. "Only to someone in the same position."

"We're not in the same position. Christos is marrying you and he watches you with an intensity that makes it clear that he wants you."

"Wanting is not the same thing as loving. Christos is marrying me because…I don't know why he's marrying me. I think I'm making a horrible mistake."

Augustina left the mirror where she was fixing her lipstick. "Passion is never a mistake, Ava. That's how love starts."

"Who told you that?" Ava asked the younger woman.

She shrugged her delicate shoulder. "I'm Spanish. We know about passion."

She ruined her sophisticated moment by giggling after she said it. "Actually, Guillermo told me that."

"I can believe it," Ava said.

Augustina offered to help Sheri with her makeup and the two women moved to another corner of the room.

"Are you sure about this?" Laurette asked. "There's still time to call it off."

No, there wasn't. She wanted to marry Christos, had wanted to from the very first time she'd made love with him over five years ago. And though she'd never had any childhood dreams of a wedding, as soon as she'd held him in her arms, she'd had dreams of a marriage. Of having Christos as her husband.

"I'm not sure, but I can't call it off."

"Are you still worried about Theo?"

"No. Christos is a great father and I believe that if I said I couldn't stay here, he'd find a way to work something out between us. I'm not marrying him because I have to."

Laurette hugged her close. "Good. I like him. I think he's good for you."

"Ha, he's bossy."

"So are you. You need a man who will take care of you."

She wondered sometimes if that wasn't part of the appeal of Christos. He was so different from every other man she knew.

"It's almost time," Maria said, entering the room. She held a small wrapped box in one hand. Theo was behind her, looking adorable in his tux.

"Mama, I just had a champagne toast with *Baba* and I didn't like it."

"That's okay."

"The photographer is going to come in here in a minute to start taking photos," Maria said. "Theo, come over here and let me comb your hair." She turned to Ava. "This is for you."

She handed her the gift-wrapped box and then stepped away. Ava glanced down at the card, which simply stated her name in Christos's bold handwriting.

"I'll give you a minute to yourself," Laurette said, and joined Augustina and Sheri.

She unwrapped the box slowly. It was made of hardwood and inlaid with gold. The design on the top of the box was the Theakis family seal, something she'd seen many times over the last few weeks.

She opened the box and the fresh scent of cedar assailed her. She closed her eyes and breathed deeply. Then she opened them and looked inside. There was an embossed notecard. She lifted it out and read it quickly.

All Theakis are of the sea and here's something to to remind you that now you are a Theakis, too.

She set the card aside and pulled out the velvet jeweler's bag beneath it. She loosened the tie at the top of the bag and pulled out the necklace inside. It was a beautiful diamond-and-sapphire encrusted choker with a platinum anchor dangling from it. There were matching earrings and a bracelet inside as well.

She caught her breath staring at them.

"*Baba* said these remind him of your eyes," Theo said, touching one of the sapphires.

She looked at her son and the women in the room and knew she was taking the right step. More than the jewels, Christos's words convinced her that, despite the fact that this wasn't her kind of wedding, she wasn't lying to herself. Marrying Christos was the right thing to do.

* * *

With the sun setting behind them, they repeated their vows on the terrace of the Theakis compound overlooking the Aegean Sea. Christos kissed Ava at the end of the ceremony with raw possessiveness, stamping his claim on her mouth to go along with the ring on her left hand that showed the world she was his.

Flashbulbs went off during the kiss and Christos felt a sense of impending doom. He'd invited several celebrity photographers, including one who would be doing a story on the wedding for one of the Sabina Group's magazines. But the public spotlight wasn't always kind, especially to Ava and him.

The flashbulbs brought back the anger he'd felt when the tabloids had broken the story of Ava's affair with Stavros.

He lifted his head and wrapped his arm around Ava's waist as they walked back down the aisle between their family and friends.

"Christos?"

"Hmm?"

"Why are you acting so…"

He glanced down at Ava. He couldn't begin to figure out what he felt, but he knew *happy* was too tame a word for it. He banished the thought of the past as he looked at her. Knew the only way he was going to find any semblance of peace was to stay focused on Ava and Theo and the future he was slowly carving out for himself.

He arched one eyebrow at her. "So…?"

"Possessive, I guess. I'm yours now," she said.

There was a note in her voice that he couldn't place and he didn't try. "About damn time."

"Do you mean that?"

"*Moro mou*, I'm not indecisive about anything especially if it involves you or Theo."

She hugged him tightly to her, standing on tiptoe and kissing him. "This is one of the happiest days of my life. I can't believe we're married."

"Well, believe it. You are my wife."

She blinked back tears, then rubbed her nose and tried to turn away. "Oh no. My makeup is going to be ruined."

Christos had no idea how to stop her tears. Didn't understand where she'd gone in her head to start crying, so he did the only thing he could think of. He took her face in his hands and kissed her. Not with the raw masculinity that he'd used to brand her in front of his friends and family earlier. But with all the pent-up and unrevealed emotions that were coursing through him.

She clung to his shoulders, holding on to him, and he realized this was what he wanted. Like the symbol on the necklace he'd given her, he wanted to be her anchor when the seas of life got stormy and she didn't have anything or anyone else to cling to.

He lifted his mouth. Her eye makeup was safe, but her lipstick was completely obliterated. Her lips were soft and pink from his kisses, slightly swollen, and he couldn't wait to get to their room.

She touched her fingers to her lips. He stared down

into her eyes, let his gaze drift lower over the long length of her neck to the choker he'd given her. It looked perfect there. He skimmed his finger around her neck, tracing the seam where skin met diamonds and sapphires. He ended with a touch of the silvery anchor.

"You have the prettiest eyes I've ever seen," he said. "They remind me of the sea." The truth was, he lost a little bit of himself each time he looked into her eyes. They were wide and held depths that he was only beginning to realize she had. This time around, their relationship was so much stronger, he thought. And though he'd never admit it to a soul, he thought that Ava had been very wise to insist they not sleep together until they were married.

She flushed a little. "I like your eyes, too."

"We're married now," he said as their bridal party joined them on the steps of the main house.

He noticed that Tristan and Sheri were standing off to one side. Tristan's body language wasn't all that hard to read as he leaned over his surprisingly interesting secretary. He was definitely attracted to her. Sheri said something and Tristan's laughter echoed in the air. Christos couldn't remember the last time he'd seen Tristan that relaxed with a woman.

"Yes, we are."

He hugged her close as a photographer bustled around arranging the group for the shot. Christos brushed his lips over Ava's ear. "I can't wait for our wedding night."

She swiveled her hips against his and then reached

up with one hand, wrapping it around his neck, drawing his head forward. She kissed him with the same possessiveness he'd shown earlier in front of their wedding guests. "Me, neither."

Tristan clapped him on the back. "Congratulations, Mr. and Mrs. Theakis! Are you sure you know what you are getting into, Ava?"

"Yes, Tristan, I'm sure. Christos is the man I've always dreamed of marrying."

Ava was drawn away by the women to fix her makeup before the photographer started taking more pictures, and her words lingered.

"A woman's dreams are fragile things," Tristan said.

So were a man's, if the ghosts in Tristan's eyes were any indication. "Are you all right?"

"Fine. I'm happy for you. You've been alone too long."

"I've never been alone," Christos said. He'd made it a point to ensure he always had a lovely woman on his arm or in his life.

"My mistake. I like Ava."

"I do, too," Gui said, coming up behind them. "And this little monkey."

Gui lifted Theo up on his shoulder and Christos felt blessed for the first time ever, not only by the friends he had in his life but by being a Theakis. With Theo by his side, he didn't feel that he was second best, and when he glanced down and saw his father smiling while he chatted with one of the Theakis relatives, he realized that he felt almost at peace.

He scowled. He didn't trust the feeling and from the past knew it couldn't last. Not for the first time, he resented the fact that he had to plan for a future that was as stormy as the seas during a hurricane. But at the same time, his reality was that, whenever he got this feeling of rightness…something bad was waiting around the corner.

"Christos?" Gui had been watching his friend's expression.

"Yes?"

"You okay, man?"

"I've fulfilled my destiny as a Theakis. Of course I'm okay."

Gui gave him an odd look, but Christos turned away and chatted with some business associates, faking an enthusiasm he no longer felt.

Ten

"Oh, Christos, this is so romantic. I didn't think you'd do anything like this."

Christos hadn't thought he would, either, but Tristan's comment that morning about how women dreamed of their wedding day had made him think about their wedding night and making it into a romantic fantasy. It had taken less than twenty minutes on the phone to get everything as he wished it to be.

"After all the trouble you went through planning our wedding, it was the least I could do."

He set Ava on her feet in the luxurious suite that he'd rented for the night. They'd leave in the morning for Paris for their two-week honeymoon. But tonight they were in Athens at one of the five-star properties his family owned. The owner's suite was large, with the best marble flooring imported from Italy, priceless works of art adorning the walls and Louis XIV furniture. Beautiful, opulent, yet it all paled compared to the woman in his arms.

She danced around the room, her strawberry-blond hair fanning out around her. There was a restless energy about her that underscored the fact that, even though he could hold her in his arms, he never really understood her.

"You're staring at me," she said, coming to a stop in front of the balcony doors.

"I know."

"Usually I'm the one who does the staring," she quipped.

"You're effervescent tonight. I can't seem to stop looking at you."

The lighting in the room was dim and candles flickered on all the surfaces. Pale-pink rose petals made a trail on the floor to the bedroom.

"Am I?" She tipped her head to the side, giving him a seductive look from under her eyelids.

He nodded. "I've been waiting for this moment since I came back into your life."

"I've been waiting for this moment since you left my life. I can't believe today has been real."

"Come over here and I'll prove it."

She smiled over at him in a dreamy way that he thought meant she might be a little buzzed from the champagne she'd drunk at their reception. She'd danced with Theo and with him, but no one else. It was as if she were sending him a direct signal that she was his.

"*Moro mou*, come here."

She shook her head. "Not yet."

"Why not?"

"You'll kiss me and I'll forget that I want this night to last forever."

"I promise it'll last forever," he said, wondering if that was the truth. His erection strained against his zipper now that they were alone and he knew that he was going to have her. At last. Well, if the first time didn't last forever, he'd make it up to her the second time he took her. He didn't plan on sleeping much tonight anyway.

She didn't say anything but kicked off her high heels and walked toward him in that sexy dress she'd changed into before they'd left the reception. The skirt danced around her legs and she put an extra swivel in her hips.

"Ava…"

"Christos…."

"Stop teasing me."

"Is that what I'm doing?"

"You know you are."

"Why don't you stop me?"

"Because you don't want me to," he said.

She stopped. "You're right, I don't. I want to tease you until you can't sit there and beckon me. Until that passion you do such a good job of hiding forces you to come to me—"

He lunged for her, pulling her tight to his body. Holding her by her hips as his mouth found hers. He plundered her lips, pushing his tongue deep into the cavern of her mouth, swallowing her gasp and tasting that champagne he knew she was buzzing from.

He didn't lift his head until she was clinging to him. "Like that?"

"Just like that. I've missed being in your arms," she said, curling herself around him.

He lifted her into his arms again, carrying her over the rose-petal path to the bedroom. She kept one hand at the back of his neck, her long fingers toying with the hair there. Every nerve-ending in his body was focused on one thing, one purpose. And each brush of her hands against him aroused him more.

He set her on the bed in the middle of the rose petals and stepped back. He reached for the dimmer switch on the wall, turning it so a low, ambient light filled the chamber.

He kicked off his shoes, toed off his socks and shed his jacket, tossing it toward the padded chair in the corner of the room.

He wanted this to be a slow seduction, their first time together in so long, but he couldn't stop his body. It was as if a red haze had come over him and all he could see was Ava and her soft curves.

All he wanted was to feel her naked skin against his and the welcoming warmth of her body wrapped around him. He wanted to plunge deep inside her and take her until time dropped away. Until there was nothing but the two of them and the kind of passion he'd never found with anyone else.

"Christos, are you coming to bed?'

"In a minute." Hell, he didn't think a minute was going to be enough time to bring him down. All he could smell each time he breathed was her perfume. All he could taste lingering in his mouth was her. All he could see was Ava.

He told himself to take it slow but slow wasn't in his programming with this woman. She was pure feminine temptation and he had her in his arms. He stepped purposefully toward her.

She sat up. "Wait! I forgot I have something special to wear tonight."

"The choker I gave you earlier would be fine but anything else is a waste of time."

"Please, Christos. It'll just take a second."

He nodded. He could deny her nothing tonight; she was so radiant.

"I left word for our bags to be unpacked."

"I can find what I want to wear. Will you wait for me out there?"

He complied and then paced the outer room until she called him back.

She was wearing some silky thing that made her so desirable he barely noted what it was.

He crossed the room and took her face in his hands, staring down at her and then lowering his mouth. He tried to harness his passion this time so he didn't over-whelm her. But the need that had been riding him since—hell, since he'd seen her at that boarding school in Florida—slipped out of his control.

His hips thrust against her as his hands slid down her back, finding the hem of the nightdress and pulling it up until he could caress her soft skin. Her thighs were firm and smooth and, as he caressed his way higher, he encountered only the smooth flesh of her buttocks.

He groaned deep in his throat, running his finger along the curves of her flesh, exploring her thoroughly. She said his name, a breathless gasp that told him she was right there with him. And then he traced his way between her legs.

"Christos…"

His name falling from her lips was exactly what he wanted to hear. "Loosen your top, Ava. Bare your breasts for me."

She shivered in his arms. Her mouth found his and kissed him just as deeply as he had her a moment earlier. When she drew back she took his bottom lip between her teeth and nipped at it.

Her hands went behind her back to the tie that held the bit of silk up. The movement thrust her chest forward. His eyes narrowed as the fabric slowly parted from her body, slipping away from her skin. "Are you sure this is what you want?" she asked, teasing him now.

He left off caressing her and caught her wrists in one of his hands, holding them behind her back.

He lowered his head and pushed the fabric fully down from her chest with his other hand. And then he stared down at her breasts, creamy and full, their tips hard and straining. He couldn't resist the invitation to take one nipple in his mouth, suckling at her. Her legs moved restlessly, one of them coming up to wrap around his hips.

He released her wrists and ran one fingertip around her aroused flesh. She trembled in his arms. Her fingers drifted down his back and then slid around front to work on the buttons of his shirt. But he was too impatient to wait for that. He set her on her feet and ripped his shirt open.

He growled deep in his throat when she leaned forward to brush kisses against his chest. She bit and nibbled, bringing him to the brink. No way could he wait another second.

He pulled her to him and lifted her slightly so that her nipples brushed his chest. Holding her carefully he rotated his shoulders and rubbed against her. Blood roared in his ears. He was so hard, so full right now that he needed to be inside of her body. The skirt of her nightgown bunched between their bodies and he shoved it out of his way.

He caressed her smooth thighs. She was so soft. She moaned as he neared her center and then sighed when he brushed his fingertips there.

He slipped one finger into her and hesitated for a second, looking down into her eyes.

She bit down on her lower lip and he felt the minute movements of her hips as she tried to move his touch to where she needed it.

He was beyond teasing her or prolonging anything. He needed her now. He carried her to the bed and fell on it, bringing her down on top of him before rolling over so she was beneath him.

He looked down into her face. Her eyes were closed for a second as she shifted her hips and rubbed herself against him.

"Hurry, Christos."

He didn't need her to ask twice. Reaching between their bodies he freed himself and covered her with his body. Their naked loins pressed together and he shook under the impact.

Now. He adjusted his hips, positioning himself, and then entered her with one long, hard stroke.

She moaned his name and her head fell back, leaving the curve of her neck open and vulnerable to him. He bit softly at her neck and felt the reaction all the way to his toes when she squirmed in his arms and thrust her hips back toward him.

A tingling started in the base of his spine and he knew his climax was close. But he wasn't going without Ava. He wanted her with him.

She moved more frantically in his arms and he moved deeper inside her with each stroke. Breathing out through his mouth, he tried to hold back the inevitable. He slid one hand down her abdomen, through the slick folds of her sex, finding her center. He stroked the aroused flesh with an up and down movement, circled with his forefinger then scraped it very carefully.

Then he penetrated her as deeply as he could. She cried out his name.

"Look at me, Ava. Open your eyes."

She did, and in that instant, as everything in his body tightened and he started to climax, he wanted to love her. Wished there was a way he could forgive the past, because he knew he held the future in his arms.

Christos rolled over in the middle of the night and felt the warmth of Ava's body. They'd made love once more before falling asleep, and he'd carefully stripped the silk slip from her body and taken the time with her he'd wanted to the first time.

He'd opened the drapes to let the light of the moon into the room, and the balcony doors so that a cool night breeze stirred the air around them. Goosebumps were visible on Ava's naked skin. He traced his finger down the line of her body.

He came to the small bump of a belly left from her pregnancy, the small trace that Theo had left on her body. The trace of a child who was at the root of their marriage—and at the root of his distrust of her. He knew he had to do something about that.

He'd tried hard over the past few weeks to allow himself to see the woman that was Ava. And to be honest, he didn't believe the woman she was today would cheat on him. But that girl in the past…he wasn't as sure about her.

She stirred in his arms, rolling onto her back. He propped himself up on one elbow and continued to caress her, finding the tiny stretch marks left by her pregnancy, and everything within him solidified. He wanted to mark every part of Ava as his own. He wanted to plant his seed in her womb. He wanted to watch her grow heavy with his child and then be there from the first breath that child took.

It didn't change the way he felt about Theo…that boy was his now, and nothing on earth could change that.

"Christos?"

"Hmmm?"

She touched his face with soft fingers and he realized that she always did that. "What's the matter?"

"Nothing."

"I wish…I wish I were the slender girl I was the first time."

"I don't."

She tilted her head. He continued tracing over the stretch marks left by her pregnancy. "Did you like carrying the Theakis heir?"

"You mean your son?" she asked.

He shrugged. "Did pregnancy agree with you?"

She looked as if she were going to pursue the topic but then stopped. "Yes. I had morning sickness at the beginning but then…yes, it was very pleasant."

He didn't ask her any more questions, lowering his head to trace the lines with his tongue. Her hands fell to his head, caressing his scalp with her fingers.

"You know what I liked best about it?" she asked in a soft tone.

"What?" He lifted his head looking up the length of her naked body to meet her sea-blue eyes.

"That I wasn't alone anymore," she said, then glanced away as if she'd said too much.

He slid up over her. Her legs parted for him so that he rested in the cradle of her body. "Would you like another child, *moro mou*?"

With his erection at the portal of her body, he knew this wasn't the time for a discussion about their family and their future. But before he drove into her and made her his again, he needed to know.

She put her hands on his chest, holding him back from entering her body.

"Would you?"

"Yes," he said, bending down to capture the tip of her breast in his mouth. He sucked her deep inside, his teeth lightly scraping against her sensitive flesh. His other hand caressed at her other breast, arousing her, making her arch against him in need.

"Should I get birth control this time?" he asked her. "Or do you want to try for another child?"

Her gaze met his. "Yes, I think I would."

She reached between them and took his erection in her hand, bringing him closer to her. "I need you now."

He lifted his head and watched her as he slid deep into her body.

She started to close her eyes as he made love to her. "Keep your eyes on mine, Ava."

He thrust slowly in and out of her body, building them both toward climax with deliberation. He stared into her eyes, wanting to see—needing to know—how susceptible she was to him. There was no room for lies in their bed and when they were close like this he believed everything about Ava.

She slid her hands down his back, cupping his buttocks as he thrust deeper into her. Staring deep into her eyes made him feel as though their souls were meeting. She started to tighten around him, climaxing before him. He gripped her hips, holding her down and thrusting into her again before he came with a roar of her name. He held her afterwards.

Ava ran her hands slowly up and down his back. He heard her breath catch and then felt the warmth of her tears on the side of his face. Propping himself up on his elbows he stared down at her and wiped the tears away with one thumb.

"What's the matter?"

She swallowed and then glanced down at his chest, at the gold medallion that swung free from his body. She caught it, tracing her finger over the pattern of the Theakis family crest.

"Ava? Tell me, *moro mou*," he said.

"I'm just so happy. I never thought you'd forgive me and we'd have this."

He bent his head and kissed her so she wouldn't be able to see the doubt that still lingered in his heart about

Theo. He wanted the peace he felt to be real and knew there was only way to make that happen.

He was going to have to have the boy tested.

Eleven

Ava rested her head on Christos's chest, listening to the solid beating of his heart. Wrapped in his arms, it was easy to pretend that the problems they'd had in the past were gone. Easy to pretend that Christos believed her about Theo and that she no longer had to prove herself to him because of the problems that Stavros and Nikki had left behind.

She tried never to think ill of them, but their marital problems were like a disease that had spread out to affect her and Christos, not just in the past, but now.

She'd come to understand a new truth about herself when she'd had Theo. And these past few weeks on Mykonos, she had learned to understand Christos so much better now than she ever could have before. And because she had her own weaknesses, she didn't want him to feel that way with her. That she was *his* weakness. Christos had given her something she wasn't sure she could have found on her own.

"Are you sleeping?" he asked.

She felt the vibration of his words in his chest and under her ear. She shifted in his embrace, tipping her head so she could see the underside of his jaw.

"No. Too much to think about." This had been at once the most terrifying and exciting day of her life. She felt that, if she went to sleep, she might wake up and find none of it had happened. That she was still a single mother living with Theo in Florida.

She tugged on his chest hair in retaliation. "Were you serious about wanting more children?"

"Yes."

"I'm glad. I think Theo will benefit from having another sibling."

"Yes, he will. Plus I think it will make our family more solid."

"Solid is no guarantee of happiness—or safety. Look at what happened to Stavros and Nikki. Who would look after Theo if something happened to us?"

He rubbed his hand up and down her arm. "Nothing's going to happen to us, but in such a case I've asked Tristan to be Theo's guardian."

"Shouldn't you have discussed this with me first?" She liked Tristan, but she wasn't sure he was parent material. He was more like the crazy fun uncle than a responsible guardian. As much as she didn't like Ari, she thought he might be a better choice.

"I made the decision before I left for Florida to pick up Theo."

"Oh," she said not really sure how to take that. "What about your father?"

"My *patera* isn't strong enough to contend with a young man. Tristan is the best choice."

"What if you're wrong?" she asked. Her heart ached at the thought that something could happen to her and Christos and Theo would be left alone in the world.

"I'm not."

"I hate when you do that." His confidence was part of what attracted her to him, but she wished at times he'd at least acknowledge that he was human and was as fallible as everyone else.

"I know. I'm sorry I didn't consult you, but there wasn't time. Would you like to ask your friend Laurette to be a co-guardian? I think that Theo will need a female influence."

"She's actually his godmother from when I had him baptized. And I do like Tristan."

"Good."

"So, having another child…"

"Yes?"

"Does this mean you finally believe me about Theo?"

She held her breath, unable to believe she'd finally had the courage to ask him that question again. He closed his eyes, rolled over so that she was under him. Her legs parted and he settled against her. His arms braced on either side of her body. He brought his mouth down hard on hers.

When he came up for air long minutes later, his hands moved over her body with intent. She was tempted to let him distract her and be swept away by the passion that flowed so easily between them. But she had to know. In a way, she already had started to believe they were going to have a real marriage, yet they couldn't unless there was real trust between them.

She pulled back, putting her hands on his face and holding him still. She stared up into his obsidian eyes that were so like the son's he hadn't acknowledged he believed was his. Sure, to Theo and the world he'd claimed her son, but she knew he had doubts. Had she shown him enough of who she really was to change his mind about her?

"Please answer me," she said at last.

"Theo is our son."

She believed him. Christos wasn't the kind of man to say things lightly. She wondered if she should ask him how he felt about her. If he thought he could ever love her. But those words weren't easy to find and she was much too scared that she might find out that he couldn't love her to ever say them aloud.

Instead she lifted her hips toward his and felt him slip inside her body. Their eyes met and held again and he took her with carefully measured thrusts until they both climaxed at the same time. She felt the warm spill of his seed deep inside her body and she wondered if giving him another child would make him love her.

But she knew that she'd done all she could. She'd just have to fill their house and relationship with love. Christos was a smart man and more intuitive than he let on. Instinctively she knew she hadn't made a mistake in marrying him.

Paris was vibrant and romantic and Ava soaked it up. They'd had dinner with Tristan's family last night and today Christos was escorting his new bride around the city to fashionable boutiques recommended by Tristan's sisters.

His mobile rang and he glanced at the caller ID before answering.

"Yes, Antonio?"

"Sorry to disturb you, sir, but Master Theo wanted to talk to you."

"No problem, put him on."

"Baba?"

"Yes, Theo?" He missed the little boy and had stopped thinking of Theo as the Theakis heir. How had that happened? When had he gone from thinking of Theo as his nephew to thinking of the boy as his son? It was as if the relationship and his distrust of Ava had nothing to do with Theo. He knew that made no sense. "How was the allergy testing today?"

"Okay, my back hurts and is very itchy."

"That will go away in a few hours. I'll have Antonio put some salve on it."

The little boy talked about other things, games he'd played with his grandfather, and Christos had a new sense of peace about the relationship. He'd asked the doctor to take a cheek swab for a DNA test from the boy while he was conducting the allergy test. He imagined he'd soon have the answers he needed to move forward in his relationship with Ava.

And he needed to know if he or Stavros was the father for insurance purposes anyway.

He wanted to believe Ava, but a part of him, that long-cynical part, was refusing to without proof.

"When are you coming home?" Theo said, a note of something in his voice.

"Not for five more days. Is something wrong?"

"I'm having trouble breathing," Theo whispered, probably so that Antonio wouldn't hear him.

"Ask Antonio for your inhaler," Christos said.

"It's in the room with Uncle Gui. I don't want…"

"Theo, it's not a weakness. Gui has seen me wheezing and using an inhaler many times. Remember when I had to use it on the yacht?"

"Yes."

"Go now," Christos said, using a firm and authoritative voice that he hoped his son would obey.

"I…"

"No arguments, Theo. Do it."

"Yes, sir." Then Theo heard him calling for Antonio.

Before his butler came back on the line, Ava emerged from the dressing room wearing a slim-fitting black gown that plunged between her breasts and had a slit up one leg. "How do I look?"

"Wonderful. You are definitely getting that one."

"Is everything okay?" she asked, indicating the phone in his hand.

"Theo was having a bit of breathing trouble and didn't want to use the inhaler in front of Gui."

"Let me talk to him," Ava said, holding out her hand.

"He's gone already. I'm waiting for Antonio. I've got it under control. Go try on another dress."

"I want to speak to my son," she said.

"Is he not *our* son?"

"Yes, he is. I'm sorry. I just have a hard time letting go."

"You don't have to let go. We're partners now," he said. As he spoke he realized how much he wanted those words to be true. The only way that was going to happen was if he started trusting Ava. Truly trusting her. And trusting her meant not relying on a paternity test.

He'd tell the company lawyers that they'd have to find a way to insure Theo without the test. The boy was clearly a Theakis.

He looked into those beautiful sea-blue eyes of hers and realized the truth that he had been running from. That he was lost without this woman. And if she left him again...betrayed him again...he'd never recover.

"Christos?"

"Hmm?"

"Are you okay?"

"Yes."

"Let me put my own clothes back on and we can leave."

He nodded and kept listening on the open phone line until Antonio came on. "Theo's fine now. Would you like me to have the doctor come back and monitor him for the evening?"

"Yes, and then direct him to call my mobile, Antonio."

"Yes, sir," Antonio said.

There was a note in his voice that Christos couldn't place. "What?"

"Your father has hired a nanny for Theo. Master Theo doesn't understand why she's here."

"Thanks, Antonio, for the information. I'll take care of this with my father."

"I figured you would."

He hung up the phone just as Ava came out of the dressing room. She had none of the clothes in her hands that she'd been trying on. "Where are your dresses?"

"I don't want anything here."

"Ava?"

"I want to go home. I'm enjoying the city and being alone with you, but I miss Theo."

Christos drew her into his arms and gave her a quick kiss on the cheek. He missed Theo, too, and he had plenty of pressing business to attend to.

"I'll call the pilot and have him ready the plane. Do you want to leave now?"

"You don't mind?"

He shook his head. "I want you to be happy, Ava."

She smiled up at him, that brilliant smile that made his breath catch in his chest. He couldn't resist kissing her. Running his hands down her back and pulling her firmly into his arms. She was his. His. He'd never had anything that wasn't given to him because of the circumstances of his birth—aside from Ava and Theo.

"Having your trust has given me a joy that I can't explain." Her optimism made him wonder if he should explain right now about the paternity test. But he didn't want to dim it. Hell, who was he kidding? He knew that she'd be angry and disappointed if she learned what he'd done and he wanted more time to enjoy the peace that had grown between them during their honeymoon.

Christos barely had the car turned off when Theo bolted from the house and down the steps. Ava opened her door and stepped out of the car just as Theo reached her. He jumped up and she caught him in her arms, hugging his small body close to hers. Tears burned her eyes as she held him close. The time spent away from her son had just felt like too long.

Christos came up and Theo immediately wriggled in her arms, trying to get to his father. She handed him to Christos and watched the two embrace. Her life felt complete, so perfect and happy that she almost was afraid to believe it was real.

How had she gotten all of this? She'd been living her single life, so sure that she'd never find a happy ending with Christos, yet here it was. The pot of gold at the end of the rainbow she'd thought she'd never see again.

Christos glanced at her, catching her staring yet again. He gave her one of those long level looks of his and she shrugged.

"I like seeing my guys together."

Theo had an arm slung around Christos's shoulder as he walked over to her. "We like seeing you, too, right, Theo?"

"That's right."

"We have a surprise for you," Ava said.

Actually they had all kinds of surprises for Theo. Ava had bought him a stuffed bear in a shop in Paris and Christos had gone wild in another toy store, buying all kinds of things.

"What is it?" Theo asked, jumping from foot-to-foot when Christos put him down.

"I'm not sure we should give it to him," Christos said, looking very intent and serious.

Ava hid a smile behind her hand, enjoying her son and his father. Just enjoying everything that this moment was bringing her.

"Please, *Baba*."

"Were you a good boy?" Christos asked.

The two of them joked around as Christos carried Theo up to the house. Ava paused there on the circle drive of the large, luxurious house and for a minute flashed back to the small, single-wide mobile home she'd grown up in. When she'd met Christos, she'd been pretending her past didn't exist and had built a world based on lies. But now she saw that some of the things she'd told herself weren't lies. Christos *was* a good man. The kind of man she could safely give her heart to.

She loved him. Heck, she'd always loved him, and acknowledged to herself that she'd never stopped. But now that love felt bigger, more encompassing than it had before, because this time she wasn't his secret lover.

She glanced down at her left hand and the large platinum and diamond band there. She was his wife.

She'd just caught up to them near the entrance of the house when Ari's Bentley pulled up.

"I need to talk to you privately, Christos," Ari said through the car's open window.

"Can it wait?"

Ava guessed his father wanted to talk about Christos's dismissal of the nanny Ari had hired. He'd told her about that on the way home.

"No."

Christos handed her the bag with Theo's gifts in it. "Why don't you go inside with Theo and show him his surprises?"

"Yes, I will."

Christos brushed a light kiss against her lips and then nudged her toward the stairs with a discreet push on her backside. Theo held her hand as they entered the house.

"What did you get me?"

She smiled at the eagerness in his voice and drew him into one of the open rooms on the first floor.

There were three long couches and some armchairs in the room.

She sat down on one of the couches and slowly opened the bag, drawing out one of the gifts. "First you have to tell me one new thing you did while I was gone."

He climbed up on the couch next to her and put the present in his lap. "I went on a speedboat ride with Uncle Gui."

"Was it fun?" she asked, hearing the enthusiasm in Theo's voice. He liked having so many men in his life, and their love of boats seemed to be conquering Theo's fear of water.

Theo's eyes sparkled. "Yes, it was. We went so fast nothing could catch us. Can I open this now?"

She nodded and he tore the wrapping off the gift box. He opened the lid and pulled out the stuffed bear she'd chosen for him.

"Thank you, Mama," he said, hugging the bear to his chest and leaning over to give her a kiss.

"What are you going to call him?"

"Hmm…Fluffy."

"Fluffy it is. Are you ready for another present?"

He nodded. She drew out another package and handed it to him. "Tell me something else you did while I was gone."

He took the long box and held it with two hands. She could tell his attention wasn't on the question she asked but on trying to figure out what was in the box. She knew he was going to love this present. It was Spy Gear.

The play set contained everything Theo would need when he pretended to be a bodyguard.

"Theo?"

"Yes, Mama?"

"Tell me something so you can open this one."

He ran his fingers over the colorful pattern on the wrapping paper. "The doctor did a test on me."

"For allergies?" she asked. "Did they prick your back?"

"Yes and he put something in my mouth and rubbed it on my cheek."

"What? Why did he do that?" she asked.

Theo shrugged. "I don't know. Can I open my present?"

"Yes," Christos said coming into the room.

"What other kind of test did the doctor perform?" she asked.

Christos rubbed the back of his neck and looked away from her and she knew the answer before he said it.

"A paternity test."

She stared at Christos, unable to really understand what he'd said. "I thought you and I had already come to an understanding on this topic." Her ears were buzzing.

"We have," he said.

"They why did you have a test done?"

"Mama, don't get mad. The test didn't hurt me."

She hugged Theo to her side and bent to give him a kiss. Christos had gone behind her back.

This was the second time she'd allowed Christos Theakis to break her heart. When was she going to learn that he couldn't be trusted?

Twelve

"It's okay, sweetie. I...I just thought your father and I had an understanding."

"What's an understanding?" Theo asked.

Ava's eyes never left her son's. And Christos saw her shrinking away from him as the seconds passed. He'd ordered the test so he could give her what she wanted, bring real trust to their relationship. And he'd decided that he wasn't going to hear the results.

But now he felt as though he shouldn't even have made the gesture. He saw the hurt and anger in her. And understood it on one level, but on another...well, he wasn't the type of man to trust blindly and she had to have known that.

"An agreement. Like the one you and I have where

you always tell me the truth no matter what," Ava said, finally lifting her gaze.

Theo put the box on the couch and stood up, looking up at him with a serious expression that he knew mirrored his own. "Did you lie, *Baba*?"

How to answer this? "No, Theo, I didn't."

"Did I misunderstand you when you said that you trusted me?" Ava asked.

He shook his head. This conversation was complicated and delicate. Not fit for the ears of their four-year-old son. He swept the boy up in his arms and hugged him so tightly that Theo squirmed. *His son.*

"Will you give your mother and I some privacy?"

"Yes," Theo said. Christos put him down and Theo ran out of the room, taking the stuffed bear with him.

Ava had her arms wrapped around her waist and was staring at him in a way she never had before, as if the wind had been knocked out of her. Even that day at the school when he'd come back into her life, she hadn't looked like this.

"Ava—"

"Don't try to sugarcoat this or explain your actions. I made it clear that I needed your trust on this issue, Christos."

"I know that. I do trust you."

"Yeah, right."

"Don't be sarcastic. You can't carry it off."

Her arms dropped to her side. "I'll be whatever I like. I'm the injured party here."

He shook his head at her. "Put yourself in *my* shoes, Ava. I saw you and Stavros together. Nikki knew he was sleeping with another woman that summer and you were the only one near him."

Those were images he'd never been able to get out of his head. Though they were fading with time.

"Put yourself in my shoes, Christos…you give your virginity to a man you think you love and your boss comes on to you and you end up losing the man you love, your job and your family."

"I'm sorry that your family didn't stand by you," he said, unable to fathom her family abandoning her, because his never would. Even when he was at his wildest his father had still kept in touch. And he'd always had Guillermo and Tristan, who were like brothers to him.

"Their rejection I expected. I never fitted in at home and knew they wouldn't want anything to do with me or Theo. Your rejection hurt a lot."

"I never intended to hurt you," he said, thinking about the pain he'd carefully disguised as anger when he'd caught her in his brother's arms. The anger that he'd used to mask the vulnerability he'd felt at having trusted her.

"Of course, you didn't. Now that you know Theo's your son, is everything magically fixed in the past?"

He didn't hesitate, because the one time he had, with her, had brought them to this moment. "I had the test performed, but I haven't read the results."

"Then why have the test done?"

"I needed proof on this so that I could trust you."

"You needed *proof*? Trust doesn't work that way. Relationships are built on a belief in the other person, not facts and tests, and I can't live with a man who doesn't trust me."

"Are you threatening to leave?" he asked. He wanted to toss her over his shoulder, take her up to his room and lock her in. Ensure that she could never leave. But on the outside he struggled to play it cool.

"You sound as if it doesn't matter to you," she said.

"Hell, yes, it matters to me. But I'm not going to beg you to forgive me for something that was necessary."

She shook her head. "What do you mean necessary?"

"You wanted me to trust you, to believe in you and I wanted to give you that. To be able to love you the way you deserve…"

"And the only way you could do that was to go behind my back and have Theo tested?" she asked.

He took a step toward her, because this time she hadn't sounded defensive or angry. She'd sounded confused.

"You wanted something from me that I'm not capable of giving."

"What do you think I want from you?"

"Blind trust."

"I didn't want blind anything, Christos. I wanted love. Full-on, head-over-heels love. The kind of stuff that you read about in old epic tales."

He rubbed the back of his neck, trying to ease the tension there. "That's not realistic."

"I know what reality is and I know what I feel. And I love you that way, Christos."

Suddenly nothing else mattered. "You love me?"

She shrugged. "Yes, I do. But I can't live with you if you are going to lie to me, especially where Theo is concerned."

She walked past him and out of the room. He just stood there, thinking about her words. She loved him. What did that mean? Was that the emotion that had been buzzing around inside of him? Was that what all the possessiveness and jealousy he felt around her stemmed from?

He realized at that instant what Ava had meant by needing his trust, because there was no way he was ever going to be able to find proof of her love unless he simply believed her.

Ava felt small and very much the little girl from the trailer park as she left Christos and went out on the balcony that overlooked the vast, landscaped gardens at the Theakis compound. The house was huge and she had no idea where Theo was, but she wanted to see her son. Wanted to cuddle his little body next to hers and just bask for a few minutes in his unconditional love.

"What are you fighting with my son about?"

Surprised, she looked up at Ari as he came out onto the balcony in his wheelchair. He was the last person she'd talk about her problems with. In fact she suspected he'd probably applaud her problems with Christos and have Maria pack her bags and drive her to the airport.

"It's none of your business," she said at last.

"Everything that affects the Theakis family is my business."

"Did you meddle in Stavros and Nikki's marriage like this?" she asked. Anything to change the topic from her and Christos.

He sighed and for a moment she saw every one of Ari's eighty-one years on his face. "No. Stavros and Nikki…they had their own way of working things out. I didn't understand them."

"Me, neither," Ava said.

"You got caught in the middle of one of their games."

Ava knew that but was surprised to hear it from Ari. "What do you know about that?"

"I know everything that happens in my kingdom."

"This isn't a kingdom."

"Stop giving me a hard time. And stop letting the past dictate your future. You married Christos and are his wife—it's time you acted as if those vows meant something to you."

She glared down at him, thinking about broken vows, and knew she wasn't the one who had started this. But then again, this wasn't an elementary-school game of blame. "I take my vows very seriously, Ari, but some things…I can't compromise to make my marriage work. It's silly and probably American, but I can't change the fact that I want my husband to trust me."

Ava wrapped her arms around her waist and turned away from her father-in-law. Had her dreams of marriage been too unrealistic? Had she somehow been brainwashed by too many Disney animated films as a young girl? She'd never thought so. She'd seen evidence of happily married people.

And all of her single friends were looking for the same thing she was. They wanted the spouse and the kids and the other crazy stuff that went along with them. Not an idealized version of family life, but the reality of it. And Ava knew that had to start with trust. Because if she and Christos had a real marriage there were going to be fights, and only with real love could they weather those storms.

"You remind me a lot of my wife."

"I thought you didn't like me," she said.

"I don't. You're too stubborn and refuse to do what I say…that's exactly how Leka was. You have that same fire and passion when it comes to protecting your son and standing up to me."

"Why are you telling me this?"

"Because you look like you are finally thinking of giving up, and that's not who you really are."

"Ari, I've tried. I can't make Christos trust me, and without that everything else is built on air."

"Why do you think he doesn't trust you?"

"I asked him to believe my word that Theo was his son."

"The paternity test was legitimate. We had to have it for insurance purposes."

"The Theakis men do whatever they want. If he'd wanted to, Christos could just have said Theo was his son."

"He's not the only one who decides these things," Ari said.

"Are you saying you're the one who asked the doctor to administer the test?" she asked, knowing perfectly well that Ari hadn't. Christos had admitted to doing the deed himself, but she wondered how far Ari would go to try to convince her to stay.

"I was going to, but I can tell from your tone that you know it was Christos."

"Yes, I do." She sighed again. She felt so hollow inside and had no idea how to get back to normal.

"It's not that Christos doesn't believe in you, Ava, it's that he's afraid to believe in you."

"I don't follow."

"When my Leka died, Christos was young—only nine. He was very close to his mother, and even when he was a young child, he and I never saw eye-to-eye. And her loss was…hard on all of us, but especially on Christos."

Ava imagined how Theo would react if she were taken from his life. It was a heart-wrenching thought and made her really feel for Christos.

"What does this have to do with the man he is now?" she asked.

Ari pushed his sunglasses onto his forehead and looked her straight in the eye. "He stopped letting anyone into his life. He put up a barrier that only those two hellions he hangs out with were ever able to get past."

She wanted to smile at the way he described Guillermo and Tristan. They were two of the wealthiest and most successful men in the world, yet to Ari they were hellions.

"I still don't see what this has to do with me."

"I think he's testing you to see if you'll stay."

She shook her head. She had no doubt he was testing her in some way. But what Ari said… "I'm not sure I believe that."

"I've known him all his life, Ava, and I haven't seen him smile the way he does around you and Theo since he was a little boy.

"I've lost one son and am not going to give up on the one I have left now that he's finally found his way back."

Ava shook her head. "You can't make him love me."

"No, but you can."

"I'm not going to. I've spent my entire life striving for things out of my reach and just once I'd like someone to put me first."

"Christos already does that with you. He cuts his days in the office short to spend more time with you and Theo. Think about that." And Ari wheeled around and left her there.

Ava sighed and made her way back to her own room. She couldn't bring herself to go back to Christos's bed. Not yet.

She wished she could believe that Christos had been motivated by love, but she didn't think she could. She'd fooled herself twice into thinking that Christos loved her, and she'd been wrong.

* * *

Ava came out of the house the next afternoon and found Christos and Theo playing in the pool. She knew that Christos had been teaching Theo to swim but watching her son jump from the pool deck into the water made her breath catch. He surfaced quickly, swam to the edge and got out again.

"Mama, watch this," Theo said.

"What am I watching?"

"Cannonball!" He jumped into the pool with a big splash of water.

Christos stayed in the water but swam over near her. Resting his tanned muscled arms on the side, he looked up at her.

"How are you?" he asked, softly.

There was real concern in his voice. Or was she just imagining it? Hearing what she wanted to. "Fine."

"Ava, I don't like this distance between us."

"I didn't put it there."

"How can I make it up to you?"

"You can't, Christos. There was only one way to prove you trusted me."

"Mama?"

"Yes, Theo?"

"Watch this."

"I am watching."

She looked away from Christos to stare at Theo. But what she saw was the fact that her son used to be afraid of the water and being here with Christos had changed that. Being with Christos had changed *them.* She'd always been afraid of who she was, but Christos had given her the strength to be herself.

"Theo, enough for today. I have to go back to work."

"Ok, *Baba.*"

Theo swam to the side where Christos was and hugged him. Ava lifted him out of the pool. Theo hugged her and then ran to the poolside table where Maria had placed lemonade and snacks.

Christos got out of the pool and stood next to her. It was the closest they'd been since their fight. "I can teach our son not to fear water, *moro mou*, but I don't know how to teach you to trust me. I know that you can't see past what I did, but the reasons were more complex than just your trust."

"Your father told me. Tried to take the blame for the test."

Christos shook his head. "I ordered the test, I did that. But I haven't looked at the results, and I won't."

Ava felt the first chink of doubt in her resolve that his forcing the test was a bad idea. She watched him walk away, seeing for the first time that they both had to trust each other. She had to believe in him when he made promises to her, and she hadn't.

Christos spent the next two days at the office trying to tell himself that he didn't need a close relationship with Ava to be happy. But he missed her. He wanted her back in his bed. At night when he came home to tuck

Theo in he'd prompt the boy for stories about his mother so he could find out how she was doing.

God, he was pitiful.

The love he wasn't sure he felt for her was now seeming more and more real. He ached to have her back in his bed, not just so they could make love, but also so they could talk about the day.

He knew only one person who'd been in love, who knew what real heartbreak was. And though he'd always been careful to keep his emotions private, he had nowhere else to turn. Life with Ava couldn't continue this way.

He left Theo's room and walked down the hall to his study. The room was filled with items he'd collected and had at one time been a sanctuary for him, but no longer. Now it just seemed so much emptier than it ever had before.

He dialed Tristan's number before he could change his mind and without calculating the time difference from Mykonos to Manhattan.

"Theakis, it's the middle of the day here."

"I'm sorry, this couldn't wait."

"What's the matter? Is it Theo or Ava?"

"It's…ah, hell, Tristan, I've screwed things up with Ava. You said something on our wedding day about women's dreams…and I've never really understood what she wants from me."

"Ask her."

"What?"

"Ask her. She'll tell you what her dreams are and then you can fulfill them."

He knew what Ava wanted and realized he'd backed himself into a corner. "She wants me to love her and trust her."

"You don't really trust anyone," Tristan said.

"I trust you and Gui."

"Now, you do. But you didn't for the first fifteen years we knew each other."

"I don't think Ava's going to give me that much time."

"Having met her, I'd agree. What's the hold-up here? Is it the relationship with Stavros?"

No, it wasn't. It was him and the damned hollowness inside that he knew was the wellspring of his aloofness. That distance he kept as a buffer between him and the world.

"No, that's not it."

"What is it then?"

He couldn't put it into words with Tristan. "Nothing."

"It sounds like you love her, *mon ami*. Don't let her slip away. She's the first good thing to happen to you since…well, ever. She's the kind of woman who can give you the home and family you've always wanted."

"I wasn't looking for home and family."

"Whatever you say."

He wished it really was whatever he said. Because then he'd order Ava to move back to his room and make their lives together everything she wanted them to be. "Later."

He hung up the phone as everything coalesced in his

head. He needed Ava even more than he needed Theo or Ari or the Theakis shipping business. He needed her because she made him feel alive. Before her, he'd been stuck in the rut that came from always running and never standing still.

Did he love her?

Yes, he thought. He did love her. She was the only woman who'd ever made an impression on him. The only woman who'd ever made him feel so many different things. The only woman he'd never been able to forget.

He needed to find Ava and tell her that he loved her. Tell her that he'd been an idiot for not believing in her. Because now he understood what she wanted from him.

He went to the bedroom she'd moved back into two days ago and knocked on the door.

The door opened and she stood there in her bare feet and bathrobe. Her face was scrubbed clean of makeup and her hair was pulled back. His breath caught in his throat as the love he felt for her swamped him.

She kept the door partially closed like a barrier between them and he realized he wasn't going to let her do this. Let her turn him into some kind of simpering fool because he loved her.

He pushed the door open and scooped her up in his arms. He kicked the door closed and carried her across the room. He tossed her down on the center of the bed and then covered her body with his own.

She wedged her hands between them pushing against his chest. "What are you doing?"

"Claiming my wife."

"You already did that on our wedding night."

"No I didn't," he said, bending down to kiss her because the words hovering on the tip of his tongue were too revealing.

He plundered her mouth and restaked his claim on her. Tried to show her with his body all the things that he struggled to find the words to say. Her hands skimmed over his chest up to his neck, wrapping around his shoulders.

"I've missed you, *moro mou*."

"I've missed you, too. But sex isn't going to make everything okay between us," she said. "I want more than this from you."

"What do you want, Ava?"

"You to know that I trust you. So I have something for you."

"What?"

"Go sit down and I'll show you."

"Show me?"

"Yes."

She got up and walked away from Christos and he watched her go. She returned with an envelope, handing it to him. "I had this done because I don't want to test you or your love. I need to trust you as well."

"What is it?"

"Another paternity test. Open it and put your doubts to rest. I know that the situation you found me in with Stavros and the lies that I'd told you about my background all contributed to what you believed of me."

"Ava, I trust you. I know—"

She put her fingers over his lips. "Just let me do this for us."

He pulled her down on his lap and she snuggled close to him as he opened the envelope and pulled out the paper inside. He didn't look at it but instead stared down at her. "This can't change the way I feel about you. I trust you with my entire heart."

"That's wonderful, Christos, but I want more."

Thirteen

"I want more, too," Christos said. "I want your love."

A tear trailed down her cheek. "I haven't stopped loving you."

"Good."

She smiled, thinking of the test results that waited on that paper. She wasn't sure what he'd say, but it was the only olive branch she had. "Good?" He still hadn't looked at it.

"I think I meant fantastic."

"Why?"

"Because I love you, too. I think I always did. But I've been afraid to let you see how much you matter to me."

"Oh, Christos, why?"

"Because…" Christos whispered in her ear. "If I didn't love you, then it wouldn't matter if you left me."

"I'm not going anywhere."

"I know," he said, shifting her more comfortably in his lap.

"Your father was sure you were testing me."

"I think I was testing myself. Can you forgive me for not believing in you?"

"Yes. I can."

He took her mouth with his, letting his hands wander over her body. He untied the sash at her waist and pushed the sides of her robe open. She shivered and undulated against him. He leaned down to lick each nipple until it tightened. Then he blew gently on the tips. She raked her nails down his back.

"Oh, Christos, I'm afraid to believe this is real."

"Doesn't it feel real?" He shifted to lay her on the bed then moved further down her body, kissing his way over her stomach, his tongue tracing over the silvery stretch marks and lingering on her belly button.

He continued moving lower until he hovered right over her center.

"Open yourself for me," he said.

Her legs moved, but he took her hands in his, bringing them to her mound. She hesitated but then did as he asked.

"Hold still," he said.

He leaned down, blowing lightly on her before drawing her flesh into his mouth. He skimmed his hands up her thighs, then lifted his head and looked up her body.

Her eyes were closed, her head tipped back, her shoulders arched, throwing her breasts out.

He lowered his head again, hungry for more of her. He feasted on her body the way a starving man would, giving her as much pleasure as he could to celebrate the joy she brought to his life.

He wanted this night when they'd both confessed their love to each other to be one she never forgot. He concentrated on driving her toward her climax. He used his teeth, tongue and fingers to bring her to the brink but held her there, wanting to draw out the moment of completion until she was begging him for it.

Her hands left her body, grasping his head as she thrust her hips up toward his face. But he pulled back so that she didn't get the contact she craved.

"Christos, now."

He scraped his teeth over her and she cried out as her orgasm rocked through her body. He kept his mouth on her until her body stopped shuddering and then slid up her.

"Your turn," she said, pushing him over onto his back.

She took his erection in her hand then followed with her tongue, teasing him with quick licks and light touches. But he was too close to the edge to let her continue. He pulled her away from his body, wanting to be inside her.

He moved her until she straddled his hips. Then, carefully, he pulled her down while he pushed into her body.

He pulled her legs forward, moving them farther apart until she settled even closer to him.

He slid deeper still into her. She arched her back, reaching up to entwine her arms around his shoulders. He thrust harder and felt every nerve in his body tensing. Reaching between their bodies he touched her between her legs until he felt her body start to tighten around him.

This time they cried out together, and then she collapsed on top of him, her head on his chest.

As they lay snuggled together, he found peace and contentment with her. Something he'd never known he'd want or need.

There was one more thing he had to do. He reached for the paper with the paternity test results, which had ended up next to Ava on the bed. Slowly, without looking at it, he tore it into tiny pieces and let them flutter out of his fingers. "Now, do you believe I love you?"

"Yes," she said.

* * * * *

Christos may have finally been tamed,
but Tristan Sabina's story is just beginning.
Don't miss the next sexy and exciting
SONS OF PRIVILEGE *story from*
Katherine Garbera,
The Wealthy Frenchman's Proposition,
on sale in February 2009 only from
Mills & Boon® Desire™!

MILLS & BOON

INTRIGUE

On sale 16th January 2009

COLBY REBUILT
by Debra Webb

Protective yet reckless, Shane Allen is unlike any man Mary Jane has ever known. Assigned by the Colby Agency to protect her, could this bodyguard prove the ultimate lover too?

WITH THE MATERIAL WITNESS
IN THE SAFEHOUSE
by Carla Cassidy

FBI agent Ryan has been sent to Raven's Cliff to protect his former lover. Amnesia sufferer Britta has no memory of him, but super-sexy Ryan intends to remind her – one touch at a time!

FAMILIAR STRANGER
by Michele Hauf

Jack had been recruited to fight the paranormal Cadre organisation – instead he fell for mysterious member Mersey. Now he faces a world of untamed passion *and* darker danger..

DEADLY TEMPTATION
by Justine Davis

Liana is determined to prove the heroic lawman who saved her life years ago innocent of corruption. Now, with time running out, Logan must put his life – and heart – in Liana's hands.

**Passion. Power. Suspense.
It's time to fall under the spell
of Nora Roberts.**

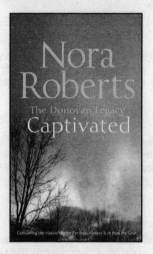

For the latest script of his blockbuster horror film,
Nash Kirkland tracks down self-proclaimed witch
Morgana Donovan and sceptically demands the
secrets of her imaginary craft.

Nash is stunned to discover that he is equally
mystified by and attracted to Morgana. Either he
is being driven mad or Morgana is telling the truth
about her powers. And the most important
choice Nash will ever make depends on
getting the answer right.

**This is the first volume in Nora Roberts' spellbinding
The Donovan Legacy.**

Available 2nd January 2009

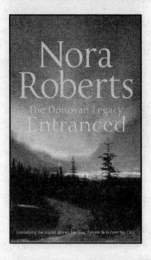

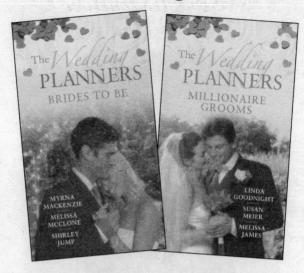

2 FREE

BOOKS AND A SURPRISE GIFT!

We would like to take this opportunity to thank you for reading this Mills &
Boon® book by offering you the chance to take TWO more special
selected titles from the Desire™ series absolutely FREE! We're also makin
this offer to introduce you to the benefits of the Mills & Boon® Boo
Club™—

- ★ FREE home delivery
- ★ FREE gifts and competitions
- ★ FREE monthly Newsletter
- ★ Exclusive Mills & Boon Book Club offers
- ★ Books available before they're in the shops

Accepting these FREE books and gift places you under no obligation t
buy, you may cancel at any time, even after receiving your free shipmen
Simply complete your details below and return the entire page to th
address below. You don't even need a stamp!

YES! Please send me 2 free Desire volumes and a surprise gift. I
understand that unless you hear from me, I will receive 3 super
new titles every month for just £5.25 each, postage and packing free. I ar
under no obligation to purchase any books and may cancel m
subscription at any time. The free books and gift will be mine to keep i
any case.

D9ZEC

Ms/Mrs/Miss/Mr ....Initials ....

BLOCK CAPITALS PLEASE

Surname ....

Address ....

....

....Postcode...................................

Send this whole page to:
UK: FREEPOST CN8I, Croydon, CR9 3WZ